D1738610

# The Undoing of a Libertine

*The Undoing of a Libertine* is definitely a book to read and devour. Mark my words, Raine Miller knows how to deliver a story that gives you the complete experience, and leaves you BEGGING for more. She's has amazing talent, and I can't wait to see what she has in store for us next. Bring on the swoon!

*Author,* **BELINDA BORING~**

A fast paced story filled with secrets, passion, betrayal, danger, learning to trust, romance and love. A gripping read that will leave you breathless and in awe of Ms. Miller's compassion while addressing a very serious topic. With her engaging characters and her rich plot you can't go wrong with *The Undoing of a Libertine.*

*MY BOOK ADDICTION~*

I very much enjoyed reading this book and will definitely read more from Raine Miller in the future. *The Undoing of A Libertine* may have dark story-lines, but the romance and sensuality is scorching hot.

*BOOK SAVVY BABE~*

Ms. Miller creates characters that I fall in love with! They are strong but have weaknesses that readers today can relate to. I enjoy how the hero is friends with Darius and Marianne, from her novella *His Perfect Passion.* I love how Ms. Miller is able to intertwine her characters into other stories…giving us more of the characters we already love and know! If you read Ms. Miller's recent work *Naked* and *All In* and enjoyed those books, then I am confident you will love her historical romances just as much!

*BETWEEN THE PAGES~*

Love, love, love this historical novel by Raine Miller. Having had read *The Blackstone Affair* first, I knew that Ms. Miller's historical romance books had tie-ins to *The Blackstone Affair* and would play a role in future books of that series. I adored Jeremy Greymont *fanning myself* -- Compelled by determination, yet loving with Georgina, and sensitive and charming to boot! As always with any Raine Miller book, I was not left disappointed. Highly recommended!

*BECCA THE BIBLIOPHILE~*

# The Blackstone Affair

Ethan Blackstone is the most swoon-worthy male character I've ever encountered.

**COLLEEN HOOVER,** New York Times *Bestselling Author~*

The title of this book is so aptly named as her characters are stripped **Naked** down to their bare feelings and what they do to one another.

**FLIRTY & DIRTY BOOK BLOG~**

I was in it from the beginning and I had a hard time letting go. The writing was excellent with dialogue a-plenty; some witty British humor and slang...loved that!

**SWEPT AWAY BY ROMANCE~**

Fast paced, page turner with smart-mouth characters. Leaves you with just enough steam coming out of your panties to keep you hanging on long enough for **All In**.

**EROTIC SMUT REVIEWS~**

**Naked** by Raine Miller is a fantastic story filled with plenty of drama and erotic romance.

**BOEKIE'S BOOK REVIEW~**

**All In** is guaranteed to hit my to-be-read pile after such an intense and addictive story. I must continue this journey of Ethan and Brynne!

**THE BOOK WHISPERER~**

This book is so good...I don't even have the words to do it justice here! Getting a wicked glimpse into Ethan's head in **All In** pretty much blew my mind. He's naughty yes, but he's also incredibly human and he loves his girl so much it hurts.

**SCANDALICIOUS BOOK REVIEWS~**

*Other titles by Raine Miller*

HIS PERFECT PASSION

*The Blackstone Affair*
NAKED
ALL IN
EYES WIDE OPEN

# The
# Undoing
# of a
# Libertine

# DEDICATION

To the Ghardians

*This precious book of love, this unbound lover...*

**—William Shakespeare,** ***Romeo and Juliet*** **(1595)**

# The Undoing

## of a

# Libertine

*Raine Miller*

# CONTENTS

# ACKNOWLEDGMENTS

For my fans. This is for you. I write first and foremost for myself, but without the amazing readers who write to me and share how one of my stories has touched them, or gave them some enjoyment as they read the words, or made them forget about life's troubles for a few hours, I wouldn't be able to do this for my living. Reading a precious message from a fan is one of my greatest joys as a writer. Thank you for that gift.

xxoo R

# CHAPTER ONE

*September, 1837*
*London*

**A** proper blow always felt nice. Satisfying as hell, he thought. And he'd needed it. Badly. As usual, the sex played out just the way he liked—driving at full hop and more on the rough side of things than not.

His preference for a hard grind had always been like that, and thankfully plenty of brokers plied their skills in the fleshly arts to suit his tastes. To get what he was after never proved a problem. Hell, the beating heart of the pleasure trade trumped in London. If a fellow couldn't find what he wanted in Town, then the toff was probably out of luck.

Jeremy Greymont leaned against the headboard and indulged in the drained flush of a man being satiated, for the moment at least. He knew the feeling wouldn't last. It never did. That was the thing when he paid the person he fucked, didn't know her from Eve, and intended to forget about her the second his prick was back under wraps in his kecks.

Looking around the room, he tried to see it for what it was. A room tastefully done up in forest-green silk wallpaper and dark oak, well appointed and clean enough. Only the best for him, right? But the trappings of decoration aside, it was just a room. A room for fucking. It was merely a room with a bed for the purpose of carnal dealings between people who exploited each other.

The exploitation was up front of course. If he thought about it, the exchange was nothing more than simple commerce at the core. A purposeful trade of good coin for the use of a body. This was about as decidedly purposeful as it was possible to be in Jeremy's opinion. And he was very careful about it. He made sure to employ a French letter with courtesans. No pox, clap, or by-blows for him. He didn't need those worries plaguing his conscience.

And once he had someone, Jeremy usually never had them again. A repeat fuck was a rarity. He sought only physical gratification. This he understood and respected. Attachments could always be avoided, but weren't much of a worry for him regardless. It was nigh impossible to cultivate a relationship if the two parties never saw each other again after the raucous romp amid the bed linens was over and done. He wanted it that way.

Jeremy had to wonder if he was even capable of loving a woman. He certainly had never felt anything akin to a romantic notion about any of the women he'd had. And he'd had many. Jeremy liked them, admired their assets, took pleasure in their bodies, and enjoyed them thoroughly, but that was as far as he was willing to go.

Upon reflection, Jeremy accepted that the hard docking he did wasn't really that satisfying after all. If he was honest, he would say it had become remote and perfunctory for him. What was he even doing here? The oddest sensation flickered through him. *Get up. Leave! Leave this place and never come back. You cannot find it here, and you don't want to be like...him.*

Jeremy had arrived at his bordello of preference to cleave off some tension tonight. Coming away from another obligatory meeting with his grandfather and feeling like an absolute shit-stick in the process, he'd needed the release.

Sighing heavily, he dressed himself, thanked his feminine companion for a job well done, and left in search of relief of a different sort.

If he couldn't fuck the demons out of his head, maybe a less private method could be applied. A copious dousing of whisky might just do the trick, he thought, while making his way out into the mild autumn night.

At *The Wicked Goat*, he settled down into communion with his own personal bottle of Scotland's best and his musings. Jeremy wanted to prove to his grandfather that he took his responsibilities seriously. He didn't intend to shirk, but at thirty years old, Jeremy was running out of time to demonstrate his seriousness about doing his duty to the family. Mere lip service was no longer an option. The time was upon him, he knew, but the idea of simply settling for anyone put him off more than once. He wanted her to be *right*. But what in the hell did that mean? Right? To be right for him or right for the role? He felt hopeless in this search. Well, not really a search, for he hadn't put forth any effort of note as yet.

Jeremy shifted in his seat, on edge again, thinking of their conversation...

*"You must secure the line of succession, son! It is your duty by birthright. Find a good wife and get an heir, and be damn quick about it! I'm not going to last forever."*

How many times had he heard the entreaties? Jeremy smirked and tossed his head back, thinking how pleased Grandfather would be if he actually did marry, and to a female of decent lineage. God, both his grandparents would be ecstatic. He wanted to make them proud of him, but the thing was, he didn't know many such women. Women of good family, that is.

Where to find a mate? Where to even start? The females he usually consorted with didn't come with bloodlines written out on parchment. He needed a virgin, and the very idea made him roll his eyes. *By Cupid's cock, what would you do with a virgin?* Exactly. Bedding an innocent did not appeal in the slightest. Not with the way he liked to fuck. Hard and fast was his only rule. He couldn't imagine doing that with a virginal maid. He'd likely frighten her to death.

Born into money and privilege, the baronetcy he'd inherit one day loomed closer with each passing year. Thus the persistent pressure to step up to his duty and secure the line could never be forgotten for long. He supposed sacrifices would have to be made all the way round, and sulking about it served no good purpose. If he could just secure someone suitable and install her in his country house to serve up an infant or two, he could continue on with his libertine ways, with very little bother to either of them. Jeremy thought he would be an easy husband, demanding only the access needed to create the legitimate heir required of him. After one was produced, his lady wife could do as she pleased. She'd have her status in society and his money to make up for any lack in attentions from him. He wasn't a monster…just a man.

As soon as Jeremy remembered how much he despised London society, his mouth turned down into a scowl that caused his lip to curl with a menace. He could barely tolerate society's requirements now. It was an imposition to show at the few events he graced each season. The thought of attending more such tortures was unbearable. The cloying looks, the vicious backbiting and jockeying for positions of power all disgusted him. And don't forget the plotting of eager society matrons trying to secure matrimony for their overbred offspring. He'd been avoiding every bit of it for years.

Now he supposed he'd have to take a serious look in order to find a bride, and force himself to attend more balls and dinners. He felt a headache starting.

"Greymont! Why so long in the face?" His friend, Tom Russell, loomed over him, his usual sanguine self apparently going about the predictable routines of drinking, wenching, and cards, not necessarily in that order, but typical evening fare for a gentleman seeking diversion.

"Am I?" Jeremy returned, taking a sip from his glass.

"God yes, man! You're veritably eking waves of blue mouldies from your person." Russell took a seat. "I hope it's not catching," he said warily.

Jeremy grinned at his friend. Russell had a clever way of turning any situation into amusement.

"I didn't know you were in. Business demands?"

"You could say so." Jeremy poured a glass and slid it to Russell.

"I'm surprised to see you in here at this hour of the night. It's early, for you." Russell eyed the bottle of scotch suspiciously. "No slippery pleasures to entertain you this eve?"

"Done that already." Jeremy looked over and shrugged, thinking it hadn't been all that entertaining, really.

"Well then, if you've had a dose of quim, you might look a bit more pleased, I'd think. What the hell's wrong with you?"

"Oh, nothing that a suitable wife and heir won't cure," he remarked dryly.

"Is Sir Rodney tightening the noose? Giving ultimatums?"

"I'm afraid so, Russell. I need to embrace matrimony and get said partner knapped. The sooner, the better. That's the gist of it."

"I s'pose," Russell said thoughtfully. "Don't let my father get wind of your predicament though," he warned. "He'll have Georgina foisted on you before you realize what's done."

That got his attention. "Georgina, your baby sister?"

"Yessss, but she's not a baby anymore, Greymont."

"She is out?"

Russell snorted in the affirmative. "I'd say so. She's already one and twenty, and her birthday comes January next."

Jeremy conjured up his memories of her as Russell prattled on.

"Georgie's never shown an interest in marrying though. She hates our father's meddlesome pushes toward the altar. Pater is quite determined to see her wed though. Says she's wild as hell, roaming about the countryside like a gypsy. He doesn't approve of her sporting habits either. Thinks a husband and babies will settle her." Russell shrugged. "But I think he just wants to be rid of her so he doesn't have to be reminded..." Russell frowned and trailed off.

"Reminded?"

"Yes. I think so. She looks so much like our mother now that she's grown a woman. She is a reminder of what he's lost," Russell said, eyes flickering left.

"Well, that's not her fault she looks like your mother, is it? And what is wrong with her sporting habits?" Jeremy asked, suddenly interested in this conversation.

He recalled Georgina Russell as a young girl. She had always been there when he'd visited Oakfield, loved to ride horses and shoot at targets, for he had seen her do both on many occasions. He knew she liked to draw as well. He could envision her with sketchbook in hand, observing and then rendering nature skillfully in charcoal. Blonde, pretty, quiet, and fiercely independent was how he pictured her. Intelligent, not silly and empty-headed like most girls of society. It had been years since he'd seen her, and Jeremy had to admit he wanted to know what she was like now.

"Nothing. At least I don't think so. Georgie is lovely—a free spirit, she's not going to sit inside embroidering cushions all day long and be happy about it. Our mother died when she was still a child, and Pater never did pay much attention to anything after

Mater left us. He'll see Georgie married and off his hands whether she likes it or not."

"Has anyone offered for her?"

"There is one, but he is odious. You know Lord Pellton?"

"Gawd! Please not him!" Jeremy did not temper his disgust. "A bloody degenerate that one, and far too old for her!" The thought of that reprobate slithering over the nubile body of Georgina Russell made him ill. What a deplorable waste of a perfectly fine woman. Jeremy actually shuddered at the vision that popped into his head.

Tom Russell chuckled. "She flat out refused. Caused a huge uproar in the household and has practically been kept under house arrest since. Our father and Pellton went to university together. Pater thinks she should be honored and keeps trying to convince her to agree to the marriage. He says if she won't take Pellton, then she must do her duty and assent to another just as suitable, for he means to have her settled as soon as possible."

"Well, your sister must have some sense if she refused Pellton. He is a sodding pig."

"True that, Greymont." Russell stroked his chin thoughtfully before his eyes lit up in inspiration. "I know! Why don't you marry her? That would make us brothers." He arched his brows at Jeremy, directing his gaze to below the waist. "You'd have to curb that whore-pipe of yours mind you. She is my sister after all. I don't know how well she'd take to your proclivities—"

Jeremy just gaped at his friend. His face must have told a story of such surprise that Russell had to pause, a wide grin settling in on his square jaw. Russell was clearly amused by his own bright idea.

Jeremy kept quiet and absorbed the suggestion even though he had no intentions of curbing anything he liked to do, now or in the future.

Russell babbled on happily, "You will have done your duty to your family, my father will get his wish, and Georgie would be far happier with you, I just know it!" He clapped Jeremy hard between the shoulder blades. "See, my friend, I have solved your problem for you!"

Jeremy's drink sloshed over the rim of his glass from the force of the blow to his back. The oaken tang of spirits wafted up his nose in a way that soothed. "I never took you for much of a schemer, Russell. And your cleverness exceeds the limits of most persons—you just act the idiot as a ruse."

"My friend, I cannot deny your charge. It suits me. I find it ever so much fun to go around being cleverer than people think I am." Tom tipped his glass in a salute and drained the scotch.

During their card play, Jeremy decided to accept Tom Russell's invitation to Oakfield for a shooting party. Or at least he used the call as his guise. His friend's proposition had intrigued him greatly. Now that the seed had been planted, Jeremy wanted to go right away.

The more he thought of Georgina Russell, the more he could picture her as the perfect candidate for matrimony. She came from a good family, would bring a respectable dowry, not too young, not too old, attractive, relatives he liked, and from what Russell said, still a lover of the outdoors, so she probably wouldn't mind skipping the endless social battlefield of London high society. That fact alone would elevate her in his esteem. She sounded like a pearl to him.

He would go and assess the situation, see her again, get to know her better. Truth be told, she caught his eye at only sixteen years old. Jeremy remembered how appealing he found her then, even before she'd grown up. What would she be like now? How would she find him? he wondered. Might she like him?

Yes, this was good. Georgina Russell... For the first time, Jeremy felt the glimmer of hope.

# CHAPTER TWO

Georgina breathed in the fresh air, detecting the earthy scent of rain seeping from the clouds. Just being out of the house felt a relief. The stark gloom of Oakfield's interior was oppressive enough, but being confined and having to recall her shame was more than she could bear today.

Her father never let her forget it. Trying to marry her off to the first man who made an offer was his way of making reparation to her. It didn't feel like reparation though. It felt like punishment for something she had not asked for, but had been laid upon her like a curse. She felt cursed in truth. She believed it. Why else would such a thing have happened to her?

Horrifying as it was, there were times she could still feel his hands groping her, the smell of his breath panting at her, the pull of her dress ripping under his hands, the weight of him, the taste of paralyzing terror in her throat. The worst had been the words. The things he'd said when he—

Georgina hugged her arms and shuddered. At least being outside felt—clean. The creek ran full before her. Its fresh current bubbled smoothly over pebbles rolled flat by innumerable surges of water and much time. She realized she would have to wade across.

The heavy air seemed to swirl with the anticipation of impending rain as she sat down to remove her slippers and stockings. She wondered if she'd make it back before the drops actually started to fall. From the feel of things, she doubted it.

*Damn. No luck for me.* Papa would be all the more displeased with her when she came home drenched and muddy, she knew. There was nothing for it though. She could see no other option. Moving quickly, she hitched up her skirts and forded across the bubbling stream. Reaching the other side without mishap, she climbed the bank and sat down again so as to don her stockings and boots once more.

Stunned silent, Jeremy peered through the trees. He would have made his presence known had she not lifted her skirts and exposed her shapely legs at that very moment. He didn't consider himself much of an intellectual but certainly possessed intelligence enough to know that if Georgina knew he was there, she wouldn't be revealing her flesh to him, and he most certainly wanted to see her lovely display right now. In fact, he couldn't have torn his eyes away from the picture of her if he'd tried. His cock would have leapt out and growled at him if he'd lowered his eyes.

He found her very pleasing. Long, dark-blonde hair paired with a well-filled figure any man would appreciate. The color of her eyes was indiscernible to him though. From his distance he simply could not make them out and it annoyed him. Jeremy found that suddenly he wanted very much to know the color of her eyes.

Georgina had indeed grown up, and the years had been very good to her. She bore curves in all the right places. Curves he could make very good use of. Curves he could worship. Those were generous breasts for all her willowy height, tall for a woman, but built gracefully.

Jeremy held his breath as she lifted a pale limb and pulled on a stocking. He kept holding it when she secured the stocking with a pink garter, wrapped around the tapering flesh above her knee. He finally succumbed to the need for air, but breathed quietly so as not to miss the show when she repeated the exquisite act with the other leg.

*God, yes!* Georgina Russell had grown into quite a morsel. It would be a pleasant task to get an heir with her, indeed. Hopefully he'd need to work at it, or on her, for a long, long time!

She appealed to him all right. His hardening prick told him so. He shifted his weight to relieve the uncomfortable tightening holding sway over his body.

Cool autumn rain began to plop down in slow, fat drops as he made his way silently back to his horse. He would move on and wait for her to emerge from the wood where she would sight him on the road.

The squall which had sprung up escalated as the minutes ticked by. Jeremy could tell the moment she spotted him though. She slowed noticeably as if unsure whether to continue in his direction.

Pulling his horse to a stop, he dismounted. "Miss Georgina Russell, I believe." He inclined his head in greeting. "Do you remember me? I am——"

"I remember you, sir." She cut him off, eying him stonily.

An attempt at lightheartedness compelled him to ask, "What's my name then?"

"You are Mr. Greymont, my brother's friend." Her eyes fluttered down and away from him, but he got a good look. They were golden eyes, glowing amber, and liquid, like the smooth

Scotch whisky he favored, swirling in a cut glass.

"Well done, Miss Georgina. I am just on my way to your house now. I've been invited for the—"

"Shooting party," she interrupted, her eyes returning back to him, but still so very solemn. That was twice now she had stopped him mid-speech. This girl before him was wary, on edge. If he didn't know better, he'd say she seemed almost afraid of him. She was a wholly different person than he recalled, greatly changed. Georgina had grown up most fair for truth, but in her manner she had definitely altered.

"Please allow me to take you home on my horse. Samson here is so strong he won't even notice he's carrying the both of us." Jeremy reached up a hand to give the great horse an affectionate pat on the neck. "He's gentle as a lamb around ladies."

"No, sir." She shook her head gently, making the cool rain dripping off her nose look absurd.

"I must insist. This rain is piss—" He cleared his throat and tried again, cursing himself for speaking so coarsely. "Um, the rain shower, it's quite fierce at the moment. You realize you shouldn't subject yourself to the wet chill longer than need be. Think of your health."

She looked hesitant, unsure, shifting her weight as she stood there sizing his offer. Probably sizing him up as well.

He knew the uncontrollable urge to convince her. "I intend to get out of this rain myself, Miss Georgina, and I cannot do that if you won't come with me. I'll not leave you here alone on the road in a downpour," he told her determinedly. "Come with me." Jeremy reached out his hand to her. "You know who I am. It's all right."

She stared at him, her eyes darting, as if making a decision to trust him or bolt back into the woods. *Just like a nervous filly.* She bit the corner of her bottom lip, probably having no idea how charming she looked in her indecision. Her lips were dark pink and full, puckered at the corner of her mouth where her teeth came together with flesh in between. *How do those lips taste, I wonder? Will I ever know? I want to know.*

Jeremy smiled gently, bobbing his arm that extended the hand. "You are safe with me."

Those were the magic words apparently.

She stepped forward.

*Good girl.* As she put a wavering palm into his, he felt warmth in their handclasp through the leather of his glove. The elegant bones of her hand fit nicely into his, he thought.

"Let me help you up," he warned before reaching for her waist. He felt her flinch slightly when his hands gripped and lifted her. Knowing her to be an accomplished rider, he assumed her confidence in finding her seat, but she didn't show much surety in her manner. He observed trembling as she bent her knee around the pommel, fashioning it an impromptu sidesaddle.

"I won't be too secure this way, I'm afraid," she murmured.

"Not to worry. I'll see that you stay on." He mounted up. Seated behind her and off the saddle, he had to draw close to her back in order to fit the both of them. She tensed at the brush of his body. Jeremy took hold of the reins, his arms reaching around her and coming to rest against her sides, level with her breasts. He clicked at Samson, and the horse moved out, seemingly unconcerned at the extra passenger.

Inhaling, he caught the essence of eglantine wafting up from her neck. The gentle scent went straight to his brain, and from there, his prick. *Not now, you idiot. A cockstand pressing into her arse won't win you any favors!*

And oh, dear Lord! His mind went rampant with imaginings of her most certainly lovely *derrière* underneath all those skirts. And it presented mere inches from one whopping erection straining eagerly to get out. *Christ, help me!*

Keeping his wits clear enough to refrain from putting his lips onto her neck was easier said than done. Oh, how he wanted to. The image of her sitting on the bank, donning her stockings, danced still fresh in his mind. He remembered those gorgeous long legs of hers. He wanted to see them again. He wanted those legs wrapped around his hips when he buried his cock to the—

*Think of something else—think of something else—anything but that!*

"What finds you out today without your h–horse, Miss Georgina?" He really needed to rearrange himself. At the crotch.

"Why do you ask, Mr. Greymont?"

"Am I correct in remembering you to be an avid rider? I don't recall you walking when you could ride instead."

"Your memory is sound, sir." She sighed before continuing. "Were it an option, I would indeed have ridden today."

"Is your horse unfit?"

"No. Nothing so simple as that. My horse waits in the stables and wonders why she's been not been taken out."

She grew quiet then, and Jeremy knew enough not to push. He waited for her to explain.

"My riding has been restricted by my father. By seeking to deprive me of those things that I value, he hopes to bend me to agreement in a matter I cannot bear to think of, let alone consent to."

"Ah, a familial dispute. I've learned it is best not to get entangled in such prickly concerns as family squabbling, especially those that involve ultimatums." But this was precisely his reason for being here, now wasn't it? His grandfather had given him an ultimatum.

"You are exceptionally wise, Mr. Greymont, I assure you," she replied wryly. "In fact, I must beg a favor from you. It is in your best interest for truth."

"You intrigue me, Miss Georgina." He leaned a little closer as he spoke into her ear, swallowing so hard she must have heard the gulping sound he made. "And the favor?"

"You must drop me off before we lead up to the house. Papa will make a huge fuss about the fact I went out walking, let alone being caught in a rainstorm. Trust me, you don't want to enmesh yourself, Mr. Greymont."

*Yes I do.* "I might be persuaded to grant your favor if you give me one in return," he bargained.

"What do you want?"

*You splayed out naked in the bed underneath me.* "I will accept the simple promise of a favor for now. When I think of something, you must grant it forthwith," he said teasingly.

"A favor within reason, Mr. Greymont," she whispered stiffly in front of him.

"Of course, Miss Georgina. I strive to remain a gentleman in a lady's presence. You should have no worries on that account." Jeremy told himself he was truthful about the "striving" part at least, as he savored the idea of the favor he might win from her.

"This is a good place to stop." She indicated with her head toward the edge of trees. "I'll go on ahead, and if you'll give me a few moments to make my way, I'd be grateful." She stiffened her back, anxious again, waiting for him to do as she asked.

Pulling Samson to a gentle stop, he offered, "Let me assist you." He leapt down and held up his arms to grip her. She hesitated, lowering her golden eyes before leaning into his strong hands. They latched on to her waist firmly, deft in bringing her to standing on the ground. He hated to take his hands away. He wished he could lower them to her hips instead and pull her right up against him so he could feel her close-up. But if he did, she'd sense a whole lot more of him than a young virgin should. And the shock to her maidenly sensibilities probably wouldn't earn him any marks either, at least not good ones.

He had a lot to learn about virgins, he knew. Best to start now, he thought wryly, having never imagined a time in his life when such lessons would be necessary.

Jeremy looked down at her, willing her eyes to lift so he could read her. She kept them downward though, her long lashes curling delicately over cheekbones sprinkled with raindrops. *Just lovely.*

She had a scar on her left cheekbone that curved up almost to the corner of her eye. It wasn't large and it wasn't horrible, but it could be seen clearly, as if to validate her humanity—the absence of perfection in her skin. Something had hurt her in that place, and she'd bled just like every other person did, and when the skin had healed, something was left behind—a mark to remind that everyone was just flesh and blood and bone.

His hand lifted, seemingly all on its own with the need to touch where she'd been hurt and to brush the rain on her skin. What would it feel like? Pulling back just in time, shocked at how close he'd come to pawing her, he forced some words out of his mouth. "You'd better get yourself out of the rain. I'd hate to think of you becoming ill."

She nodded slowly.

"Until later then, Miss Georgina," he offered, hoping that "later" wouldn't be too long in coming.

She curtsied elegantly then raised up to face him. "Mr. Greymont, thank you for your assistance, and the favor." Next she turned to Samson and held out her hand. When the beast nuzzled forward, she stroked the gray velvet of his nose. "And thank you, noble Samson, for carrying me home."

Those eyes of hers did him in. Jeremy got lost. He knew it the instant they lifted. Unable to speak, he just stood there, watching her talk to his horse, very happily waylaid in those pools of glittering gold.

"I am in your debt." Turning abruptly, she fled the copse of trees, hurrying toward the rear entrance of the house.

Jeremy didn't know if that last part was meant for him or for Samson, but he didn't much care. Her voice mesmerized him.

Laced with a hint of huskiness and emoting pure sensuality in the most innocent way, the sound drew him in. He wanted to just sit and listen to her talk. For hours. And he didn't want her to go yet.

Jeremy sucked in air as a stab hit him in the chest and he had to watch her leave. Eglantine still hung in the wet air where she'd just stood.

Georgina displayed herself as lovely and alluring and proper. Jeremy felt a definite attraction, but there was something that didn't ring true with her situation. He knew this without a shadow of a doubt. Georgina Russell was not as he remembered her. Neither spirited nor confident. Something plagued her, a burden of some kind. He would describe her as an anxious beauty now. Jeremy was sure he didn't imagine it.

"We'll have to just find out what is bothering the pretty lady, won't we, Samson?" he said to his horse.

Samson nickered and nudged Jeremy on the shoulder.

# CHAPTER THREE

*And when we think we lead, we are most led.*
—Lord Byron, *The Two Foscari* (1821)

Georgina shivered in her clinging, wet dress. Her whole body tingled, and she registered her breath coming faster than it should. She had known him precisely the moment she'd spied him on the road. *Jeremy Greymont.*

Here at Oakfield. And why was he here? He hadn't come for a visit in years. An uncomfortable stuttering, emanating from the region of her chest, seized her for a second before it could be willed away.

Just as charming as she remembered, and handsome. Not handsome by society's standards though. He carried too much of a roughness for that distinction, from the intensity of his gaze to the unshaven shadow he wore. His clear blue eyes showed much more lurking underneath that manly, rugged visage of unsaid wants, mystery, a darkness, something a little wild and unchained in their depths. His sandy-brown hair was a bit longer than he used to wear it, unruly and falling over a heavy brow, complementing those azure eyes of his perfectly.

For all his refined manners and dress, he possessed a certain *bons vivants,* a hale quality that surged from him with every gesture. He was male strength and power all wrapped up in a very tall, broad-shouldered, muscular package.

And that voice of his! He spoke with an irreverent drawl that gave off a clear devil-may-care attitude but somehow managed to refrain from bridging into disrespect. Georgina found his manner of speaking to be charming. Too charming for his own good, probably.

She rang for a bath and perused the gowns in her wardrobe, ticking through them rather harshly until she rested her fingers on a shimmering sea-green silk taffeta. She had yet to wear the dress. It had been ordered before and delivered after. Georgina remembered dates like that now. Like every event in her life now measured against that one experience in time.

She laid out the gown carefully on her bed. The color looked nice—watery and cool, like the rain today that had wet them both. She shook her head to free the vision but went right back to thoughts of Jeremy Greymont anyway, despite her desire to steer clear of him.

As if charm needed to be a factor of consideration for him. She could not imagine he lacked feminine admiration. No, that man wouldn't even need to employ charm. He'd have a plethora of ladybirds swooning over him without ever having to open his mouth. Jeremy Greymont was very pleasing in her view. She'd have thought he'd be married by now, what with his eventual title and wealth. The women must have to be beat back with a stick.

In the saddle with him had been a struggle. The silence deafening over the creak of the tack, the clop of Samson's hooves, and the soft whisper of rain.

Georgina's every sense had been heightened by being pressed so close to him. His body had been hard like marble, but warm. And he smelled good. Being up in that saddle next to Jeremy Greymont had felt strangely safe though, like nothing bad could ever happen.

"Your coat is a right mess, sir." The valet took his master's coat with a wince.

"Please don't fuss, Myers. We both know you live for the joy of putting my clothes to rights." Jeremy unbuttoned his waistcoat and then his fine, white shirt, shrugged out of both of them at the same time, and let them drop. "How was the voyage?"

Jeremy didn't miss Myers's patient sigh as he retrieved the garments from the floor. "It was satisfactory, sir. You could have spared yourself the rain had you rode in your coach."

"Ah, I could have, but am so very glad I did not ride with you in my coach," Jeremy said smugly.

"Sir?" Myers asked, distracted by the clothing in desperate need of his attentions, but responding anyway, as the loyal man he was.

"Nothing, Myers. Don't you worry your head about it. Just lay me a hot bath and work your magic on my dinner dress for tonight. There is a lady here I wish to impress."

Myers ignored him. Probably didn't even hear most of what Jeremy had said. It didn't matter. Myers would fit him out smartly even if it was raining mud at a country frolic on the heath.

"Georgie, look who's come to visit!" Tom Russell called his sister over to where they stood. "Surely you will remember my friend, Jeremy Greymont, from Hallborough Park. He's come for the shooting." Tom turned to Jeremy. "Greymont, my sister, Georgina, now all grown up."

Jeremy bowed, unable to keep the teasing from his voice.

"Miss Georgina, how do you do? I must say, I did not recognize you, *so* different you look from the last time we met."

If he thought she looked lovely glistening in raindrops, he was even more impressed with her fitted into a marvelous green dress, the bodice of which caressed her breasts in the way his hands wanted to. Her rosy scent floated up his nose, calming and enticing at the same time.

"Mr. Greymont." She curtsied. "Welcome back to Oakfield." She lifted her face, sending him a silent "thank you" for keeping their meeting today in confidence.

He flashed a wink to let her know their secret was safe. A burst of gladness warmed him. He liked the idea that they were keeping secrets together, and the pretty smile she returned.

"Thank you for the welcome. I look forward to the restorative freshness of the country. London has many qualities, but I think most would agree that freshness is not among them."

"Do you live in London now, Mr. Greymont?"

"I split my time between Town and my home, Hallborough, along the coast in west Somerset."

"Can you spy the sea from your house?"

"Indeed. The view is quite stunning. Sometimes all the way to the Welsh coast across the channel if the sky is clear. It makes for quite a sight. The local artists find it a favorite scene to capture."

Jeremy liked that Georgina seemed so interested in his home, and all of a sudden, a vision of her standing out on the second-floor balcony, staring out to sea, popped into his head. He could see her dress blowing back, framing her legs, and her long hair whipping in the ocean breeze. And she looked so very natural standing there on his balcony, in that pretty imaginary vision. Like she belonged. He took a sip of wine to give himself something to do, for he suddenly felt very self-conscious of every word he spoke and every movement he made.

"Well, it sounds very beautiful, Mr. Greymont. You paint a

nice picture of your home for me to imagine."

"Do you still sketch, Miss Georgina? I do remember you liked to draw at one time."

She smiled at him. Not a huge smile, but one of genuine warmth. So warm, in fact, he felt it, too. Her smile warmed him.

"You have a good memory, sir. And yes, I do still."

That lovely warmth of feeling Jeremy had enjoyed so well dissipated just as quickly as it came once the announcement for dinner was made.

One of the other guests pushed forward to claim the honor of escorting Georgina to the table. She had no choice but to assent.

Lord Edgar Pellton, Baron, from someplace or another in Avon, was indeed a guest here and sniffing after Miss Georgina Russell in hopes of making her his next baroness. The man was rich, titled, and in need of an heir. He'd been married before, but lost his wife in childbirth, along with an infant daughter. It was said that Pellton didn't mourn the loss of his wife for even a day, angry that she hadn't seen fit to give him a son, and returned immediately to his notorious ways with those who shared in his penchant for orgiastic bacchanals. Behavior quite ridiculous for a man far into his fourth decade, in Jeremy's opinion.

After his arrival, he'd unfortunately discovered Lord Pellton's attendance for the shooting party along with him.

*What a goddamn letch!*

Jeremy watched Pellton stride up to Georgina, his waistcoat buttons straining against the bulge at his middle. His features were sharp and mean, like a rat trying to steal from the larder, wriggling in where he didn't belong and having a go at taking something he didn't deserve. Pellton sure as hell didn't deserve someone as lovely as Georgina Russell. Jeremy could scream that from the mountaintops with undisputable certainty. And Jeremy was positive he detected a slight shudder from Georgina when Pellton offered his arm. And he couldn't imagine how Georgina's father would even consider sacrificing her to such a beast. How those two disparate men had maintained a friendship was beyond Jeremy's fathoming.

Jeremy tugged at his shirt cuff and set his jaw as the uncomfortable stirrings of jealousy coiled inside him, and he didn't feel at all relaxed sitting down to dinner, despite the time he'd prepared for it and Myers's efforts with the excellent new suit he'd worn.

To be placed next to Georgina was a small consolation. Jeremy looked at her hands, so finely made, and remembered the feel of holding one in a clasp. The moment she'd stepped forward and agreed to let him take her home, there had been firm strength in those elegant lady hands of hers.

"I trust you are no worse for wear after your very wet walk this afternoon? You certainly don't look it," he said admiringly. "Were you able to return undetected?"

"I went unnoticed, Mr. Greymont, and able to avoid...um...trouble, for a time at least." She directed her eyes, still downcast, to the dinner companion on her other side—one Lord Pellton, who, at this very moment, nearly drooled over his plate as he stared most luridly at the bodice of her lovely green gown.

Jeremy found Pellton's open staring crudely offensive and thought it would be a miracle if he managed to get through the whole fortnight of the party without sticking his boot up the idiot's arse.

"I am glad then, Miss Georgina, that I had opportunity to assist you today." He willed her to meet his eyes. When she finally did, he spoke carefully. "Something I would be honored to do for you, anytime."

Georgina returned a slight nod before lowering her amber eyes once again. "Thank you. You are a kind gentleman." She got quiet for a moment. "Your horse, Samson, is a beautiful creature."

*So are you.* "I'll tell him you said so, the next time we talk," he returned.

"Do you converse with your horse, Mr. Greymont?"

"All the time, Miss Georgina. I find him the most sensible gent of all my acquaintance."

"I know what you mean." She gave him the briefest of smiles and grew quiet once more.

Jeremy thought she looked sad, and he wondered what had happened to make her thus. He could admit that he found Georgina Russell very attractive and would be more than willing to bed her, but strangely, he wanted more than just a tumble. He found it suddenly essential to see her really smile, to have her golden eyes smoldering at him, teasing him. He wanted her to be happy. He wanted to be the one who made her happy, something he'd never cared about with anyone ever before. And if Jeremy knew one thing it was this: the fair Georgina Russell did not hold happiness in her heart.

# CHAPTER FOUR

*She fair, divinely fair, fit love for gods.*
—John Milton, *Paradise Lost* (1667)

Gold and yellow, a smattering of vibrant orange-red, filtered above her head. The leaves were beginning to reveal their colors. A faint breeze rattled through the autumn pendants, making them shimmer in the light.

A beautiful sight, but Georgina could not appreciate any of it. Not the fine September afternoon, nor the glorious color showing amongst the leaves. She was miserable and didn't see any way to escape her present problems. The argument with Papa this morning had been awful. He would not give up on persuading her to accept Lord Pellton's offer of marriage.

*"A peer of the realm offers marriage to you, Georgina. A title, status, security, and you would decry all of it in favor of rusticating into spinsterhood for all to ponder why? I'll not allow such a thing, my daughter! This house will not fall to scandalous gossip. Never!"*

Papa was ashamed of her and could hardly bear to look her in the eyes. Of course he was. She *had* shamed her family. Marrying her off would prove the easiest way for him to be rid of her. If he could sweep her under the rug with a good marriage, the Russell name would remain upstanding.

But marriage to Lord Pellton would not be good. Not for her. More like a nightmare.

Papa had told her this morning that Pellton was tiring of her reticence and would likely withdraw his offer if she didn't show him some encouragement. Georgina had responded that he'd be wise to withdraw for encouragement from her would not be forthcoming in this lifetime or any other.

To punish her for not yielding, her father had yet again forbidden her to ride, so she had to make do with a walk on the grounds instead.

Georgina wasn't trying to be difficult or make trouble, but she just couldn't bring herself to do it. Lord Pellton was a lecher. She hated the way he looked at her, like he dreamed of her unclothed—and vulnerable. And she didn't believe he would be a kind husband.

A shudder passed through her body. She imagined he thought of the ways he would like to have her, and she would have to submit to it because he needed an heir, and it would be his right to do as he wished. He probably wouldn't leave her alone until she produced one. And to live with him and call him husband? The very idea made her physically sick.

Truth be told, he frightened her. Something about him reminded her of the other one, bringing back a horror she didn't fully remember, but still only wished to forget.

Lord Pellton didn't see her as a person. She knew that much by the way he treated her and looked at her. To him, she was just a thing to be used until she provided what he wanted. She couldn't do it, she just couldn't. She was ruined now anyway. Georgina was no fool. She knew herself. She was well aware that marriage to a man like Pellton would…kill her.

Georgina did not hear the sound of boots upon the ground,

well, not at first. She was awash in troublesome thoughts of her dilemma that didn't seem to diminish the more she pondered.

*Sweet Christ.* Jeremy took in the view of her from behind and knew he was in trouble. More accurately, that in a few moments would be making a complete horse's arse out of himself.

Sitting in a tree swing that looked like it had hung for many years from the great oak, Georgina absently rocked from side to side, using her foot as an anchor. Her dark golden hair had been bundled into a soft mass with plenty of errant curls escaping the attempt at containment. He wanted to pluck out the pins that held those locks. He wanted to see it tumble down her back and frame her face.

Then he would take a curl and lift it to his nose so he could fill his head with the soft whisperings of eglantine. After that, he would fist handfuls of the silky stands and pull her to his lips, in effect trapping her in his embrace. From there he would plunder that appealing mouth of hers, using his tongue to taste and claim the warm depths. Envisioning her mouth caused him to imagine his cock being surrounded by her sweet lips. He could just see them closing in around the head of his prick, right before she slid him to the back of her throat and sucked him dr—

Her head whipped around to glare at him. "Mr. Greymont? You startled me! I did not know you were there."

Georgina's indignant reprimand splashed his warm, erotic fantasy with drops of icy, cold reality, killing the thing instantly.

*Caught red-handed, you bloody idiot! Go ahead. Now is the time to make that horse's arse out of yourself!*

"I—I was walking back from the shooting and saw you," he sputtered. "You looked so peaceful in your musings there in the swing." He cleared his throat. "I—I was reluctant to disturb you."

*Like you're doing right now. Fool!*

She stared at him, saying nothing.

"Miss Georgina." He bowed. "I apologize for the disruption and for startling you. Please forgive me."

He gave a slight shake to his head, hoping it might clear his brain of all the wicked thoughts. It didn't. Those naughty fantasies weren't even nudged slightly down and out.

"It is a small thing, sir. Consider yourself forgiven." She turned back the way she had been facing before, her backside to him once again.

Yes… That lovely bum of hers, resting lusciously atop the seat of the swing, just begging to be stroked. He would use both hands to grip the cheeks as he slid up to—

"Mr. Greymont," she admonished, "are you still there?"

His rampant conjuring interrupted for a second time, he jerked. *Good God, man, get a hold of yourself!*

"Yes, I—I—I was just about to ask if I may escort you back to the house, Miss Georgina. It's probably not the best for you to be out here with the shooting going on. Yes? Please—please allow me." He came around to the front of the swing and offered his arm.

Georgina eyed him thoroughly, probably wondering what flustered him and why he kept stammering like a half-wit. God, if she knew the truth, she wouldn't think him "kind" or a "gentleman." She'd most likely smack him in the chops. The idea of her trying to cuff him brought on a smile and a rush of more erotic fantasies. Of how he'd trap her hands and turn her so he could bend her over and get to her from behind—

*Stop! You are such a bastard.*

Thankfully the sweet Georgina could not read his naughty thoughts, for she smiled at him. Not much of a smile, more of a rueful expression than anything, but he was beginning to know this was typical of her. Whenever she did grace him with a smile, it was really only half-beam, and as arousing as hell.

In fact, everything about Georgina aroused him. She affected him profoundly. His body got tight and hard, his tongue tangled in the most annoying way, prohibiting coherent speech, and yet, he could not keep away regardless of how foolish he behaved in her presence. He was drawn like a bee to a glade of sweet blossoms.

"Very well, sir. I am past my time anyway and may expect certain chastisement from my papa for going out in the first place." She got up from the swing and took his arm.

He gulped and cleared his throat again. "Surly not, Miss Georgina. Your father probably just wants to keep you safe from harm, yes?"

He loved the way she felt so soft next to him. He could smell her, too, and again the scent affected him viscerally, his kecks becoming uncomfortably cramped in the crotch.

The sarcasm rang clear in her answer. "Things are not always what they seem, Mr. Greymont. Remember that."

"Now that sounds downright ominous, Miss Georgina."

"It does, I know. You are right, sir. But still, it would be prudent to tread carefully, for your own sake."

"I consider myself duly warned then." He grinned saucily at her. "I think you are trying to scare me off, but you should know that I don't panic easily, especially when my mind is set."

"So you say, Mr. Greymont." She curtsied. "Thank you for the escort." She turned abruptly and left him.

Jeremy watched her go, unable to redirect his eyes. The allure of her hips swaying in cadence with her gown caused his cock to twitch. Like the thing wanted to chase after her. Which, of course, was spot-on really. As he rearranged himself so he could walk without limping, he thought about what she'd told him. *"Things aren't always what they seem."*

*Isn't that the cry of the day!*

# CHAPTER FIVE

*Bring me my bow of burning gold:*
*Bring me my arrows of desire:*

—**William Blake,** *Milton* **(1804)**

Rainy weather was fine for shooting birds, but rather a
hindrance to the pursuit of nature walks, rides, and
other activities a young lady might prefer to
embroidery or crocheting lace. Georgina needed to get outside and
into the fresh air. Three days of being forced indoors had left her in
a less than easy mood, and although needlework had its place, she
was profoundly sick of it.

Moving determinedly toward the clearing, she could see the
target that the gamekeeper, Mr. Alberts, had set up for her as she'd
requested. The bows and extra equipment would also be ready for
her. The gruff gamekeeper had always been kind to Georgina,
doing little favors for her way back when she was small even,
when he knew she would like it. She appreciated his efforts, for
she knew Mr. Alberts to be very busy with the shooting going on.
More than once, he'd lured Lord Pellton away when the man had
come trailing after her during house parties like this one. Georgina
made a note to procure some of the special tobacco he liked for his
pipe.

She threw up her hand to shield herself when a pheasant flew out from the underbrush right in front of her. The start made her heart pound. She hoped the men wouldn't venture in this direction for the hunt. Surely this little glade was far enough away from the birding going on that she wouldn't be bothered. It abutted a ring of sycamore which melted into light forest beyond it and was one of Georgina's favorite places to shoot her bow. But what if all the birds had fled to this quieter sanctuary and the hunters decided to follow? It would not be safe here in the glade if they did.

Georgina shrugged and continued further on the path, rationalizing that Mr. Alberts would remember she had arranged to come here and could warn the shooters off if they decided to come this way.

A flash of gold flickered in movement directly ahead at her ultimate destination of target shooting. She heard the whoosh of an arrow splitting the air. Georgina realized that she was not alone, and for the second time, started, freezing in step. She felt every thump of her heart, clamoring deep inside her chest, and hated the fact that every stray sound or movement made her jump like a mouse. Now. Would she be like this for the rest of her life?

Someone had preceded her to this clearing. Georgina slowed and moved forward cautiously, staying quiet and out of sight.

It was a man. And he was using her bow to shoot at the target Mr. Alberts had set out for her. Or attempting to try at least. The lack of hits could attest that the man was a terrible shot.

Drawing closer, Georgina was able to discern exactly who had horned in on her sport. Jeremy Greymont. There in his dark-gold jacket, a bright-green neck-cloth, his hair a bit tousled, standing out as a tall twist of contrasting light against the dun of the landscape. Georgina stilled herself so she could observe him in action. Watching Mr. Greymont sight up the bow, with possibly the worst form she'd ever seen, was amusing. So much so, it distracted her from questioning why he was even here at all. He should be off shooting with the other men, shouldn't he?

"That's not how you sight a bow," she announced in a loud voice.

He snapped his head around, the blue of his eyes catching the light.

"You're holding it wrong." Georgina could see him flushed red in the face as she came forward.

"Am I?"

"Yes, you are. An English longbow should be held in tight to the shoulder, with your stance perpendicular, and a bracer employed to steady the bow arm."

"I've had no proper instruction." He dropped his head in greeting. "Miss Georgina, I deduce that you must have requested this equipment be made ready for your exercise today, and here I have intruded upon your arranged activity." He gave a sheepish grin. "Forgive me. The thing is, I've always admired archery, but for myself never took it up or got taught the standard form..." He trailed off, his voice faltering a bit, the following silence awkward.

Georgina stayed quiet and took in the scene.

Mr. Greymont must have felt compelled to cover the silence because after a moment he went right back to justifying exactly why he was here and not off shooting at birds with the men. "My shotgun jammed. I thought to give up birding for the day, and upon my return came upon the glade here, saw the bow and target, and couldn't help being curious. Before I knew it, I was—"

"Taking up my bow? Trying your hand?" Georgina answered for him. The strangest inclination to rescue Mr. Greymont from his own embarrassment surprised her. Why in the world should she care if he was embarrassed or not? But for whatever reason, it bothered her seeing him struggle to explain himself.

"Yes. You have well and caught me at it, Miss Georgina."

Georgina stifled the urge to laugh at him. Mr. Greymont standing in the glade, arrows strewn everywhere but in the rings of the target, his slightly rumpled appearance in perfect harmony with the scene of destruction, reminded her of a child attempting to hide a stolen sweet, with the evidence smeared all over his face. The picture of him was too much. A smile cracked, and then a giggle escaped. Georgina had to cover her mouth to keep from losing control. She didn't want to be rude.

"Ah, I amuse you."

"In this instance, sir, I am afraid, yes." Georgina bit the inside of her lip to still the persistent urge to laugh.

Mr. Greymont grinned back at her though, a naughty look that told her he wasn't all that bothered by her amusement at his expense. "I s'pose I deserve it. I am, after all, a dreadful shot, the proof displayed for all to witness, my dismal talent with a bow." He held out his arms wide. "I assure you, I can do much better with a gun." He shook his head back and forth slowly and released another grin. "I plead mercy, Miss Georgina."

"And mercy you shall have, Mr. Greymont. I'll never disclose my knowledge of your...ah, skills, as a bowman." Georgina cocked a brow at him. "But perhaps you'd better take a brief lesson in the basics of proper form, you know, should you find your curiosity getting the better of you again at some other house party you might attend in future."

"Miss Georgina, I heartily accept your offer. How do we begin?" he asked, far too easily.

"You want me to instruct you, Mr. Greymont? What say you I am no better at hitting the mark than you are?"

"I would be honored to take any bits of wisdom you care to scatter my way, Miss Georgina. And I know you're skilled because I remember you shooting at targets when you were just a girl. Your accuracy was true then, and you've had years and years to hone your talent. I'd bet my horse you're a crack shot by now. At the very least, a Lady Paramount worthy of master status, or in your case, mistress." He winked at her.

Mr. Greymont had a naughty streak. What was he playing at? Could an educated man really be so inept at a sport that must be compulsory for someone of his class? He knew enough to know that a "Lady Paramount" was the person appointed to preside at tournaments and had ultimate say. And he definitely looked a little too eager in Georgina's opinion. Smiling at her, waiting on her answer, like he'd anticipated her offer before she'd made it. He held out his hand to her. The breeze rattled the leaves in the trees above them.

"No need to bet your magnificent Samson, Mr. Greymont. I'll do it."

Georgina deliberately clasped her hands behind her back, deciding that two could play at this game, whatever it was, and that sharing in some company could be no harm. It would even be a pleasant change to have a companion while she was out here shooting. Jeremy Greymont was safe.

"Before we can start, all these arrows must be collected first," she told him, her eyes missing nothing as she observed the scattered points. Jeremy caught another amused grin cracking from the corner of her mouth.

God, she was a delight to look at. With her hands clasped behind her back, the most pleasant result of lush breasts pushed forward as if in welcome was much admired. Today she was gowned in a rich brown velvet that wrapped around her lush curves like melted chocolate. He'd bet she tasted just as sweet as the decadent dessert if ever he could get his tongue anywhere onto her skin. The mere thought of tasting even a sliver of her sent the stuff behind the front flap of his kecks to throbbing. Whatever else was at issue between the two of them, Jeremy found himself hugely attracted to this woman. He wanted her.

"Mr. Greymont, I do believe you have emptied the quiver," she teased as she bent down to gather up points.

*I'd love to find my way into your quiver.*

"Have I? How many arrows to a quiver?" Jeremy kept his face straight as he asked the question, even though he knew the answer. No, he was enjoying this playful banter with Georgina Russell too much to come clean about his archery skills not being quite so terrible as he intimated. Jeremy wasn't being entirely truthful, but what harm was there in this? His gun *had* indeed jammed, and by chance he'd come upon her archery equipment laid at the ready. What better way to get to know Georgina than begging for help with his shooting technique?

So in the glade he'd waited until she'd arrived. Jeremy couldn't have just sat in the grass. He would've looked a tremendous sap, so he had shot arrows to fill the time while he waited for her to show up. With as little focus as possible. But with Georgina to help him, hopefully standing very close so he could breathe in her lovely scent some more, his bowman skills might take a swift turn for the better.

All in all, Jeremy would say that things were working out rather well. Today was the first time he'd seen Georgina cheerful and light. And Jeremy quickly decided that a smiling, happy Georgina was well worth any effort on his part.

"Two dozen fills a quiver, and not a hit among them!" she sang back at him.

The laugh Georgina had been suppressing up until now came forth with a clear burst into the autumn air of the glade. Jeremy could tell she had been trying to hold back from laughing outright at him, for she was a lady after all, but the happy sound of her was so lovely, Jeremy felt grateful to have been the person responsible for making it happen. Suddenly struck with the notion that her laughter was a gift, he paused for a moment. Strange. He shook off the sensation and kept retrieving arrows.

"Miss Georgina, I believe you are finding my lack of accuracy to be a great source of merriment. And actually, I did make a hit, but the arrow did not stick. It came off from the target."

"Ah, well, there's a name for a point that does that. It's called a—"

"Let me guess!" Jeremy blurted, holding up a hand to stop her. "You call it a bounder."

"No, not a bounder." Georgina shook her head slightly.

"A jumper then."

"Wrong again, Mr. Greymont." Her lips twitched.

"A springer? Tell me it's called a springer, Miss Georgina." Jeremy was enjoying himself too much to stop.

"Well, you are certainly full of creative ideas, I'll give you that, Mr. Greymont, but I am afraid you are still incorrect. The proper term is 'bouncer.'"

"Ah, bouncer. Right. Bouncer makes good sense, for the arrow bounces off the target without holding fast. Very good."

Georgina gave him what could only be described as a tolerant look. "So, if we were to assess your performance thus far, we could say you had one bouncer and the all rest were a miss."

*I'm here alone with you, and I'd call that a direct hit.* "But you won't tell on me, will you?" Jeremy said knowingly, loving the fact that they could share in another secret.

"No. I will not expose you as I've already said." Her eyes swept down to the grass.

"Why won't you?" Not understanding why he asked her such a thing, Jeremy just knew he wanted something from her. A gesture on his behalf. What? He couldn't really say, and the question left his lips as easily as a spot of fluff pulled by the wind.

Georgina blushed beautifully before answering. "Because, I think you are—"

She paused and lifted her eyes to meet his. Jeremy felt his body tense in anticipation of what she would say of him. The snapping sound of leaves rocked by the wind filled the silence.

"—in great need of my help, Mr. Greymont!"

And then the beautiful Georgina laughed. A sound not loud or boastful, but soft and sweet and gentle, like a caress down his neck that travelled straight to his heart and warmed it, spreading slowly from the inside out.

*You have that right, Miss Georgina Russell. I desperately need your help.*

Jeremy bowed with a flourish before stepping forward to hand over the last collected arrow. "That's the last, and I am ready for my lesson."

He made sure to get a brush of her hand with his as he passed her the arrow. The place where their hands touched tingled under his leather glove. And as Jeremy gave himself over to her for archery basics, he truly felt some goodness, some enjoyment, a blast of happiness, some delight—whatever the hell it was—it felt nice. Jeremy felt damn wonderful for the first time in a long, long while.

# CHAPTER SIX

*What reinforcement we may gain from hope;*
*If not, what resolution from despair.*

—John Milton, *Paradise Lost* (1667)

One week and innumerable wicked fantasies later, Jeremy's card game suffered abominably due to distraction. His attempts to sleep at night during that same week hadn't fared much better, what with his wicked imaginings getting the better of him when he was alone.

The distraction was the lovely woman across the room from him, of course. Jeremy had been watching her for the past half hour. So he had seen how her father seemed oblivious to the leering of that lewd bastard, Pellton.

Just this morning Jeremy had been witness to more bad behavior on Pellton's part. As he had left his own room, he saw a young maid exit Pellton's, her rumpled clothing askew, furtive glances all around, and a hand to her hair to smooth it. All testaments to what Pellton had been doing with her in the night. In Jeremy's opinion, such behavior was the lowest of the low. Using servant girls, particularly in the confines of a host's home, simply wasn't done. And if he considered that Pellton was trying to woo the daughter of said host in addition to his infidelities, there seemed no end to the man's dreadful manners.

Pellton was forever begging Georgina for strolls in the garden and for games of cards. Jeremy had done his best to rescue her from those incursions because whenever Pellton got near her, Jeremy felt his ire blossom. A visit to the library had been especially timely only yesterday. He'd gone in there to find something to read, which was unusual in itself…

Jeremy knew he needed something to do in his room at night besides think about what he'd like to be doing with Georgina between the bed linens.

He also knew Oakfield's library was well appointed. Jeremy felt confident he'd be able to find something of interest in its vast collection, but when he stepped in, he got the surprise of an interest very different from that of a good book—the sight of Georgina reading. Her back faced him as she reclined on a lounge chair with one leg draped over the chair arm. Her pink slipper pointed down to the floor, exposing a lovely stockinged ankle and underskirts aplenty.

"Thank you, Fannie, you may set it on the table," she said without looking up from her book.

"I've been called many things over the years, but that name, never," he answered, unable to refrain from teasing.

Georgina peered around the side of the chair and, pulled her leg off its perch so fast the book slid from her lap and dropped with a thud. "Mr. Greymont! I do beg your pardon. I—I believed you to be the maid with my tea." She bent down to retrieve her book off the floor.

"Obviously." He smiled at her. "No apologies necessary, Miss Georgina. And I am sorry I don't have any tea to bring to you." He held up his empty hands. "I've just come to find a book."

"Obviously." She smiled back, a hint of mischievousness lighting up her face.

Teasing him again. It was so easy with her. Being around her, talking, sharing a meal, taking the air, anything, everything was just so damn easy with her. Effortless. He had to force himself to say something. Otherwise he'd just keep standing here and staring, like the besotted idiot he was.

"You looked very captivated by your tome. Please continue on, Miss Georgina, and don't let me disturb you. I'm just going to search the shelves back there." He indicated with his thumb.

"Very well, Mr. Greymont." She gave a serene nod and turned back to reading her book. This time, her leg kept primly on the seat of her chair, unfortunately for him.

Jeremy wandered over between two shelves and began his search for something to read. He heard the maid come in with Georgina's expected tea a few minutes later, and he heard when she closed the door behind her when she left.

He pulled down a thick volume and opened it. *The Last of the Mohicans: A Narrative of 1757,* by the American writer, James Fennimore Cooper. Jeremy had heard about this novel. He checked the date on the title page. The story had caused quite a stir in Europe since its publication in 'twenty-six. He knew the setting for the story took place during the Seven Years' War, when France and England battled for control of the colonies in America and where the French had called upon the native tribes to fight against the British. The protagonist viewpoint was that of its Indian hero, and it was this facet of the novel that caused such a rumbling among those obsessed with the order of the classes. Jeremy flipped through pages until he came to an illustration that looked wildly interesting. It showed a man and a woman in the background watching in horror as an Indian warrior wrestled with a great bear standing on its hind legs. Right down his alley. His unconventional mind was piqued by anything radical. Jeremy knew this book would suit him perfectly.

His choice made, he tucked it under his arm and made ready to leave when he heard the door open again.

"Aha. I've been searching everywhere for you, my dear. It was only when I spied the maid leaving did I think you might be in here."

The voice had a slithery cant to it, and Jeremy knew who it belonged to the second he heard it. Pellton. The vulture.

"What are you reading, dear Georgina?" Pellton demanded.

"Poems. I am reading poetry, my lord," Georgina answered back in a stiff voice.

Jeremy stayed behind the shelf, out of sight, and listened. He heard Pellton set himself down on something and say, "Read me one of the poems out of your book. I wish to hear your voice, Georgina darling."

"Sir, you should not speak to me in ways so familiar."

"But why shouldn't I speak familiarly to you? I intend to marry you, and the sooner you accept the fact, the better."

"No, sir. I have given you my answer, and it is an emphatic—"

"Your refusal does not concern me overmuch." Pellton spoke right over her words. "I know that in time we will come to an understanding. You see, my darling Georgina, you have no other suitors, no prospects other than me. And your father wants you to marry me, doesn't he?"

"No!"

"Yes, he does. In fact, he appears quite eager to get you off his hands. I know I'm not mistaking his intent regarding you. I only wish your dear mother were here to see you become my bride."

"Do not speak of her! Lord Pellton, if my mother were alive today, I would not be in the sorry position I am in at present. She would never make me marry against my will, no matter the circumstances." Georgina sounded angry now.

"Circumstances. Yes, circumstances have a way of changing everything, don't they? You look so like your mother, Georgina..." Pellton mumbled the rest inaudibly, but then the sharp sounds of rustling broke over the mumbles. The noise alerted Jeremy to peer out from behind the bookcase to see what offense Pellton was perpetrating now.

"Release me at once, sir," Georgina demanded, pulling her hand back from where Pellton gripped it.

"Is there a problem?" Jeremy called loudly, stepping out into the middle of the room.

Both of them turned their heads to the sound of Jeremy's voice at the same time. Jeremy couldn't be sure if Georgina remembered he was in the room or not, but Pellton sure as hell was surprised to see him.

Jeremy pointed his gaze to where Pellton was clutching her. The weasel sneered at him. Georgina yanked her hand free with a jerk and glared at Pellton.

"Yes, I do have a problem. I suddenly feel like I might be sick! Excuse me." She turned away and swept out of the room.

Jeremy cocked an eyebrow. "That was quite the feat, Pellton. You made Miss Russell sick."

Pellton squinted his eyes and struck just like the viper he was. "Oh, bugger you, Greymont!" he spat and then walked out, leaving the library peacefully quiet once more.

Jeremy went to where Georgina had been sitting. Her book lay on the side table and was still open to the place she'd been reading.

He picked it up and read the page...

It took a great deal to rile Jeremy, but it didn't require much when Edgar Pellton was involved. The ridiculous toad irritated the hell out of him just by breathing. Mostly when he fawned after Georgina like he was doing right now! The scene was nearly an exact replay of yesterday in the library.

Pellton had Georgina trapped on a chaise, where she was

attempting to read another book. Jeremy also saw how Georgina turned away from the oaf, affecting a cut, when he'd tried to engage her in what was no doubt, again, some topic inappropriate for polite conversation.

Good for her, Jeremy thought, when he saw Georgina cut Pellton. The line of her neck looked so fine turned in profile, away from her tormentor. But Jeremy wasn't the only person who noticed. Mr. Russell had also been watching his daughter. And he took her to task for what he saw her do.

Mr. Russell asked to speak with her and then firmly backed her into a corner where he began to quietly chastise her for insulting a guest.

Jeremy saw how Georgina's face grew stricken, how she crumbled under the displeasure of her father. After a few moments of this, she put a hand to her mouth and fled the room in tears. Mr. Russell looked about to have an apoplexy, before going to pour himself a double whisky. Pellton looked rather pleased, a spiteful little smirk cracking out the seam of his serpent lips.

Jeremy couldn't believe it. Her misery was apparent, as was Pellton's debauchery. Why in the hell would any father push a daughter into marriage with such a beast? Pellton would mistreat her. Everyone must have heard the whisperings of his depraved leanings. Or maybe Mr. Russell did not know. Jeremy knew John Russell preferred the hunts and house parties of country life to the social doings of London. He guessed it was possible Georgina's father did not know the reality of Pellton's nasty predilections.

Jeremy gave his card game another five minutes before excusing himself. Ten more passed before he actually found her.

She sat in the solarium, on a bench amid the tropical green leaves of plants that could never survive the English climate if exposed to the natural elements. Her tears had stopped, but now she looked broken and defeated. Even in her misery, Georgina was beautiful to him. She wore a silvery blue dress tonight, the shine of the fabric glowing in the lamplight.

"Not enjoying the evening, Miss Georgina?" He spoke quietly so as not to startle her. "I saw you leave." He came closer. "You appeared distressed." He sat down next to her on the bench.

She kept silent at first. They just sat next to each other, contemplating in the quietness of the exotic plants that surrounded them, and their clean, earthy smell.

It seemed like an age before she spoke. "Wouldn't you be?" Sad, hazel eyes lifted to glitter at him.

Jeremy tilted his head in question.

"If you were on display like a prized bird to be bagged by the best shot? In this case, the 'best shot' is repulsive to me. I hate it!"

"What do you hate more, the part about being on display or the quality of the candidate trying to 'bag' you?"

"There is only one candidate, and Papa does not care for my feelings against his suit."

"Have you agreed to anything?"

"No, and I don't plan on it either, but I am afraid Papa will find a way to force me." Her composure crumbled then, and the tears came. "I can't bear it if he gives me to Lord Pell—"

Jeremy didn't hesitate to pull her into his arms. He held her close and felt the quivering coming from her body, right through their clothes, straight to his heart. God, she felt good. And in that instant he knew.

*She feels right.*

Everything about Georgina felt right. Jeremy wanted to breathe her in. He wanted to kiss and touch her all over. He wanted her naked underneath him and their skin hot and pressed together. He wanted her crying out his name when he made love to her. Yes, he wanted all of those things, but even more than that, he wanted to protect and reassure her. It stung his heart to see her so distraught.

"He won't," he murmured into her ear.

Georgina stiffened. The shock of being in his embrace was the cause, but she gave in to it almost immediately, indulging in how wonderful a feeling it was to be held by Jeremy Greymont, to be safe and comforted, at least for this one moment in time.

She stayed in his arms and let him hold her. He smelled divine, slightly sweet like cloves and shaving soap, and she liked the way he rested his chin atop her head. His hand brushed up and down her back. His warmth radiated into her chest, and for the first time in years, she felt truly cherished by another person.

It took some moments before she realized exactly what they were doing, and the impropriety of it. She pulled back from him and felt the loss of his embrace immediately, the warmth and strength of him dissipating into the night air to combine with the exotic breath of the plants.

"Do you feel a little better? Please say that you do. I can't bear seeing you so sad." He fished out his handkerchief and brought it to her face. "Allow me?"

His kind gesture brought on fresh new tears that rolled down her cheeks in silent streams.

Without saying another word, he carefully dabbed the wetness away, first one cheek and then the other. When he finished, he pressed the handkerchief into her hands and his lips to her forehead. "There," he whispered.

Mr. Greymont's lips were soft, the brush of his whiskers less so, as they touched her skin. He gave her such a gentle, lovely kiss. Georgina wanted to dissolve in the solace of the moment. *It is more than you deserve.*

She shouldn't allow him to even do it. 'Twould only make things harder to bear. Georgina tilted back and looked at him. Mr. Greymont's eyes burned in return, a simmering hunger discernable even in the dim light of the solarium. They focused on her mouth.

An unsettling flare of heat hit her behind the ribs. She needed to go. His attentions were too much to take in right now. Mr. Greymont's kindness was genuine, but she sensed he held back somehow. A whiff of danger permeated the moment. She had to get away. Now!

"Please forgive me, Mr. Greymont, for my outburst. I am much better though, thanks to you. I'll not forget your kindness to me this night." She stood up abruptly. "I must take my leave now."

"Don't go! Stay? Talk with me?" he blurted, grasping her hand.

"I must go, for I am suddenly very exhausted and not at all good company right now." She looked down at his hand gripping hers. It felt hot.

"Yes, you are. Yours is the best company." But even so, he released her, looking a little guilty as he stood up and bowed. "As you wish, Miss Georgina, but please agree to meet me tomorrow— at your oak tree swing, two o'clock? I want to talk to you again. Will you come?"

His gentle entreaty was impossible to resist, and she trusted him. Regardless of the tension between them right now, she knew she'd be safe in his company. "Very well." She nodded. "Good night, Mr. Greymont."

She walked out, leaving him there in the solarium, flexing the hand he'd gripped so tightly. It tingled in the same way her forehead did, in the place where his lips had kissed.

It wasn't until she was in her bed that she remembered his words when he'd held her in his arms. Mr. Greymont had said, "He won't," in reference to her father forcing her to marry Lord Pellton. *But how can he know?*

Georgina pondered the mystery of Jeremy Greymont in her bed that night. Thinking about how easy it had been to be held close enough to scent him, to feel his hard muscles bracing her, to be stroked along her shoulders by his gentle hands.

Interestingly, his nearness didn't frighten her at all. She felt just the opposite. Comfort, solace, and security were what he offered, along with something more enticing that she didn't really understand, but drew her in all the same. In fact, she clung to that security without even knowledge that she was doing so.

Georgina still had his handkerchief, and it smelled of him—a faint hint of cloves and starch and his own crisp sharpness. The scent floated in her head until sleep claimed her. A last rambling thought swilled in her mind before fading away. *What does he wish to talk about?*

# CHAPTER SEVEN

*The reputation which the world bestows*
*is like the wind, that shifts now here now there*
*its name changed with the quarter whence it blows.*

—Dante Alighieri, *Divine Comedy* (1308)

The swing had been a favorite of her mother's. One of the earliest memories Georgina had was of being held in her mother's lap upon this very swing.

This place was in fact, very special. Her family used to have picnics right here on this spot. Tom would climb the tree, and Papa would read poetry to Mamma. Mamma would braid wildflowers into Georgina's hair and once wove a fairy crown to place upon her head. On that day, everyone had pledged their fealty at her coronation. All hail the Fairy Queen of Oakfield! Georgina couldn't recall any other intimate family picnics after that one. It must have been the last.

She grasped the rope of the swing and gave it a push. She watched the plank seat twist and rotate until it stilled and had to be flicked again.

They were lovely memories, but from a long time ago. Another time. Another life. Everything was so different now. *So very different.* And a stroll down the bucolic memory lane of her childhood didn't serve much use in the realm of the harsh reality that was her life now, did it?

Georgina arrived at the oak tree early today. She found it a good place to think. And she intended to be composed this time, too, unlike every other time she was in Mr. Greymont's company.

He was an intriguing man, and there was a quality to him that soothed her. He was easy to be with. Last night, when he'd comforted her, she'd felt like she could stay in his arms forever. The notion surprised her, but when she thought back on it, she realized that his physical presence was never unwelcome.

She reacted to Mr. Greymont in a way she had never done for anyone else. But then, the way he'd looked at her in the solarium, after he'd kissed her and wiped away her tears, she'd seen a hunger in him, clear as day, and that had rattled her.

She had admired him for years—as the charming friend of her older brother. He had been friendly and complimentary to her as a young girl, taking notice of her accomplishments in a polite, but proper manner.

That was then. Now he looked at her a little differently. His propriety was never in question, but he didn't look at her like she was a young girl anymore. He looked at her as a man did at a woman. Somehow, the thought of him looking at her like that did not anger her as it should. In fact, everything about Jeremy Greymont, and her reaction to him, felt different—

"There you are!" Clawlike hands and hot breath assaulted her from behind. "I've been searching for you again." He turned her.

"Lord Pellton! Unhand me, sir!" She struggled to free herself from his groping and pawing.

"You tempt me mercilessly, my little rosebud," he slurred in her ear. His grip held strength despite his years, and he easily pushed her up against the trunk of the tree.

Georgina felt the rough bark dig in to her back and then panic upon realizing he'd trapped her. Pellton had her pinned between his bulk and the great tree. Her struggles to get away from him only served to press her body deeper into his—the very last thing she wanted. *Oh, dear God!* In horror, she watched as he lowered his head to bury his face into the *décolletage* of her gown, his movements frantic as he began his assault.

"I have tired of waiting on your resistance, my dear," he said, slathering his mouth over her skin. "There's no point to it you know. You *will* belong to me and need to learn your role. A little taste of what will soon be mine won't hurt. It shall help to speed things along." He huffed the words at her chest.

"No! Sir, please let me go. Stop! This is unseemly! Noooo!" She thrashed her head back and forth in an effort to dislodge him.

"Fighting me will only make you taste sweeter," he crooned evilly, one hand covering a breast and squeezing. "You are a wildcat, my pretty."

His words, the smell of him, the weight of his body pressing against her, sparked absolute terror in her brain. She remembered words that had been told to her before. *I am going to fuck you now, my wildcat. Keep fighting. That's it. Fight me while I fuck you...*

Georgina no longer knew who or what attacked her. She just knew she must fight to get away. Fight or die.

She fought, kicking and scratching and clawing and hitting with all of her strength, thinking the whole time that it couldn't possibly be happening to her again.

"Get away from her, you bastard!" Jeremy Greymont's words met their mark with deadly intent. The sound of him alone got Pellton's attention, but the shotgun bearing down on her tormentor added the extra incentive to follow the command.

Pellton froze against her as she panted against the tree, her face turned as far away as possible, his breath making her want to vomit.

"But she is my betrothed, Greymont." He slowly turned to face Jeremy, his eyes wide. "I am entitled to her. And how dare you threaten me with a gun!"

"I dare." Jeremy held his gun steady. "Miss Georgina, have you agreed to marriage with this ape?"

"I have not!"

"Are his attentions welcome to you?"

"By God, no!" She bolted away from the tree to stand behind Jeremy.

"Then be on your way, Pellton. You cannot be assaulting maidens. It is loutish for a gentleman, let alone one who calls himself 'Lord.' But then, you've never been bothered by the constraints of propriety."

Pellton flushed red, an ugly scratch welting along his cheek and jaw. "Maiden, you say? Hardly a maiden!"

*Oh, please...nooooo!* Georgina found herself dropped to the ground, wishing the earth would open and swallow her whole right in this minute, terrified to hear the exchange between the men. Lord Pellton must have heard gossip about her from somebody. Her mind scrambled as she fought for understanding of why he would say such about her. *He knows! Somehow, he knows.*

"You attack her character as well as her person? God, Pellton, what kind of a monster are you? Be gone—off the property if you know what's good for you." He cocked the gun. "Now."

"You'll be sorry for this, Greymont!" Pellton sputtered, his voice shrill.

"No, I won't." Jeremy threw back his head and kept the gun trained on Pellton. "I am sick of watching you leer at her over dinner. And now this? It's enough to make me puke!"

"Whyever for, Greymont? She's got your prick twitching as well. I can see it in your eyes! You can think of nothing but how badly you want to fuck—"

Jeremy silenced the foul words with the gun barrel pressed an inch from Pellton's nose.

"Time to go, Pellton. Not another word out of you. I don't

know how much longer I can hold my finger still. I'm feeling a bit tense at the moment. Hunting accidents are an all-too-frequent occurrence these days, what with firearms being so unpredictable."

Pellton breathed hard at Jeremy from behind the barrel of the shotgun, his eyes bulging.

"This gun might jam though. I had some trouble with it last week. You could always take your chances and keep flapping your mouth, Pellton," Jeremy taunted. "Or not. Either way, you're buggered, *my lord*!"

Georgina sobbed from a heap on the grass, praying Lord Pellton would just go and for the torment to cease. She didn't look up, and she couldn't bear to see what was happening between the two men.

Lord Pellton must have taken Jeremy's threat to heart because he never said another word.

Jeremy tracked Pellton's departure, never taking his eyes away as he watched the letch slink off. It gave him a moment to will his racing heart to slow its thundering inside his chest. He heard the hysterical sobbing of Georgina on the ground at his feet, the sound slicing his heart like a dagger.

"Shhhhhhh. No harm done. He is gone and won't hurt you again." Jeremy dropped to his knees, gathering her up. "I am here, and you are always safe with me. Always."

Georgina clung to him in a panic, trembling, burying her face in his chest, her hands gripping his jacket. She shook so hard the vibrations moved his body along with hers.

"I won't let anything happen to you." Jeremy rubbed her shoulders and upper arms and just held her, wishing there were something more he could do. Long minutes passed with her in his arms before she cried herself out and her trembling finally ceased.

Pellton had clearly terrified her. Jeremy tensed again, remembering what he'd seen Pellton doing to her. The pig had been grappling her breasts with his hands and mouth. How dare he touch her! The idea of another man putting his hands on Georgina made him want blood for payment.

"What can I do for you?" he asked as gently as he could, hating that she was scared.

"You've already done it! You saved me and made him go. I don't know what he would have done." Georgina lifted tear-filled eyes to meet his. "I was so afraid—thank you a thousand times, Mr. Greymont. You are a remarkable man to do—"

"Let me get you home and I can go to your father and tell him about Pellton." He cut her off and pulled her up to standing.

"No! You must not!" she begged, shaking her head and digging her heels in when he tried to lead her forward.

He whipped his head around to stare at her. "But your father must be informed of his low character and know of what he tried to do."

She hung her head. "You will pay for it if you persist in this. Don't you see? They'll look to you."

"Look to me for what?"

Georgina widened her eyes at him. "You don't know?"

He didn't answer but felt certain he did indeed know very well.

"They will look to you as a husband for me. I cannot believe that Tom didn't say anything about it. I am sorry, Mr. Greymont, it is not of my doing."

She composed herself and looked him square in the eye. "My father wants me married and gone. He doesn't much care to whom, obviously. He will be angry that Lord Pellton has left us." She put her hand on his arm. "But you can get away if you leave now. You should go, Mr. Greymont. Just take your leave, and get as far away from this cursed place as you can. No one will ever know about today. I won't say a word to anybody."

Jeremy held her gaze throughout her speech, even surer of what he must do. He looked down to where her hand rested on his arm, and then slowly up to her face, still tear streaked and red. Portions of hair had come undone from the loose knot she wore and trailed wildly in the soft breeze. He wanted her back in his arms, those soft curves tight up against him. Everything became so crystal clear all in an instant. He wanted her. Such a simple truth in the emotion, he thought. Wanting a person. For him, that person was Georgina, and no other would do.

"I still need to talk to you, but I realize you are upset and this is not the best moment. I'll leave you with this. Would you like it if I were a candidate for your hand?"

"Are you?" she whispered, her eyes rounding in surprise.

"Do you want me to be?" he whispered right back.

"Mr. Greymont, regardless of what I would like, you don't want to be a candidate, trust me."

*Yes I do.* Determination fueled him. "I am calling in the favor you promised me the day I arrived. Tonight. You must meet me in the library at midnight. I'll be waiting for you."

She started to shake her head.

Taking both of her hands in his, he worded his request carefully, but firmly. "It *is* important. Come to me, Georgina. My intentions are nothing but honorable. You have naught to fear from me, I give you my word. I only wish to talk to you."

He brought both of her hands up, observing the fine bones of her fingers, before kissing each palm right at the center. Then he entreated with his eyes, locking onto hers.

"As you wish." She dipped her head elegantly, turned, and walked away, leaving him under the sheltering leaves of the ancient oak.

He stood frozen, powerless to move, only able to watch over Georgina until she found her way safely inside the house.

Jeremy was positively savaged with worry for her. Yes, he was fussing already. Might as well don a nanny's apron and cap, he thought, wryly. The urge to hover and stay close by was difficult to curb. In fact, Jeremy had no intention of curbing the impulse. What he wanted to do was flay Pellton and snarl at anyone who looked at *his* Georgina in a way they shouldn't. Then, he'd take her sweet, innocent form into his arms and kiss her senseless. Or until he was senseless. Hell, he was already senseless! *Yes, she will be* my *Georgina.*

Was he really going to do this?

*Yes, you are.*

Jeremy needed a whisky right now, or three. He felt surprisingly steady in the nob, considering what he would be doing come midnight. Hellfire and damnation! Courtship is torture on a fellow, he thought.

# CHAPTER EIGHT

*His love was passion's essence—as a tree
On fire by lightning, with eternal flame
Kindled he was, and blasted.*

—Lord Byron, *Childe Harold's Pilgrimage* (1812)

Honesty was the only option open to her. Georgina knew she would have a difficult time denying Jeremy anything that he asked. She also knew she couldn't betray him either. He was too worthy and good. She'd have to tell him the ugly truth before he asked her the question. And then he'd no longer want her. He'd be repulsed and embarrassed, and she hated do that to him, but couldn't see any other way.

Life felt so very unfair at the moment. It had not turned out at all how she'd imagined when she was an innocent and still whole, and dreamed of the fairy tale. Dreamed of the brave knight who battled dragons and rushed in to sweep her to safety. Her life was no fairy tale. Although Lord Pellton could fill the role of a dragon, she thought wryly. No, the knight of her dreams married her and took her away to his castle where he loved her for the rest of their days.

Making her way to the library with a heavy heart, she could guess what the honorable Mr. Jeremy Greymont would be asking her, and she also knew what her answer must be.

Georgina quietly entered the library to find Jeremy pacing impatiently. He faced the clock as it closed in on midnight. The click of the door latch caught his attention, and he turned abruptly.

Her heart stuttered painfully as she drank him in. His sharp blue eyes fastened on to hers and softened. Still in his evening clothes, his hair was a little tousled, as if he'd been dragging a hand through it. Pieces of sandy brown skittered over his brow. His lips stood out smooth and full against the shadow of beard that surrounded them. They were the same lips that had kissed her forehead and her palms. *What a beautiful man you are, Jeremy Greymont.*

He kept still for a moment, his stare raking over her fast before coming to rest upon her face. She'd worn her hair down but tied together onto one side, and had covered up with a blue brocade dressing gown over a lacy nightdress.

She suspected he liked how she looked because he swallowed deeply before speaking. "Thank you for meeting me, Georgina. Please sit down?" He indicated a chair for her.

Seeing the swallowing and the admiration in his eyes, she felt even more regret for what she must tell him. She took the seat, lifting her eyes to him. "Mr. Greymont," she whispered in greeting, wanting his admiration for her to go on, but knowing he wouldn't feel it once she explained why she couldn't accept his hand.

He cleared his throat. "You told me today that your father has imposed the requirement of marriage for you. I confess I did know of his intentions to see you wed. Your brother told me when I met him in London. And the idea intrigued me. I have admired you for years, but you were too young before, and I was not of a mind to settle down then. But now, my aspirations have changed." His voice trailed off as his eyes swept over her again.

She looked up at him, still standing, so tall and strong before her and thought he was the most handsome man she had ever known. And then she felt the pang hit her in accepting that she would probably never see him again after this night.

He sat down in the chair opposite to her. "I had to come to see you again and learn more about you. Being in your company has not been a disappointment. Rather, it has been quite the opposite. Georgina, I think you are perfect for me." He reached out and gently clasped her hand. "My grandparents raised me, and my grandfather, Sir Rodney, will leave a baronetcy when he goes. He is getting on in age and wishes to see the line secured, impressing urgency for me to wed and get an heir for Hallborough Park, our estate in Somerset. So you see I also have the necessity of marriage on me."

Georgina felt the urge to laugh at the absurdity of fate. Jeremy wanted to marry for the purpose of getting an heir just like Lord Pellton did. *But he's not like Lord Pellton.* How could two men want the same and her reaction be so vast in difference? Easy answer, that. One man was good, and one was bad. Jeremy saw her as a person, while Pellton thought of her as something to use. Jeremy was kindness and comfort. Pellton was lecherous and frightening.

He gathered up her other hand so that now he held both of them in his. "If I could bring about such with you, it would not be a burden in any way. It would be a privilege. I would be honored to have you for my wife." He straightened in his seat and swallowed. "Georgina, will you—"

"Jeremy," she interrupted, "don't." She bowed her head. "Do not ask the question." The regret in her voice sounded so pitiful, even to her own ears. She tugged her hands out of his clasp.

He resisted her withdrawal for just an instant before letting her hands go. "What is it?" he asked.

"I cannot marry you because I am not fit to be wife to any man," she whispered, praying she could get through the rest of the explanation when he demanded it.

"Because of Pellton today? I don't care about him, and I stopped him before he could...hurt you." He stroked her cheek with a knuckle. "No one will ever hurt you again. I'll protect—"

The door burst open, and both of them turned to see Mr. Russell stride into the room.

"What is the meaning of this? Greymont? What are you about young man—dallying with my daughter in the dark of night? It is bold of you!" Mr. Russell glared at Jeremy, but Georgina could detect the triumph in her father's stare.

Jeremy jumped to his feet, bowing his head in deference to the older man. "Apologies, sir. Mr. Russell, I can assure you I have only the most honorable intentions toward Miss Russell."

"It's a good thing, Greymont, for you have compromised her and I'll accept nothing less than an offer."

"Of which I am fully prepared to put forward. I called Miss Russell here tonight to ask her the question directly. I would have gone to you next, sir." Jeremy turned smiling eyes on her and held out his hand.

She felt tears well up, making her vision swim, shook her head, and devastated the man she wanted but could never have. It wasn't in Georgina's destiny to have him. Fate had stepped in and demanded payment.

"I cannot marry you, Mr. Greymont. It is impossible."

"Why can't you?" Jeremy asked, puzzled by her refusal, a frown slashing his brows.

God, her heart hurt. This must be the pain of it breaking. "I told you before, I am not fit—"

"Georgina! Hold your tongue, girl!" Mr. Russell shouted threateningly from the doorway.

"Papa! I won't mislead him. I will not do it. Not to him." She felt such anguish in this moment. It felt like she had left her body and looked down on herself as she spoke the horrible words that would kill her chance for a happy life.

"What is it? Why do you refuse me? Georgina?" Jeremy sounded different now. Doubt had crept in.

"I—I am not—"

"Goddamnit, girl, silence yourself!" Mr. Russell exploded, red-faced and shaking.

"No, Papa! I cannot. He deserves to know what he would be getting in a marriage with me!" She faced her father bravely, knowing she would pay later for this defiance.

Jeremy sounded truly worried now. "What would I be getting, Georgina?" He swallowed hard, his throat flexing.

She turned to him and took a deep breath. "I can barely look at you and say the words, so great is my shame. But you deserve better than me. Much better."

"What would I be getting, Georgina?" He repeated the question, this time with the sharpness of daggers flying across the room.

She gulped a deep breath and said it quickly, before she lost her nerve. "You would be getting a ruined bride—who's no longer chaste—and unable to—unable to bear the touch—to do her duty in marriage. I cannot do it. I am as I said before, not fit for you. I am ruined."

She saw the sting flash in his eyes and a flinch as he comprehended her ghastly confession, and she had to cover her mouth. Georgina's pain was naught compared to the ache of hurting him, but she could do nothing else. Her heart squeezed up tight, closing itself off.

The hysterical idea of flinging herself down to the floor and begging him to marry her anyway, despite her disclosure, flashed as a possibility. But that was simply a panic reaction. She could never do such a thing to Jeremy. He deserved someone who could be a true wife to him and give him the heirs he needed.

This hurt. So badly. The anguish terrified her in its intensity, but that must mean it was a worthy sacrifice—she was doing the correct thing. Yes. This was how it must be. Georgina would sacrifice her happiness to ensure his. Knowing the loss of Jeremy Greymont would be always be felt with great regret, but also knowing in her heart, that this night, she had done the right thing in letting him go.

# CHAPTER NINE

*When we two parted*
*In silence and tears,*
*Half broken-hearted*
*To sever for years...*

**—Lord Byron, "When We Two Parted" (1816)**

Jeremy felt the breath leave his body. It eked out of him slowly, letting him feel the loss at its most painful depths.

Georgina's sorrow-filled eyes had glowed at him in the dim of the room, and he'd never forget how she'd looked. Like a princess. So soft and alluring in her nightclothes with her hair spilling down over one shoulder. A tragic, but exquisite princess in his eyes.

Right before she had said the words that broke his heart, he'd felt the coldness of dread seize that beating muscle which gave him life, felt it turn brittle, so that when he did hear those terrible words, it just splintered all apart in an instant. Like an icicle dropping onto a rock and shattering into oblivion, as if it had never been, at one time, whole and shimmering.

His chest ached. He felt sure there must be a blade still embedded there after slicing him open, slowly being turned to ensure a maximum degree of suffering. He knew the need to lash out at something.

Georgina fled the room first, a desperate attempt to hold on to her composure for dignity's sake, her final words to him being, "I am so sorry, Jeremy. Forgive me." And then she turned away. Turned from him and was gone.

Mr. Russell followed his daughter out, having the grace to look shamed for his duplicity as he departed.

The keening of the library door closing on its hinge screamed through the silence of the cold room. But even the chill of the room could not compare to the coldness in his heart right now.

Being so close to getting what he desired and having it snatched away was cruel.

*I cannot marry her. She will never be mine. I'll never hold her in my arms or sleep with her or be inside her. I'll not touch her body or kiss her or make any babies with her.*

His body gulped in some breath, and he dropped to a chair, his legs unwilling to hold him up. Jeremy couldn't believe it. Georgina was supposed to be the girl for a libertine rip like him. He'd found her amid the bleak matrimonial landscape he thought never to make much sense of, let alone have to wade through. She was good and beautiful and gentle, but not weak. She'd have tamed him, made him decent, an upstanding citizen, worthy of respect. She'd been his miracle. Perfect.

No. He gritted his teeth until his jaw ached. His image of her had been perfect, not her. Georgina was flawed just like everyone else. Now he knew why the girl he remembered from long ago was so changed.

*Not chaste.*

Why had she said she could not bear his touch?

*Ruined.*

Well, someone had touched her well and good. Who in the goddamn hell had she fucked? And why? Her lover hadn't offered marriage? Maybe he was already married, this man who'd had her.

Or below her station. Jeremy thought he might be sick. Right here on the Turkish carpeted floor, amid the leather tomes of Oakfield's elegant library.

*What in the hell will I do now?*

He had been so sure of everything. Sure he would have her. Sure she would have him.

The pain cut too deep, rendering him incapacitated for coherent thoughts, so he just keep repeating the same truths over and over in his head, willing his mind to accept what his heart could not.

Jeremy packed his things quickly, determined to go at first light. Myers could head out in the coach behind him. He was going to London anyway. He had to get away from here before he did something stupid, like go up to Georgina's room and seduce her. Oblige her to accept his touch and see if she still felt like refusing his offer. He could go up to her room right now and cause a commotion. They'd be found in her bedroom together, and that would be all society required. He wouldn't even have to fuck her. He'd sure like to though. Maybe it would tamp down all this ragged anxiety he'd been holding in.

He could make Georgina marry him. He could force it right now. Her father didn't seem to mind much about the quality of the candidate as long as the bastard offered marriage.

Jeremy crashed down on the bed, feeling like a five-year-old and fitting because his best toy had been snatched away by a playmate. No, he wouldn't go to her room. That would be supremely stupid.

*She doesn't want you.*

In the dark, cold gloom of an otherwise comfortable guest chamber, Jeremy embraced sanity and faced the brutal truth. He couldn't take advantage of Georgina like that. He remembered the broken look on her face when she'd told him. He could never do such a beastly thing to her. It would put him right on par with Pellton now, wouldn't it? And she'd said she was incapable of doing the one thing—the only thing really—that any woman he called wife must be able to do. Accept him into her bed.

There *was* something that needed doing before he left this place though. So just before dawn, Jeremy pounded on the door with vigor, his fist ready.

When Tom Russell opened that same door, groggy with sleep and standing in his nightshirt, a punishing right hook shot out and connected squarely against Tom's jaw. Jeremy's hand stung from the strength of the blow he delivered.

"What in the bloody hell was that for?" Tom sputtered, rubbing his maw.

"Fuck you, Russell! You knew about Georgina and led me here! Damn you to hell, you bastard! What kind of a pathetic friend are you anyway?"

"What has happened? Greymont? Tell me!"

"I offered for her last night, and she has refused me. Said she was no virgin and could not fulfill the duties of marriage. Now why in the hell is that? Can you tell me true, Russell? No lies or fabrications this time. The truth will do nicely, you conniving, bloody prick!"

Defeated, Tom dropped his head. "I'm sorry. 'Tis only because I hold you in esteem, and know you've always liked her, that I thought you might be able to overlook her—her state of shame. She is blameless in it, Greymont. Blameless I tell you, but rather the victim."

Jeremy froze, coldness seeping into him, like ice water poured down his back. "What? Did someone do her wrong?"

Tom nodded. "Nearly five months ago. She had been out riding and stopped to water her horse. She doesn't remember everything, which is probably a blessing. A man she didn't recognize passed her, greeting politely, but then doubled back, taking her unawares. He covered her eyes with something, but she remembers a red coat, she is definite about that. When her horse wandered home alone, I went out and found her."

Tom looked frayed, recalling the details. "It was very bad what he did to her. Vile, cruel...very bad..." Tom sat down wearily. "She must have fought with all of her strength because he beat her brutally before doing his worst. I hardly recognized it was her when I saw what he—"

"Stop! I don't—I don't want to hear any more!" Jeremy dropped his face into his hands and scrubbed back and forth. *It hurts to know! I cannot bear to hear it!*

His mind reeled wildly at the images which came to him anyway. Georgina fighting and losing, her hurt and terrified— "Wait! Who did it to her? Tell me you caught the piece of shit that hurt her."

Tom shook his head. "We tried but turned up nothing. We thought the red coat might indicate a possible regimental on leave or deserting, but we never got even a hint of a trail on the bastard. All investigating had to be done furtively for Pater is determined to keep her attack a secret. He is petrified of bringing a stain to our family name. 'Tis why he wants her married and gone from here. Pater thinks he is protecting her—that a respectable husband and her own children will cover up what's happened to her. No one knows but you, Greymont."

"I think Pellton knows."

"No." Tom was adamant. "He can't possibly. He is only here because he needs a young bride for want of an heir, like you. Father's known Pellton for ages and thinks my sister is out of her mind to turn him down—and the title of baroness as well. Georgie won't have him though, which is good for I don't think he'd treat her well." Tom looked reflective. "I thought for sure she'd accept you though. She likes you. I know she does! She's always spoken of you admiringly over the years, Greymont, you know?"

"I did not know, and I am very sorry for all she has borne. She deserves much better." *A better man than I.*

Tom spoke hopefully. "May I see if I can change her mind about accepting you? I can go to her right now and make her understand how marrying you would be—"

Jeremy stopped him, holding up a palm. "I cannot marry her now, Russell. Surely you can see that."

"I understand," Tom said, sadly. "You want a virtuous bride."

Jeremy looked to his friend unbelievingly. "That's not why, you idiot."

"Well, what then?"

"Are you that stupid and insensitive, Russell? Your father certainly is! Trying to give her to a man that will mistreat her, especially since she has been brutalized and cannot bear the touch of a man, by her own word!"

Tom still looked confused, and Jeremy wanted to hit him again.

"My purpose in marrying is to get an heir, remember? Your sister refused me, saying she cannot fulfill the duties of the marriage bed. She was very clear. She told me she cannot do a wife's duty. Now, if she cannot do that, then there will be no child! Is that clear enough, you witless dolt?"

"Yes," Tom replied, chastened. "I recognize your position, and I apologize for leading you here. It was wrong of me. You were my one good hope for her, Greymont, and I thought you might—" He stopped himself, offering his hand. "Sorry for everything, my friend."

# CHAPTER TEN

*I do not know how elastic my spirit might be, what*
*pleasure I might have in living here...if the remembrance*
*of you did not weigh so upon me.*

**—John Keats, "Letter to Fanny Brawne" (1819)**

S ir?"

Jeremy looked up at the concerned face of his man of business, mind completely blank, realizing he hadn't been listening to a word, but could hardly feel embarrassed by his breach of manners, for he'd been doing it a lot lately. "Paulson?"

"Yes, well, I was just reminding you of my absence commencing tomorrow," the man said haltingly.

"Absence?"

"Yes, sir. The appointment for Mrs. Paulson with the specialist doctors. I am to take her to them tomorrow."

Remembrance nicked the skin of self-preoccupation, flooding Jeremy with shame. The cast of Paulson's eyes carried the burden of worry. "Oh, yes, of course, Paulson. I do remember you told me. Please. Off you go." Jeremy swept his hand in a motion.

Paulson looked solemnly back, saying nothing, but no doubt assessing everything. Jeremy hadn't quite been himself lately, and

Paulson was no dolt, even if he was far too polite to ask why his employer had become a brooding wretch.

The man was hardworking and clever—phenomenal with the ledger books. Jeremy couldn't imagine where his business would be without Paulson running the day-to-day of things at the London office. The man was carrying a heavy load, both with his employment and his personal life. Paulson had a lovely, but sadly, ill wife, an asthmatic, at the mercy of her lungs' poor condition, and from all indications, worsening.

"My man, don't give this here another thought. It'll all be waiting when you return, you know," Jeremy told him.

"Yes. Thank you, sir. I am grateful for the time." Paulson lowered his eyes, and the silence grew awkward. He shifted on his feet and spoke again. "I'll be back to the office by the end of the week," he said finally, lifting his eyes.

Jeremy could see the worry in them as plain as day. The ache of a man watching his wife slip away and helpless to stop the slide. The pain and fear of losing his mate. Love was such a cock-up, so cruel at times, he thought.

Jeremy rose from his desk abruptly and walked over to the coat rack. He took Paulson's coat and hat down and walked them over to him. "Yes, yes, of course you will," he said dismissively.

Paulson took his coat and hat, his head bent again.

"Now here, please take yourself home to Mrs. Paulson at once, and give her my very best wishes for a good outcome this trip," Jeremy said more gently.

"I'll tell her you said so, sir. She hasn't forgotten your kindness from the last time." Paulson hesitated just before he went out, pausing at the doorway to say something maybe, but then thought better of it. He dipped his head, donned his hat, and took his leave.

Gloom descended, cloaking the room instantly behind Paulson's closing of the door. Jeremy sat back down at his desk and took stock of himself. He sat there in his office for a long time.

He wasn't feeling much joy at the moment, but his true troubles were scant compared to Paulson's, and being sorry for oneself was disgustingly pathetic.

Making a decision, he got his own coat and made ready to go out. Dinner at his club would be a good place to start. And later? He'd just have to see how he felt then.

Jeremy's mood complemented the cold drizzle. London was comforting in its familiarity, and he hoped his activities tonight could help him to stop thinking about her.

The past month had been utter hell for him. And he couldn't forget. Her face, her eyes, her scent, even visions of what had happened to her swam through his head constantly. Those visions were the worst of all. Imagining some beast violating her and then abandoning her injured on the heath, like a scrap of unwanted cloth, stained and ravaged. *Ruining her for me.*

What was she doing right now? *Does she ever think of me?* He certainly thought about her. Thoughts of Georgina Russell occupied all of Jeremy's idle time. And much of the time he was supposed to devote to work or business. Tom told him that Georgina had always spoken fondly of him and that she liked him. *I'd bet she doesn't like me now.*

The look of Georgina when she told him was something he would never forget as long as he lived. So beautiful and yet so ashamed. *You left her behind, and she doesn't want you.*

In his suffering, Jeremy felt dreadful, but as a man, still had the baser needs to satisfy. Needs that he intended to meet this night with a real flesh-and-blood woman. It was time to move on without her, and this was the first step in making that happen.

His imagination and his hand around his cock could only take him so far, and were about as gratifying as thin gruel set down before a starved man.

*The Velvet Swan*, a high-class bordello in Covent Garden, would be his salvation. Jeremy didn't come here often, but tonight when he'd left his club after dining, he had given the address to his driver. For no good reason it had seemed like the only place for him to go. As soon as Jeremy stepped in through the red door, he found himself greeted warmly by the abbess. Heavy perfumes and the smoke of tobacco pipes mixed with the earthy scents of all the swiving going on. Swiving, tupping, docking, shagging. By whatever term, it all meant the same—fucking. Plenty of souls were busy fucking in this house tonight, and Jeremy was here to do the same.

The abbess, Therese Blufette, was a woman to be admired for her beauty as much as for her skills in business. She had always treated him with a certain fondness that went beyond the typical client relationship, and he'd never understood why. He couldn't be any different from the thousand others who spent their coin on flesh.

As he followed her into the salon, she looked pale and thin to him. Being French, she had that lovely darker complexion many European women favored and a fine figure still, for a woman of her more mature years. After he settled in with a drink, she approached him.

"Mr. Greymont, I am pleased you have come to see us. It's been a long time."

He tilted his head in acknowledgement. To be honest, he felt dead inside and wasn't up for chatting nonsense with the abbess tonight, regardless of his admiration.

She seemed to sense his reticence though and got quickly to the point. "I wish to speak with you about a private matter, one I think you will have an interest. If you would be so kind to call for me once you've enjoyed the company of your companion, I would be ever grateful, sir."

He raised an eyebrow and nodded once. She had piqued his interest, and he figured whatever she wished to tell him couldn't be too ridiculous. She seemed an intelligent woman after all. "As you wish, Madame."

Madame Blufette looked very relieved, some color suffusing her pale cheeks at his agreement. She thanked him graciously and left the room.

After she'd gone, Jeremy viewed the merchandise pragmatically, finding what he liked right away—that being hazel eyes paired with blonde hair. *Bloody perfect...*

Jeremy followed his alluring companion, who called herself Marguerite and spoke English with a sultry French accent, up the stairs.

Upon reaching the landing, he knew surprise to see a face he recognized, but had hoped never to see again. Off to the right with his back to him, Lord Pellton and another man, younger, but clearly sharing a physical likeness, were engaged in negotiation with Therese Blufette. Jeremy seized the opportunity to slip by unobtrusively and unnoticed.

A huge guard stood his post at the very end of the hallway. Thick, muscular arms folded over a wide chest the size of a tree trunk—a very old tree. Bordellos had to employ sergeant-at-arms sorts such as him in order to function. The merchandise was valuable and deserving of protection when badly behaved clientele got out of hand, which was often when strong drink mixed with stiff cods and a houseful of quim.

The guard eyed Jeremy directly, giving him the once-over as was his job. Jeremy offered a sharp nod, and the big man responded in kind.

Marguerite stepped into their destined room and Jeremy followed, closing the door behind them. She stood waiting on him, a slow smile spreading as she opened her pink dressing gown, revealing smooth, naked flesh for his pleasure. Dark-budded nipples hardened as he looked her over. Pert breasts, long legs, and a pretty quim all waiting for his hands and his mouth and his cock. There for the taking. He told himself to get it over with. That he'd feel better when it was done.

Jeremy closed his eyes as he reached for her, hoping to make it easier.

It did nothing to help him forget…

…Sitting on the side of the bed, Jeremy held his head in his hands, elbows propped on restless knees. "I can't do this now. I need to go from this place."

"Is it me? Would you like a different girl?"

*Yes, a different girl, named Georgina.* "No, it's not you. You're fine, luv. It's me. I shouldn't be here. I am not myself." *And I can't get hard for anyone but her, apparently.*

"Your heart is taken by another?"

Jeremy sighed. *Yes.* "Trying to forget is harder than I thought it would be." He shook his head, incredulous at baring his soul to a prostitute. Putting the money on the side table, he smirked up at her. "Don't tattle on me?"

"Never, sir." Marguerite pulled on her robe, looking at him in wonder. "She is a lucky woman to have got you. Can I beg you to stay for just a few minutes?"

"Why?"

"The men in the hall—I don't wish to go with them again, and I might avoid it if I am engaged with another patron."

"I know the elder one. Do they come here often?"

"Just last night. The older man is uncle to the younger. Our abbess, Madame Therese, is not glad for their patronage. They've caused trouble before, hurting girls."

"What happens?"

"They seek a *ménage*, one woman for the two of them, and their touch is harsh and painfully given. None of the girls like to service them, so the price goes higher. They feel they are being robbed, thus their treatment is even more punishing."

"Was it you last night?" Jeremy asked gently, feeling sorry for her.

Marguerite nodded. "I am saving money so I can go to France, to Calais. I have a sister there. I only agreed to go with them because of the coin. I told myself it was worth it."

"They hurt you. I saw bruises on your skin." Jeremy felt suddenly sick thinking of Georgina suffering rough treatment at the hands of Pellton if she'd accepted him for a husband.

"I survived it, and besides, they indicate they will have no need to continue coming here. They boasted that soon they will not have to pay for their wicked pleasures for the elder intends to marry, and once he has the girl, they can both use her as they wish and she can do nothing about it. The nephew even bragged that he had tried her out and found her most satisfactory for she fought him and he liked that about her. I cannot imagine why a lady of society would agree to marry into such a family." Marguerite shook her head, pondering the mysteries of the rich and entitled.

Jeremy felt the hair on the back of his neck stand up. *It was Pellton's nephew who raped her. That is why Pellton knew she wasn't a virgin!*

"Marguerite, did they seem sure that the elder would marry the girl?"

"He appeared confident and boasted that when he wed her they wouldn't have to pay for their *ménages* anymore."

Feeling cold, freezing fear engulf him, Jeremy prayed for rationality to overcome the sudden need for vengeance swimming through his blood. "Thank you," he told Marguerite, thinking he owed her a great debt. "I now know why I was supposed to come here tonight."

He fished open his money purse and pulled out some bills and a card, handing them to her. "Take this, Marguerite. Visit this address and see a Mr. Paulson when you're ready. Give your name—I'm sorry, what is your surname?"

"LeSavior. Marguerite LeSavior."

"Right," he said, thinking the angels must be laughing down at him right now. A "savior" she certainly was. "You'll have comfortable passage to Calais whenever you want. Go to your sister. Make a life. You deserve better than this."

"Why would you do such a kindness for me, sir?"

"Because I have the means to do so and it is no hardship for me to help you, but mostly because you have helped me. More than you can ever know, Miss Marguerite LeSavior." He bowed. "Thank you," he said to her at the door, thinking that if he ever had a daughter she might just have to be styled with the name Marguerite, at least for one of her names.

When Jeremy let himself out, he saw Pellton at the end of the hall, following behind a courtesan, entering a room, the nephew trailing behind. Jeremy got a good look at him and knew what he saw. Pellton's nephew wore a coat, notable in color—notable in that it was a deep, dark red.

Turning his head, Jeremy saw that the big guard also watched the two men. His stare looked, for lack of a better term, malevolent. Marguerite was correct in her claim that the establishment reviled Pellton and his nephew.

Once their door shut behind them, the guard turned his piercing eyes onto Jeremy. He lifted an eyebrow as if to suggest, "that was fast."

Jeremy shrugged. "Sometimes it's just not in the fates."

The guard gave a nod and a sympathetic grunt. Male to male, they were in perfect understanding.

Jeremy decided he could trust this man. "Say, I was wondering, do you know the name of the younger of the party that just went in?" He jerked his head toward the room Pellton and his nephew had just entered.

"And why would you want to know that?" the guard asked in a gravelly, accented voice.

"He and I have some unfinished business," Jeremy gritted out.

"What is the nature of your business?" The guard narrowed his eyes.

Jeremy looked levelly, his eyes stabbing the man. He felt rage in the very pit of his guts. Voicing his reasons required considerable effort, his emotions surging, threatening to overpower his acute, calculating judgment.

"He took something. Stole it brutally away and hurt a person very dear to me." Jeremy nodded at the guard. "I'm going to see that he pays for what he did."

A slow, malicious grin formed on the guard's face. "A man must do as his conscience demands of him," he said. He paused thoughtfully before putting out his hand. "I am Luc, and would be delighted to help you, sir."

# CHAPTER ELEVEN

*It is the end that crowns us, not the fight.*
—Robert Herrick, "The End" (1648)

Summoned to her father's study, Georgina thought this couldn't be a good sign, but regardless wasn't able to muster up much anxiety in any case. The past weeks had worn heavy on her.

Once Jeremy departed Oakfield after his disastrous proposal, Georgina felt the loss of him keenly. Tom had told him everything, so Jeremy knew the "why" of her disgrace. She also felt her will to resist her father's machinations fading away. Papa was still determined to marry her off, and aching for a man she wouldn't have was of no comfort. A wonderful man who'd made her feel like a true woman, desired and cherished. For a short time, at least.

She'd held a tiny flicker of hope that Jeremy might still want her after being told the hideous truth, but no, he had not. He'd gone quickly and probably felt like he'd dodged a bullet.

She could still remember the flash of disgust in his eyes when she'd shared her shame. Like dung had been thrown at him.

No, the future Sir Jeremy Greymont, Baronet, of Hallborough Park and Somerset, would have no use for a soiled, ruined bride, and that's exactly what she would be to him.

For all her heartache, Georgina thought pragmatically and saw a bleak future. There wasn't much spark left in her anymore to care though. With little to look forward to and nothing to lose, she hoped to leave Oakfield, unseen and quietly. Apart from Tom, nobody really wanted her, so she shouldn't be missed once she left. As soon as she found the means and the way, she was getting out. Out of Oakfield, out of England, out of life as she had known it.

She knocked on the door, reminded of the audiences to this very study, after *it* had been done to her.

The humiliation and more so the fear that the monster might have impregnated her had simply paralyzed her father. Mr. Russell could think of little else and had continued to inquire obsessively if she experienced any signs, for or against a pregnancy. And she'd answered him, mortified and shamed anew each time he'd asked the question.

Then finally, one small blessing, a lifeline in a sea of drowning horror, fell her way. Her courses arrived, and she could finally answer her father definitively and stop the dreaded questioning once and for all. What a relief. For the both of them.

"Come."

She stepped in. "Papa, you wished to see me?"

Nodding solemnly, in his way, Mr. Russell looked her over thoroughly, like he was trying to solve a conundrum. Shaking his head, he finally spoke. "I don't know how you've managed it, girl, especially the way you treated him when he was a guest here, but it seems that luck favors you. He still wants you."

An icy chill slid up her spine. "What do you speak of, Papa?"

"He is back and willing to overlook what transpired last time. His offer for your hand in marriage has been put forth yet again and on *this* occasion, you *will* accept him."

*Oh dear Christ and the angels! Lord Pellton has returned.*

She backed up. "No. No, please, Papa. Don't make me!"

"Georgina, enough of these dramatics," he said tiredly. "It's time to grow up and face your duty. His offer is respectable. You will want for nothing, will have a place in society, and shall bear a title, for Christ sake! That's more than your mother got. You will be called 'Lady.'"

"Oh, Papa!" She covered her mouth and turned from him. The walls were closing in on her. She felt small and powerless, completely at the mercy of others, with no voice of her own. She asked on a shuddering breath, "How can I do this?"

"You can, and you will. You are a Russell and must do your duty to your family and then to your husband, as is a woman's obligation."

She answered him with silent sobs, thinking she would start praying for a short earthly life. If she agreed to this, her life would be over anyway.

Mr. Russell's voice softened, and he drew up behind her. "I know you've suffered, my daughter, but I believe this is best. A life of your own, and once they come, your own children to care for. In this way you can forget your—your past indignity. That man needs a son, and you are of a fine and noble family. He honors you. There is no shame in being a wife and mother, Georgina."

She felt truly broken and tired, the will to resist crushed down to the point that she just didn't much care anymore. Lord Pellton's first wife had died in childbed and maybe she would, too. Whatever waited for her if she agreed must be her fate. What did it matter? Nothing mattered to her, not any longer. Feeling dead inside, she moved her head up and down woodenly.

"Success at last!" Mr. Russell blurted. "You've made the right decision, Georgina. I'll just go give the happy news and bring him in for a private audience with you." He put a hand on her shoulder and squeezed.

"He—he is here, now?"

"Yes. He arrived an hour ago, special license in hand. Says

enough time has passed and will not wait any longer for you. The ceremony will be in the parlor, tomorrow morning, and then you'll depart for your new home after the wedding breakfast. We can set back the date of your betrothal to the time when he was here before. Let it be known you were secretly engaged all these weeks. The maids should start on your packing right away. I'm sure you'll have your own maid waiting for you when you arrive to your new home."

Mr. Russell sounded positively giddy as he chattered about what needed to be done. She hardly paid attention to him, but did notice when the room grew quiet.

A sudden thought entered her mind. Right here, right now, was the last time. This moment was the last time she was a free person, operating under her own will. Because very soon, Lord Pellton would come in through that door and claim her. She would belong to him and would have to serve him. Her life would no longer be hers. It felt rather like a death, she thought.

She focused on the painting above the fireplace. It showed a seascape set along a craggy coastline. The storm-tossed waves at sunset, the glowing orange sun about to dip below the horizon. She'd always liked it, the colors and the subject. The painting could be a metaphor for her short life—this moment was *her* sunset, her end.

The door opened. She heard boots.

Standing frozen, she stared at the sunset in the painting, utterly unable to move.

He walked purposefully toward her, his steps hitting the floor in hard beats, growing closer and closer. She could hear his intense breathing. When he came within striking distance, he stopped behind her. She scented…cloves?

That couldn't be right. There was only one person she knew who smelled of cloves! Her spine stiffened, afraid to think of him. *Jeremy?*

"Can you not look upon me, Georgina? I want to look at you, for your face is the only thing I can see in my dreams all these weeks since we have been apart."

She turned to him, feeling suddenly light-headed and thinking that the painting wasn't of a sunset after all. It was a sunrise. Yes, most definitely. A glorious sunrise.

# CHAPTER TWELVE

Georgina started to drop, and Jeremy reached out his arms instinctively. He got to her just before she hit the floor. Her head lolling back, limp and lifeless in his arms—he realized she'd fainted dead away.

Carrying her over to the chaise, he laid her down carefully, supporting her neck. He poured water from the pitcher and wet his handkerchief to press against her cheeks and forehead. Her skin looked pale, and she felt thinner to him. She hadn't weighed enough when he'd lifted her. Please don't let her be ill, he prayed, feeling himself break into a sweat. He should have never accepted her refusal last time, should have been with her all these weeks.

An errant thought popped into his mind that she looked just like Sleeping Beauty from the fairy tale. Caressing her face, he said, "Wake up, Sleeping Beauty. Georgina, please wake up!" He shook her a little, still calling her name before he couldn't wait another second. Cupping both sides of her face, he tilted her so he could reach her mouth and brought his own down close. Jeremy's lips met Georgina's lips. Velvety. Warm. So sweet.

Time stopped dead, or maybe he'd just died and gone to heaven. He was kissing an angel, and he could smell roses. The touch of her breath brushed into him, the taste of her infused his blood with incredible need. Cradled in his hands, he kissed her over and over. And for a beautiful instant, all was well in the world. It truly felt like it because she opened her eyes just then and spoke to him.

"Is it really you?" Her voice sounded deep and a little rough.

"You fainted," he said, stupidly. "I kissed you, and you woke up. Are you well?" he croaked, feeling like he might need to lie down himself.

"I—I thought you were going to be—" She shook her head as if to clear it. "I never thought you'd come back here, or want me."

"I can't do anything else, and I don't care about—what has happened in the past, other than you being hurt by it. I *do* want you. I want you, Georgina. Marry me. Be with me."

Pulling back, he bore his eyes into her, willing her to agree. He watched her amber eyes turn sparkly with tears.

He could resolve himself to begging if he had to. He'd made her cry. "Please?" Bringing his forehead down to rest against hers, his arms wrapped around her back, pulling her close. "Marry me."

"But why—" She struggled to sit up.

He helped her up to sitting. "No buts! I don't want to talk about—"

She stopped him with her fingers pressing down on his lips. "Jeremy, you deserve someone better than I. Someone who can be a true wife and love you in a way I probably cannot."

He kissed those sweet fingertips before replying. "Better? Better than you? There is no one better! And you don't have to love me. You just have to put up with me. I'm not very lovable anyway, I don't think." *Now that's an encouraging thing to say to the girl of your dreams. You are such a profound arse!*

He took her hand in his and pressed it against his cheek. "I s'pose I'm an idiot for saying such a thing to you. Asking a girl to marry you and then telling her you're not lovable and won't she please just say 'yes' anyway. It doesn't really bolster my chances that you'll accept me, does it? But I am a supreme idiot. I find that has been a common theme whenever I try to talk to you."

Georgina frowned at him, the space between her eyebrows crinkling. "You're no idiot, Jeremy." She shook her head slowly, still with great somberness. "And why do you say you are not lovable?"

"Well, I am selfish and self-indulgent. I have not practiced much restraint in my life, and I am bound to slip up sooner or later. But I am willing to take that chance, and if I have you to help me, Georgina, I am sure I could be a better man than I have been."

"Your assessment of yourself is an interesting one. I have not seen you behave selfishly or act indulgent ever. As for your lovability, I'm sure you're wrong there, too, Jeremy." Her eyes drifted to the side.

"I'd like very much to be wrong about that one," he told her.

"And so you have come back," she said.

Georgina moved her fingertips ever so slowly along his jaw, and it took all of his strength to keep still and not devour her with kisses. He wanted to kiss her again. He wanted her safely married to him and in bed where he could kiss her senseless and make love to her for hours and hours.

"As if I have a choice, Georgina. You have wound me into knots. I am so entangled in thoughts of you I could not find my way out if ever I desired."

"Then why did you leave before?" She dropped her hand and her voice changed. She lifted her chin a bit, her eyes sparking. "You left right after Tom told you what happened to me. You didn't want me then."

Jeremy knew shame for his actions before. Georgina was no shrinking violet. Her memory worked just fine. She had not forgotten how he'd run out the night she'd told him.

"I am so profoundly sorry for leaving you then. I made the worst decision—I was a fool, I know. But you're wrong. I did want you. Have always wanted you. My wanting you was never in question." He swallowed deeply. "I was afraid—" Jeremy stopped himself and shook his head once. "No. I'll not say another word until you agree to have me," he said, feeling his jaw harden.

"Afraid of what, Jeremy?"

"You might not have me if you know the reason. You've been traumatized and much harm has been done you." He reached forward and touched a fingertip to the scar beside her eye. "He did this to you." He worded it as a statement, needing no confirmation. He knew the scar came from her attack.

Georgina's eyes flickered away again, but she nodded her head, yes. Her throat pulsed as she swallowed. And he realized something else about her. She felt shame at what had been done to her. *It's not your fault, sweet Georgina.* It killed Jeremy to know she suffered still, and he wanted nothing more than to erase it from her mind.

"And every time you see the mark, you will remember what was done." Her voice trembled. "I cannot bear that, Jeremy."

"No, Georgina." He pressed his lips to the scar. "I will not. When I see it I will be reminded of your bravery, and be so grateful that you survived such a thing. No shame in that, sweet Georgina. None of what happened to you was your fault."

"Jeremy, it is my visible scar, but I fear there are more, worse ones in here—" She clutched at her heart. "And here as well." She touched her forehead.

"Then let me be the one to help you put them away. Let me comfort and protect you. I want to so badly. And none of what happened in your past alters my affection for you. Know that, Georgina. My affections for you are unchanging in spite of that knowledge. I only wish to keep you from hurt."

"Then why did you leave before, Jeremy?" she fired back.

Georgina wasn't going to take him without an explanation. He realized she was demanding to hear the "why" behind his hasty departure of a month ago. And he was going to have to tell her. *Damn me.*

"You *will* promise to marry me first. I can be stubborn, too!" Jeremy declared, supposing he might as well go in up to his neck. He set his jaw and leaned forward quickly, figuring if he had to impel her, he would use every wile he could muster to further his cause. He took her sweet lips again and not very gently this time. This time he gave her a kiss of claiming.

Rapture, pure and simple, was all he felt. That hot jolt at his groin fired right up the second he touched her mouth. His lips moved over her softer ones, and he nudged with just the tip of his tongue, trying to get inside her, if even in only a very small way.

Her lips parted to let him in, and when his tongue met her lips he didn't know how he'd ever be able to stop. The firm exploration of her lips dragged on, for he was unable to pull back. She melted right into him, taking his tongue in, letting him know her.

Georgina was made for kissing, for loving. If he could just get her to accept him, he could make it right with her. He knew he could.

Jeremy had gone over and over his position in his mind the whole way here. Yes, there were hurdles to cross, but he didn't see any other option for them. He wanted Georgina. He had to have her now. Protecting her from Pellton and his nephew wasn't even in question anymore. Georgina was going to marry him and be safeguarded from those depraved monsters. They'd never get within shouting distance of his wife ever again. Jeremy could make that much happen at least.

He kept telling himself he could be patient with her. He could be so gentle and careful Georgina would be eased into bearing all that dutiful, heir-producing shagging. Lots and lots of shagging.

An area in which he excelled. He could be a gentle lover for her. He could be that man.

Jeremy kept his mouth close to her lips. "Georgina Russell, you will not deny this sentiment between us. I know you feel it, too. I know, because you would not let me kiss you like this if you didn't feel something. I don't want to live regretting you for the rest of my life. You are the woman I want. Honor me. Be my wife and belong to me. Let me care for you. It is all that I want—to take care of you. I want you for the mother of my children—our children that will be cherished and beautiful."

She held his gaze for a long time. Such a solemn expression she wore, telling of ancient wisdoms and womanly secrets as she sized up his offer, like she was peering into the future.

"You have to trust me," he coaxed. "I want you, Georgina. The past is only that—behind us—over and done with. We can start a new life and forget about what came before. Don't be afraid to trust me."

She blinked slowly and then said the words he most wanted to hear. "All right, Jeremy. I will marry you."

His mouth went forward again, a celebration of sorts—another kiss. A kiss to seal their bargain. This time he was just a bit more demanding of her than before.

Her lips parted and took in his tongue. He swirled it over the perfect smoothness of the inside of her sweet lips. He nibbled on her lower lip, grazing with just the lightest touch of teeth, thinking he could kiss her for hours. If she stayed soft like this, he could. She let him in so sweetly, and her scent stirred him in a remarkably familiar way, but he couldn't understand how. Like he could lose himself to abandon but understanding that she controlled him utterly.

She pulled back, flushed and glowing. Taking a deep breath, she commanded, "Now you'll tell me. You gave your word. Why did you leave before? I have to know the reason." Her breath was a little heavy and got that husky sound he adored.

A glimpse of the spark of her fiery spirit returned as she eyed him. He loved when she was feisty, loved her strength and independence.

"Georgina, it was because I was afraid you'd be unable to bear my—my touch—the touch of any man because of what happened to you. And you would have to bear my touching you." He lowered his voice to a whisper and spoke gently. "For I must get an heir. Ours must be a real marriage…in every way."

She didn't say anything, just looked at him with those serious, amber eyes.

"You know, when I take you to bed, and we are together as a man and a woman," he prompted, knowing she must hear the truth.

"I—I understand. I know what you mean, and I am still afraid of just that." She blushed but didn't look away.

He watched her golden eyes get sparkly again. God, she had such bravery in her! It must be very hard to speak of this with him, but she did it with such genuine dignity, he was humbled.

Coming in very close, he gave a gentle kiss right below her left eye, atop her scar. He kept his lips near and spoke the rest. "But I was miserable when I left, and without any hope of you. I—I will never hurt you like that. I'll be so very careful when we are together. I know it'll be all right. It'll be something good between us." He kissed below her right eye. "If the way you let me kiss you is any indication, I think we've got nothing to worry about."

"What if I cannot—" Georgina touched his lips a second time, probably to make him focus on her words, but she needn't have worried for he was taking in every word and gesture. Jeremy couldn't get enough of her and probably wouldn't ever get enough, rejoicing in simply being close to her and knowing he could protect her and keep her safe.

"You can," he assured, unable to refrain from kissing her fingertips, nibbling and pulling them partway into his mouth. She tasted divine to him. "I *know* you can."

"How do you know? What if there's something wrong with me?"

"There is *nothing* wrong with you." He stroked a silky lock of hair at her crown. "I know you can do this because you're so courageous." He cupped her face and held it. "Georgina, I could never hurt you. Trust me to take care of you. I only want to make you smile and happy. The rest will come in its own time and in its own way."

"And you still want me like that? Even after knowing what happened—"

"Shhhh. Hush." Jeremy didn't want to even think about what she had endured, and he certainly didn't want her remembering, so he cut her off with a kiss instead to her sweet lips. His hands held her head steady while he plundered with a gentle, but determined pressure. Georgina let him. She even opened her mouth enough for him to get his tongue along the inside of her lips for a taste. And oh, the taste of her, soft and sweet like a ripe pear. "Does that answer your question about me wanting you? I am mad for you, and your past does not change that fact."

"If you say it is so, I suppose I must believe you mean it."

"Yes, you must because I do mean it. Now, I seem to remember that you've already agreed to have me." He winked. "All that's left is for you to trust me. Georgina, sweetheart, can you trust me?" He pulled his head back so he could see into her eyes, begging her to have faith in him. "Will you?"

Her eyes searched his, moving back and forth between the two. "Yes." She mouthed the word.

He couldn't hold back the smile that broke out widely. "Now I'm quite sure you just said, 'yes.'"

She nodded in her gentle way and whispered, "Take me away from here."

"Tomorrow. Tomorrow morning I will do just that."

She went into his arms fully, and he welcomed her sweet body pressed against his chest. He could feel the softness of her breasts and nearly groaned. A huge sigh puffed out of him. Feeling suddenly, blissfully exhausted, he knew he'd finally find restful sleep this night, after weeks of aching wakefulness.

"I know Tom is not here for the vows, but we can invite him to Hallborough for a visit if you like. I think he'll be delighted. He wants you to be happy. And you don't have to bring much—just yourself. We'll order you a whole new wardrobe in Somerset— whatever you like. I'll have my housekeeper, Richards, find you a maid and anything else you require."

He knew he was babbling as the words tumbled out of him excitedly. He pulled back to get a good look at her. "Can you tell I want take you home as quickly as possible? Is that all right?"

"It is very much all right," she told him, her pretty golden eyes softening in a way that was both demure and vivid at the same time. And aroused him wildly.

Jeremy responded with a smile. A smile that cracked wide, threatening to split his jaw open. He couldn't have cared a whit if it had. He was thinking about what he now knew. *She will be mine. I* will *have her. Sweet Georgina will be mine.*

# CHAPTER THIRTEEN

*How silver-sweet sound lovers' tongues by night,*
*Like softest music to attending ears!*

—William Shakespeare, *Romeo and Juliet* (1595)

*I'm marrying him in the morning.*

In the midst of packing up the last of her things, Georgina kept telling herself of this fact in hopes that she might come to believe it. As hard as it was for her to accept, Jeremy seemed determined to make her his wife. Georgina had no doubts of his ability to be a good husband, but she was full of misgivings about her role as a wife. When he wanted to bed her, for instance. How would—

Georgina felt her stomach flop, like a rock had been dropped down her throat. What would it be like with Jeremy? When he put himself inside her… She hugged her body, rubbing up and down her arms.

He'd said she must trust in him, and that he would never hurt her. So that was what she must do. She would trust the man who had come back for her. Who said he wanted her, no matter her past. *How can he be so sure?*

The soft knock at the door got her attention.

She checked the time on the clock—just past eleven. Would

Jeremy dare to come to her bedroom? *He might.*

Georgina pulled on a dressing gown, belting the robe of golden yellow before padding to the door.

"Who is there?"

"Only me," he answered.

Georgina felt her heart speed up at the thought of Jeremy just behind the door. Knowing full well that he should not be there, and that she should not allow him entrance, she loosened the bolt and opened her door anyway. And there he stood. As handsome as ever and unabashedly bold Her betrothed stood at her door seeking entrance as if it were the most normal thing in the world to come to her bedroom in the night.

"I saw the light coming from under your door and figured you were awake. Still packing?"

"Yes. I was just putting the last few things—"

"Let me help you," he blurted.

"You—you want to come in?"

"Yes, please."

Georgina stood aside to open the door all the way, and in he walked. Jeremy wasted no time in shutting and locking the door behind him, sealing them in her bedroom together. He leaned upon the door and faced her.

"I had to see you." He looked solemn before her, not his usual easy disposition.

"Why?"

"I just needed to see that you were safe and still determined to marry me in the morning. We were both very busy today." He nodded toward the window. "Thought I might guard the window to keep you from bolting in the night," he teased, but with a straight face.

The teasing words relieved her instantly. "Jeremy. I pray you do know that I would never do such a beastly thing—leave you hanging at the altar."

His eyes got a devilish gleam to them. "I need reassurance that you won't." He held out his arms.

Georgina couldn't resist such an offer. Standing before her, still dressed in a dark suit, but missing the neck cloth, his hair a little disordered from dragging it back with his hands. The hair dragging was a habit she had observed in him more than once, and one she found very charming. That, and the fact that being in Jeremy's arms was the most comforting place she'd ever known.

When his arms closed around her, drawing her against his body, she could feel the hard strength of this man who she would soon call "husband."

Laying her head on his wide chest, she just breathed him in. The cloves and the soap he favored mixed with a trace of Scotch whisky, filled her head. She found the elixir very soothing and realized the blended scents of his unique fragrance were already familiar to her. The notion struck that he was doing the very same with her—breathing in her scent.

Jeremy rested his chin atop her head, draping his arms around her, settling his hands on either side of her waist.

They stayed that way for a long time.

"Are you reassured yet?" she finally asked.

"A kiss or two might seal it for me."

She laughed softly and looked up at him. His clear blue eyes laughed back.

"I'm not sure if that's a good sign. I ask you for kisses, and you laugh at me."

She smiled wide.

"But I love the sound of you laughing. And now you're smiling, so I must not be too far off the mark."

Georgina pushed her face up closer to his. She looked at his lips, full and just a little bit parted. She wanted to kiss him. Closer. She offered her lips up to him.

He accepted her offering, bridging the short distance between them without hesitation. This time his kiss was very soft. Slow. Careful. He drew his mouth wide and covered her lips with his. He held their mouths together in the gentlest caress. Instead of just smelling the scotch on him, she could now taste it, and decided she liked the tang.

Jeremy pulled back first. He brought a thumb up and drew it down her lower lip achingly slow. "So sweet. The first proffered kiss from you. I want to remember you like this and never forget."

Georgina suddenly felt like she might cry. The way he looked at her, and touched her, and spoke to her tugged at her heartstrings. He made her feel special in a way she'd never experienced and filled her with the desire to please him. "Why did you really come?" she asked.

"To see you. Spend a little time together. To let you know how much I want this." He combed gentle fingers through her hair again. "We'll be married in the morning, and tomorrow night we'll be…home. It's rushed, I know, and I don't want you afraid of me. I thought, that in this way, it might ease the path for you."

"Oh." Despite the shock of what he'd just told her, she was remarkably calm. Did he expect to claim a husband's rights? Tonight?

"You want to stay the night, in here, with me?" she asked, looking up at him again, now feeling awkward in their embrace and having no idea what to do.

"Yes. If you'll let me. I thought we could be together, and when you get drowsy, you may go to sleep. And I'll be with you. I just want to help you get used to me." Jeremy bent toward her for another kiss, seeking her mouth with his. He moved slowly over her lips, joining them together in a soft burn of moist flesh. His hands moved up to hold her face to him. "That is why, my sweetheart. So tomorrow night won't be such a…new…thing between us," he breathed against her mouth in between searching kisses that turned her inside out and left her weak in the knees.

After another kiss, he pulled back slightly and asked, "So, may I stay?"

Georgina could only nod at first. The words came hesitantly a few seconds later. "I trust—I trust you, Jeremy, and I know you will be...kind, as you always are to me." Her chest was pounding so hard she was sure he must feel her. He had a point. Getting this over with would make tomorrow easier and show him she intended to do her duty. But by the gods, how could she let him—

Before she could think about it too much, she stepped back, walked to the edge of the bed, turned and faced him, untied her golden dressing gown, and opened it, exposing the sheer shift she wore beneath and feeling as naked as if she wore nothing.

Jeremy's eyes widened, and he tilted his head forward. "What are you doing?" He sputtered the question even as his eyes swept over her body, probably clearly visible through the thin fabric.

Georgina lifted her chin at him. "Getting ready for y–y–you to t–take me to bed." She realized her mistake too late.

"You thought—" He shook his head and frowned. "No! That's not what I meant! That is not the reason I came in here tonight. You are mistaken, Georgina," he admonished, looking appalled and maybe even somewhat hurt by her assumption.

*Oh God! He didn't mean to bed me.* Mortification filled her, and suddenly everything became too much. The emotions of the past day overwhelmed her and took hold. She buried her face in her hands and turned away so he wouldn't see the tears.

Jeremy was there in an instant though, cradling her from behind, as comforting and as strong as ever, the heat of his body bracing through the layers.

"Shhhhh. I'm so sorry for upsetting you. You must think me the worst sort of man. That I would come to your rooms and demand such of you." She felt his breath on the back of her neck, filtering through her hair as he moved his hands up and down her arms in a soothing way.

"I misunder–s–s–stood you, J–Jeremy. I did not want to deny you that you might think me unable—unable to be a g–g–good wife..."

"Hush now. I wouldn't think that. I know you'll be a good wife. This is all my fault. I pushed myself in here." He took her hands gently away from her face and turned her around to him. "Forgive me for distressing you. I really did have good intentions. I—I wouldn't expect you to—" He pressed a soft kiss to her forehead and stroked over her hair and down her neck. "Georgina. When we are together, in that way, we will be bound by the vows of matrimony."

"But that will be in the morning," she reminded him, wanting to dive under the bedcovers and hide.

"Yes. In the morning. But not right now. I just want to be near you and see you through the night." He took the two halves of her dressing gown and overlapped them. "As much as I love the luscious view of you in your pretty nightdress, we'll just wrap you back up so the carnal beast in me won't be too sorely tempted."

He tied her belt closed with purposeful fingers. And Georgina's heart melted anew at his chivalry. She wiped the tears off her cheeks, thinking she must look frightful.

"A beast? Really, Jeremy? I never think of you like that. And I never will." She shook her head at him.

"Give it some time, sweetheart. I've no doubt you'll see my beast. It'll come 'round eventually," he shot back with plenty of sarcasm.

He still held her loosely, his hands resting at her waist. Georgina sensed that he needed to touch her, and did not mind in the slightest.

"I truly doubt it. Others may be beastly, but not you."

He looked at her in puzzlement and cocked his head. "You are the only person, Georgina, who holds me in such lofty esteem, and I can't for the life of me know the reason. I figure your opinion of me can only go down in direct proportion to the amount of time you spend in my company." He winked. "All the more reason to wed you quickly, before you discover these things on your own."

Georgina couldn't help the roll of her eyes. "Didn't you gain entry into my room tonight by begging to help me pack up the last of my things?" She diverted their conversation to a safer topic and ignored his last comment.

"I did indeed, my lady." He bowed his head. "What did you have left?"

"Just my books and drawing supplies."

"Show me."

They spent the next half hour wrapping up the few books and sketches she wanted to bring. Georgina observed him while he packed her things. She saw how he handled each item with awareness, considering the placement in the cases with thoughtful care and respect. He didn't just cram the things in carelessly in order to finish the job.

There was so much more to Jeremy than she had any inkling of, and she wondered what it would be like to truly know him. To learn his secrets. To know his likes and dislikes, his habits and his strengths. To discover his faults. Everyone had them. She sighed, thinking he would learn hers soon enough, and hoped he wouldn't be too regretful in choosing her.

It was strange to think about how they were pledging themselves to a lifetime partnership in the morning, with still so much unknown about one another.

Georgina was glad for the simple task of packing up the last of her things. It diffused the awkwardness of before and helped put her embarrassing misstep behind them.

"Ah. I'm glad you're bringing this one." He held up a small volume. "I actually wish to read it."

"Which one is that?"

"*The Works of Robert Herrick.*"

"Why Herrick, Jeremy?"

"Well, for one, I think you like his poems, and I feel I should make an effort to share in something of interest to you. It seems like the husbandly thing to do. I don't know, am I wrong? Is that not what a husband does to be agreeable? I have no experience." He smirked in his charming way that made her heart catch.

"For myself, I know I'd find it agreeable if my husband read poems to me." A sudden vision of her father reading to her mother flashed in her head. "My parents used to. You said 'for one reason,' Jeremy. What's the other reason?"

"I think Herrick's prose is good. I liked what I read before."

"When did you read him?"

"The day I came upon you in the library. I picked up your book after you left it behind when Pellton drove you out."

"You did?"

He nodded once. "I brought it to my room and read some pages that night. I put it back the next morning where you could find it."

"I hope you'll read to me sometime. I like listening to your voice."

He chuckled. "Well, we have that in common then, for your voice hypnotizes me."

A powerful yawn consumed her. She covered her mouth and mumbled, "Pardon me. I suppose it has been a long day."

"You are tired, sweetheart."

"I fear you are right," she answered, stifling another yawn.

"Time for bed then. We have another long day ahead tomorrow." He led her over to the bed and pulled back the covers. "In you go," he said easily.

Georgina took a deep breath and unbelted her gown for the second time tonight. Strangely she didn't feel worried for him to see her in nothing but a shift. She was pragmatic enough to understand he'd being seeing any part of her he liked after tomorrow, so what did it matter tonight? But he didn't even look at her. While she was settling under the covers, he'd already turned away. He went around the room putting out the lamps instead.

Jeremy extinguished all of the lamps save for the one by the bed. Then he removed his boots. He stretched out next to her on the bed, but stayed on top of the covers.

"May I read you one poem? It is not long," he asked hopefully.

"Yes, Jeremy, please."

Georgina turned to face him on her side. Jeremy did the same.

Studying his hands as he held the book, Georgina thought his long fingers splendid of form. She thought about those hands and fingers of his touching her skin in intimate places. *Tomorrow he will touch me with those hands.*

Jeremy began to read. The sound of him travelled the distance between their bodies, his rich voice speaking the prose with artful flow...

*Delight in Disorder.*

*A Sweet disorder in the dress*
*Kindles in clothes a wantonness:*
*A Lawn about the shoulders thrown*
*Into a fine distraction:*
*An erring Lace which here and there*
*Enthralls the Crimson Stomacher:*
*A Cuff neglectful, and thereby*
*Ribbons to flow confusedly:*
*A winning wave (deserving Note)*
*In the tempestuous petticoat:*
*A careless shoe-string, in whose tie*
*I see a wild civility:*
*Do more bewitch me than when Art*
*Is too precise in every part.*

Robert Herrick, *Hesperides, 1648*

Jeremy lifted his eyes from the page over to her face. "I even understand it," he said. "Fancy that."

"Tell me."

"Well, he means that he finds greater beauty in a woman when she is in gentle disarray, rather than having her dressed in perfect, ordered arrangement."

"Do you agree with him?"

"Yes...I'd say that I do." He touched a finger to her cheekbone. "It reminds me of you."

Georgina didn't say anything. She just looked into his deep blue eyes. She couldn't. There were no words she could form that would prove adequate for all he'd done since coming to her room tonight. All he'd ever done.

"That first time...when we met in the rain. The night in the library when you came at midnight, wearing your hair down. Right now, in this bed, lying next to me." He caressed with his finger. "You are never more beautiful to me than when you are like this. As you are right now."

Georgina leaned in to kiss him, feeling it was the most natural response she could give and knowing there was nothing—no words at least—that she could say after such a beautiful declaration. Instead, she drew as close as possible with the blankets still between them and brought her lips to his. He kissed her back, sweetly and soft.

He stayed next to her in the bed, never pressing for more than a kiss or a chaste caress. Jeremy's gentle, slow kisses and trailing fingers drawn through her hair filled the minutes. She could tell how much he liked touching her hair, and thought it felt wonderful to have him do it.

So they spent their first night together in this way. She floated off to sleep eventually, comforted by his presence and hoping he drew comfort from her. Georgina couldn't help thinking about what tomorrow would bring, as well as the future with this man who'd come for her just this morning. The person who would guide her life from this point on. The father of her children. The man who said he wanted her and did not care about her past.

She never felt Jeremy leave her bed. When she woke early the next morning, he had already gone. Georgina could still feel his presence clearly though. The lingering trace of spice from his scent was all over her.

# CHAPTER FOURTEEN

*That sweet bondage which is freedom's self.*
—Percy Bysshe Shelley, *Queen Mab* (1813)

Myers brushed imaginary lint off Jeremy's jacket while he stood at the mirror remembering the night before. He thought about how Georgina accepted him into her room last night. Trusting him. He'd felt wretched when she'd misunderstood his reasons for coming. Even in her distress, she would've let him take her to bed and have his way. As much as he looked forward to bedding her, Jeremy was determined not to foul up the start of his marriage. He prayed to God for mercy in letting him please just do this one thing without gross misstep. He'd get her signature on the wedding certificate first as was right and proper. Georgina deserved as much, and Jeremy was determined she would have it.

She couldn't know the real reason he'd gone to her room and stayed the night. And he didn't plan on telling her the "why" of it either. After learning Pellton's true motivation for marrying Georgina, Jeremy couldn't get to her fast enough. He'd never known such fear or the need to protect so fiercely. He hadn't thought too much beyond getting her out of Oakfield and under his protection. It had taken all his strength to wait the few hours needed to procure the special license to wed, dashing off several letters of instruction in the process. The moment the marriage document was in his hand, he'd steered Samson in her direction, and by God if the lovable beast hadn't sensed his urgency, delivering Jeremy to Georgina's doorstep in record time. Myers didn't even arrive at Oakfield until well after dark in the coach. Jeremy believed luck must be courting him because so far all things had neatly fallen into place. He was dressed for his wedding, had won the pledge of his bride, and had a coach to take her away in.

Last night he couldn't have stayed away from her for any price. And if he'd been forced to, he would have remained awake all night outside her door to ensure no one came to try to take her from him or hurt her. Jeremy did not trust Pellton, not one iota, and as for the nephew, he couldn't even bear to think on him for even a moment without feeling bile rise up his throat.

But last night... What a treasure. A gift he'd remember until his dying day. Jeremy would never forget how she looked when she opened her robe. Her body was like a dream—a very erotic sexual dream. Long legs, curved hips, and full breasts he couldn't wait to sample. It had taken all his strength to cover up that luscious body. But even more than her physical attraction, he'd not forget how wonderful it had felt to sleep beside her, to watch over her while she slept, knowing she was safe and that she'd belong to him always. Early this morning, he'd reluctantly left her bed before the servants rose for the day. The sight of her sleeping form etched in his mind still caused his stomach to flip a little.

"You'll do quite well, sir." Myers stepped back to affirm his handiwork. The dark blue of the new jacket contrasted with a gold and blue waistcoat nicely, complementing his own coloring even in Jeremy's opinion. "You do a credit to your lady. In such a suit, you look very fine."

Jeremy looked sharply at his valet. "And the man under the clothes? Do you think he will do credit to the lady, Myers?"

Myers lifted wary eyes to meet his master's. "Without a doubt, sir."

"Do you speak truth to me?" Jeremy shocked himself by asking such questions. Opinions of paid servants did not factor into the equation. He should not care what others thought of him.

"Always, sir. You do right by those under your care, and I have no doubts you'll do the same for your lady," Myers said in his unperturbed way, reaching forward to straighten the hem of the jacket that sat perfectly level already.

The man must be in disbelief at his master's foray into the seas of matrimony. Jeremy was as well. He couldn't imagine doing anything else though. He was marrying Georgina, and that was that. In the next hour, he would gain a wife and become a husband.

"I'm glad you're confident," he returned wryly. "Say, have you seen my bride this morning?"

"Yes, sir."

"How did she look to you?"

Myers actually cracked what appeared to be a smile. The man hardly ever showed emotion. He'd been with Jeremy since he'd finished university. A former medic in the British Army, his more mature steadiness ever in effect, he rose to any occasion with a minimum of fuss, but was clearly enjoying the show today.

"She looked elegant and very beautiful on her father's arm. You are to be congratulated, sir."

"No, I meant how did she *seem*? I know very well of her beauty," Jeremy barked back, frustrated.

"Seem, sir?" Myers arched an errant brow, obviously savoring the moment.

"Her countenance, you devil!" Jeremy exploded, feeling like a schoolboy on Saint Valentine's Day. "Damn it all to hell, never mind!"

"Miss Russell appeared to me as the epitome of grace—"

"I said, never mind." Jeremy cut him off with a wave of his hand. "And just in case you've forgot, wear a thick coat, Myers, for you're riding in the open up with Ned. The interior of my coach will be for Mrs. Greymont and me alone," he said imperiously.

"Yes, sir." Myers bowed his head.

"Well, let's go get me wed then. You'll stand for me, as witness?" Jeremy gentled his tone in asking the question.

Myers's face brightened for just a second before returning to his typical mask. "It will be my honor, Mr. Greymont."

In the end, Myers was correct. Georgina presented herself a resplendent bride, solemn but steady, and so very beautiful. Her eyes found his the second he entered the room. She gave him a gentle smile, soothing his anxiety away in an instant. He winked at her.

The Reverend Goode read the words that bound them together until death as he married them in the formal parlor at Oakfield. Mrs. Goode played the music on the piano. The vows Jeremy spoke felt like the first "true" oath he had ever pledged in the whole of his life. He suspected it was Georgina who made that difference.

In her mother's wedding dress of creamy, blush, silk brocade, she looked a vision, nearly bringing Mr. Russell to tears, so great was her likeness to his dearly departed wife, he had declared.

Attempting to make amends to his daughter, John Russell praised Georgina's beauty and gifted her with her mother's pearls. His gestures were too little, too late for Georgina though. Jeremy could see that the father had lost the daughter when he was worried more for their good name than her torment.

Georgina's dowry was generous, although Jeremy cared little about the price they settled, his aim only to insure that his wife would never again be at the mercy of someone who did not cherish her as they should. He could admit there was some pleasure in bleeding her father for additional funds. If he was good at one thing, it was negotiation in business, and in this instance his persistence proved fruitful.

Before their departure, Jeremy took the additional opportunity to speak to Mr. Russell alone, informing him of what he'd learned in London about Pellton's evil intent and his belief that he was connected by blood and knowledge with Georgina's attacker. He did not spare him any of the gruesome details and was not a little satisfied to see how John Russell blanched in horror to know he would have given his daughter to such an animal and for what purpose.

So, with much relief, Jeremy got his new wife off in the coach. She shared in the relief as well. She didn't say so, but he could tell.

Georgina seemed more than ready to leave her old home and set out for her new one, in Somerset, at Hallborough, with him.

*He knew about Georgina the whole time. He endorsed it. Would have abused her. My child. Anne's own daughter!*

John Russell felt his blood run cold as he recalled something his wife had once said. *"I've never cared for the way Edgar Pellton looks at me, John. There's something unnatural in that head of his. His poor wife, how can she bear him?"*

John had soothed his wife with kisses and said it was because she was so beautiful that Pellton couldn't help but be stunned by her. What man wouldn't want her? She was the fairest prize of the county, and Pellton was no doubt a bit jealous of John's great fortune in winning her.

John Russell remembered something else, too. Pellton *had* coveted his Anne. He'd wanted to marry her. Once in their university days, when deep in their cups, Pellton had let slip that he intended to call Anne Wellesley his wife one day. When Pellton left on his tour of Europe for a year and a half, John stayed in England. He courted and fell in love with the lovely Anne Wellesley during the time that Pellton was away.

Luck favored John then. He won the hand of the most wonderful woman in the world. His beloved Anne. Pellton had joked good-naturedly over the years that his friend had stolen the girl of his dreams right from under his nose.

Anne Russell was a superior woman—one that did not suffer fools lightly. She knew what stuff Pellton was made of then and no doubt would have known now.

John felt ill enough to lose the sumptuous wedding breakfast they'd all just enjoyed. How could he have been so stupid? So blind? Betrayal was such an ugly thing. Especially when it came at the hands of a trusted friend. Realizing he had erred in every way he could have done with Georgina, John knew the most profound shame for his actions as he stood there watching his little girl leave her home, and him, for good.

*Anne, I'm sorry. Please forgive me the folly of shame when it should have been justice for our daughter.*

John Russell clutched at his chest and peered down the drive. His son-in-law's coach was very small in his sights as it carried their daughter away with him. Thank God for Greymont! And John meant that down to his marrow. He would not forget to offer special thanks for that young man when he prayed tonight.

It was funny how one's opinion of a person could alter on a turn. John had never been too impressed with Greymont in the past. The boy came off rather coarse and arrogant in John's opinion. A tad too libertine for his liking, but he had to admit, his new son-in-law did seem very devoted to Georgina and unconcerned with her past despite full disclosure of what had happened to her. Tom had vouched for Greymont's worthiness when he had enticed him to visit in September. His son maintained there was no one more honest or loyal, and Tom's word was good enough for John.

The father drew comfort in the belief that Jeremy Greymont would treat his daughter well and keep her safe. He'd give Georgina everything she deserved, affection, children, and security. Anne would have approved.

Today Georgina looked so like Anne in that dress. But her farewell to him had been stiff and awkward. She'd offered him an empty embrace, lacking any warmth of feeling, and she had not been able to look at him. John had seen her turn back for one last glance at the house though, probably vowing never to return. His little girl had nothing but contempt for her father now. And rightly so. He deserved every bit of it and more.

John endured a new wave of nausea and shut his eyes tight. Pellton wanted with Georgina what he'd not been able to have with Anne. She was the spitting image of her mother! Anne was spot-on then, and her opinion held just as true this day as on the day she'd made it. *"There's something unnatural in that head of his."*

Friend no more. Lord Edgar Pellton had just gained an enemy. An enemy with vengeance surging through his veins. John Russell made a vow, right there on the steps of Oakfield. He would make this right, for Georgina and for Anne, who wouldn't expect anything less from him where their children were concerned.

Straightening his coat, John Russell gave a small nod directed at the sky and went inside his home. He had much to do. First he would write to his son and call him home. Tom could help in this and would want to avenge his sister. He should also arrange a meeting with his solicitors to assure his affairs were in proper order just in case.

And then?

Well, he'd do the only thing he could do. He'd serve a heaping dish of cold revenge to the one who'd bloody well earned it.

# CHAPTER FIFTEEN

*Our doubt is our passion and our passion is our task.*
—Henry James, "The Middle Years" (1893)

The rolling landscape slowly changed from fields stippled with forest to windswept coastline the closer they moved toward the sea. The Bristol Channel spanned just thirteen miles of open water from the Somerset coast to Wales—a bordered natural bay extending from the mouth of the great Severn River. The area bustled with laden ships setting into coastal ports, some legitimate, and others much less so, fishing cutters and passage out of England.

Jeremy pointed out places of interest as they came to them. Georgina listened quietly and asked the occasional question. As the miles mounted, he'd drawn ever closer to her in the seat, until he'd managed to get her tucked under his arm and leaning upon his chest.

Georgina resting next to his beating heart, relying upon him for strength, puffed him with pride. He memorized the weight of her, and the shape, adoring how she fit to him. The steady sway of the coach affected the motion of their bodies rocking together gently.

There were lots of other ways to rock a body, and the visions swimming in his head weren't at all "gentle." No, he was awash in carnal yearning for his new bride. He wanted her so badly, underneath him, taking him in, a willing vessel for his hard, driving flesh. He wanted to claim her body as his, to protect and care for her. He wanted to meld with her and incinerate all that horrible shit that'd been done to her. But what if he just scared her more and reminded her of her pain?

This was so difficult, the path he had set for them, and there was no guidebook to help him along. He was the masculine version of a whore, who liked it rough, with a bride whose only experience at sex was a savage rape.

Could there be any more disparity between them?

He also felt a little guilty about claiming a husband's rights tonight with their marriage so rushed. But not that guilty. He wanted her more than he could ever recall wanting a woman, and now with the vows read, he found it difficult to think about anything else. Years of sensual indulgence weren't that easy to put aside.

Yes. He would have her tonight, and hard though it may be, he was determined to be more tender and sensitive than he'd ever done. *God help me.*

"Would you speak of Hallborough, so I can know it just a little?" Georgina looked up at him, so trusting and perfectly serene in his arms.

Unable to resist what lifted toward him, he kissed her rosy lips and then traced them with his thumb. "I love kissing you."

"Thank you," she whispered.

"For kissing you?"

She shook her head. "For wanting me."

His answer to that was to bestow more kisses, and it was a long time before he could pull himself away to speak. "That's never been a problem for me." He traced her lips slowly, circling the same path over and over. "I noticed you years ago really, when you were just a young thing. Waiting for you without even realizing it. Thank *you* for agreeing to take me on, *Mrs.* Greymont." He rested his chin on the top of her head. "I like the sound of that—the 'Mrs. Greymont' part. Someday you'll be Lady Greymont."

"I know. That's what Papa said to me yesterday. I thought he was talking about Lord Pellton the whole time and why I fainted when I realized it was you who had come for me."

Jeremy could only respond with a snarl, a scowl curling his upper lip. His teeth clenched over his jaw, and he felt his neck grow taut. "He'll not come near you, or he'll be sleeping in a coffin, the bastard!"

He wasn't sure what to do about Pellton and his nephew. The guard from the bordello, Luc, was now a paid informant. And he had a name for the shit bastard, too—Simon Strawnly.

Jeremy's ultimate priority was to protect his wife, both her person and her reputation. He couldn't allow further pain to touch her and intended that she never discover the identity of her attacker. Acting like a crazed bull whenever Pellton's name was mentioned might not be the best means of concealment though.

"Sorry, sweetheart. That was unseemly of me, but I never liked him." He grinned, feeling rather sheepish.

"On that we do agree, and I'm sorry I mentioned his name. I won't do it again. Tell me about your home?" she asked again.

"It is *our* home now, and it is lovely. Hallborough Park overlooks the sea at Kilve. From the sea path you can look across the channel and see the Brecon Beacons in South Wales if the sky is clear. The Quantock Hills lie behind us. The flowers on the heath are spectacular in summer. You can hear the waves. I think the sound of the sea is one of the most comforting in all the world. We'll take our walks along the beach, and at night we can watch the stars shine over the ocean from the house. I've arranged for your horse to be brought along with Samson, and you'll be able to ride as you wish. Have you ever ridden along the sand?"

"No, but it sounds so wonderful."

"Our neighbors, the Rourkes, are good friends, Darius and Marianne. They are recently wed, only since summer, and I think you'll like her. I know she'll welcome you very kindly. Marianne likes to sketch landscapes, and I've seen your sketches. You're very good. The two of you will have that in common."

"I can't wait to meet your friends. What of your grandparents, Jeremy?"

"They live in London nearly all the year, but I'll take you to meet them soon. They will adore you, Georgina, if only for the fact that you married me. When Grandfather gets a look at you, he'll worship the ground you walk on. We'll also go for the Season each spring and take our place, and the business is there of course, but for now I just want to have you all to myself at Hallborough."

As she looked up at him, her amber eyes clear and bright, listening to him rambling, she just looked so beautiful, he had to touch her. A finger reached out and started at her eyebrow and drew around her face in a complete circle. On the second pass around he traced her lips, remembering how sweet they tasted.

"You'll be the princess of Hallborough Park, and I'll protect you, and adore you, and make gorgeous babies with you. How does that sound?" He watched her face for anything akin to discomfort at his frank suggestion, but didn't find it. She just smiled in her unruffled way.

"Perfect, and makes me feel like I am a princess for truth. You make me feel like that, Jeremy. You are Sir Jeremy, the gallant knight who rescued me."

*How about the knave who can't wait to get the beauteous princess into his bed!* "I am glad, sweetheart. I'll try valiantly to remain worthy of your esteem, dear lady." He bowed his head.

"Always, Jeremy."

He prayed her confidence in him would hold true later when the time came to take her to bed. He didn't feel at all like a gallant knight. More like a licentious cad.

His honorable intentions toward Georgina had left him in a state of varying degrees of arousal for weeks. Jeremy hadn't been with a woman since the night he'd met Tom Russell in London. And he felt it—right down the length of his aching cock.

Jeremy breathed in the smell the sea the moment he stepped out of the coach and found it fortifying. Dusk was just beginning to darken the sky, and the sound of the surf hummed at the shore far below.

With a dramatic flourish, Jeremy helped his bride to exit and led her to the staff awaiting them on the front steps. The dark-gray stone of Hallborough Manor rose up silent before them, buffeted by the evening ocean breeze. The house had been extensively remodeled sixty years prior in the revivalist Gothic style, its tall pointed window arches pointing heavenward, evoking a kind of ancient spirituality among the natural elements of sea and earth and rock.

The housekeeper, Mrs. Richards, and his steward, Mr. Mills, received the couple warmly, having prepared for their arrival fastidiously. The torches ablaze outside, the chandeliers shining through the windows from the inside offered an earnest welcome and were so very comforting to Jeremy. He wanted Georgina to love this home as much as he did.

A quick introduction to staff and a very brief tour was all the time they had before the dinner hour was upon them.

Cook outdid herself on the regal dinner set out for the newlyweds. There were scalloped oysters in a white soup, flaky croquettes, and roast venison among a dozen other dishes they hardly touched. They served each other as was the custom, and Jeremy poured the wine. He noted that she drank two goblets and thought that was probably a good idea.

They stared at each other over their plates, Jeremy imagining how gorgeous she would look tonight and wondering how to do this without scaring her. He refilled her glass a third time and offered the lemon custard tart with a smile. Georgina returned the smile, accepted the wine, and declined the custard tart.

Now that he had her safe from Pellton and Strawnly, he still had another problem. Jeremy wasn't completely sure how to curb his rough nature when in the throes of the act.

He'd always liked his sex unconventional and had never tried or had reason to rein himself in. A little rough, dominating, experimental, he'd done just about everything possible with his cock and mouth and fingers in and on a woman's body. He'd done plenty of fucking, all with people he felt nothing for. He'd never made love to a woman though. In that realm, he was a doe-eyed virgin.

The added complication of Georgina's brutal assault made her all the more fragile. He knew he couldn't be how he'd been before. Not with her. That kind of sex was over for him.

*I can do this.* Despite telling herself repeatedly like a chant, Georgina wasn't so sure. She had agreed, signed her name, and left her home under the protection of her husband. Yes, husband. She had a husband. A husband who expected to be welcomed into her bed to begin their marital duties. *I can do this.*

She thought of Jeremy and what she knew of him. He was kind and gentle. Very gallant. Amusing, too. Just last night he'd held her in bed, and she'd never felt safer than she had in his embrace as she drifted to sleep. Surely he wouldn't hurt—

"Your bath, ma'am." The maid spoke softly.

"Thank you, Jane." Georgina presented her back, grateful for the interruption into her runaway thoughts that could lead no place good.

Jane helped her out of the gold gown she'd changed into for traveling and into a steaming bath behind a paper screen. The girl was young, probably not more than eighteen, but surprisingly efficient for an inexperienced lady's maid. Mrs. Richards had introduced Jane as her niece, explaining that she would fill in until such time as interviews for a proper maid could be arranged. The girl seemed scared to death, and Georgina's heart went out to her. The poor thing had probably been threatened with punishment if she displeased the new mistress.

"Are you new to this house?" Georgina asked through the screen.

"Yes, ma'am. I arrived just yesterday, but I haven't come from far away. Just the next village over." Her voice caught slightly.

"Ah, but it's not what you're used to is it?"

"Not really, ma'am. I left behind seven brothers and sisters at home." She trailed off and then thought better of it because she spoke the rest faster and louder. "But I am pleased to serve you however I may, Mrs. Greymont." The girl was honest at least, and Georgina liked that.

"I can see that you are. I am sure everything will be well met, Jane. Worry not. This house is new to me as well."

"Yes, ma'am." She sounded brighter as she moved off to put away the garments Georgina had removed.

The hot water felt good, soothing and loosening her muscles stiff from being confined in the coach for hours. Jeremy hadn't demanded anything during the long ride other than to hold her next to him and to kiss her. Georgina smiled, remembering how Jeremy had said he loved kissing her. His kisses were very welcome. No worries there. If only this bedding dilemma were as simple as kisses, she'd be much more at ease.

Georgina took a bar of violet-scented soap and drew it up her arm, returning to thoughts of her new husband. A perfect gentleman the whole trip, but intuition told her he wanted more and held himself back from displaying it. He knew what had been done to her and didn't want her frightened of him. He said so. He came to her bedroom last night to get her used to him. That was his intention. *Because he plans to come to your bed tonight and this time it won't be merely for sleep.*

They had discussed it last night. He said when they were together in that way, it would be within the bounds of matrimony. Well, that was now. Jeremy was coming in a short while to do all those things he wished to do with her, and she must allow him. *Dear God, help me to do this.*

She had been in so much pain…after her attack. Her body had ached in every place, and there had been injuries to parts of her that made her worry she mightn't be able to grow a child due to damage. *Please don't let it hurt like that.* The doctor had reported her well recovered though, and Georgina prayed he was right, for she truly wanted her own children. To be a mother and hold her own babies was a dream she held in her heart.

Georgina thought of her mother, Anne, and felt the pang of missing her gentle embrace and wisdom. She felt so lost and confused. There was nobody to whom she could share her fears about what was to happen tonight. Who could she have spoken to about such things? Her father? Her brother? Not likely. They both just kept telling her that marrying and starting a family was the best cure for what she'd borne and would help her to put the past away.

*Please don't let it hurt like before.*

Georgina finished with the soap, rinsed herself, and stepped out of the bath. She dried her skin briskly with a thick towel to ward off the chill.

"Your nightgown, ma'am." Jane draped a sheer yellow gown over the screen.

Georgina reached for it and drew it over her head. It was made of the thinnest cotton gauze but fully gathered at the sleeves and neckline which dipped low. It would be easy work for him to push it off her shoulders and bare her breasts. Might he leave her gown on? She shook her head with a firm shake. Somehow she knew Jeremy would wish it off. Strangely the thought of him seeing her body didn't bother her too much. She was more worried about all of the other things he would do to her body.

*Please help me to do this duty to my husband.*

"Your hair, ma'am. Shall I brush it out for you?"

"Please do." Georgina nodded and sat down before the dressing table, willing her nerves to settle. She watched Jane in the mirror, carefully removing the pins that held her hair up, one by one until at last her hair fell free. It tapered to a point at the middle of her back where Jane started the brushing. She began at the end and worked her way up slowly without painful tugs and snags. She might be an inexperienced lady's maid, but she knew how to brush out long hair.

"You have lovely hair, Mrs. Greymont. It is very soft."

"You have a lovely touch at brushing it, Jane. Your sisters must have long hair, for you know how to do it gently."

"Thank you, ma'am. I have two sisters and am well acquainted with the brushing of long locks." Jane moved through each section of hair until every strand had been tamed. "Would you like a braid, Mrs. Greymont?"

Georgina shook her head once. "I think not, Jane." She couldn't, and wouldn't say any more to a servant. It wasn't proper, but it didn't stop her from thinking about why she wouldn't have it braided. Georgina would leave her hair down because she knew Jeremy liked it best that way. He enjoyed touching and fingering through it as he had done last night.

"Well, I'll say good night then, ma'am. Please call for me if there is anything I may do for you." Jane bobbed a curtsy and let herself out of the room.

Georgina listened to the sound of retreating footsteps and then silence. She got up from the dressing table and moved to stand before the fireplace, slowly counting to one hundred in her head. It was the only thing she could think to do in order to keep her feet planted firmly on the floor and from running out the door.

*I can do this.*

Jeremy's heart thudded hard in his chest to the point of causing physical movement. Nervous was what he was. He could never remember feeling like this before sex, but here he was, nervous as a hare at a dog race. What was Georgina thinking right now? She must be nervous. How could she not?

It was hard to tell when he stepped into the well-lit room because she had her back to him. She was glorious all the same. Standing before the fire, Georgina appeared more beautiful than he had ever seen her. She wore her blonde hair down, the soft curls flowing over her shoulders and down her back. Her nightdress, pale yellow and thinly translucent, pooled at her feet. He could just make out the shape of her mile-long legs and other gorgeous parts in the backlight of the fire, like the perfectly rounded curves of her beauteous bum.

He stopped. Waiting, looking, admiring. It was all he could do.

She turned around.

His arms shot out, and he heard himself whisper, "Come to me."

Savoring every step, he watched as she walked toward him, her breasts swaying beneath the thin gown with each stride forward and then softly bouncing every time her foot touched the floor. *Mother of God!*

Once he could draw her into an embrace, he finally felt able to inhale a breath. He closed his eyes in thankfulness, so great was the relief to at last have her against him—safe and warm and smelling of sweet-scented soap.

"I love your scent. It's soothing and stirring at the same time."

She didn't say anything, just nestled closer.

He felt the softness of her breasts pressing onto his chest. *Bed. Need to get to the bed...*

Before he could think too much, he just scooped her up and carried her to the massive bed, where he laid her out and then put himself in next to her. Better to just start, he thought. Get them to the place where things would play out, and stop worrying. She was soft in his arms and submitted to him leading the way.

"You are beautiful all the time, but right now, in this moment, there are not words for how you are." He spoke softly, stroking the back of his hand along her cheek and then her neck and across the low neckline of her gown. His fingers curled up until just the middle one was left trailing down between the valley of her breasts and then back and forth over the exposed part of the swells.

She surged into the finger touches and closed her eyes. He felt her chest moving, her breathing increasing its pace. "Gina, are you nervous?" *Like I am.*

She nodded solemnly, her eyes still closed. "I don't want to disappoint you."

"You couldn't possibly, and you don't look nervous. You look like a goddess to me." He nuzzled soft kisses at her throat, very close to her ear. "But are you remembering things that hurt you?"

"I don't want to remember," she said.

"It won't be like that." He kissed her lips. "I hate the idea of you afraid."

"But you don't frighten me, only the memories do." She lifted her eyes, glittering with emotion, and he could see there was bravery in them, too. "Make me forget, Jeremy."

*That's my girl.* "I am. I'm going to replace that evil. With something good, something you'll want to remember."

He dipped down to her lips again. Very gently he put a hand to the back of her head and pulled her to him, thinking that her body felt like a paradise he wanted to explore forever.

Her soft curves and hollows, her scent, the golden color of her, the sounds of her body moving against his, the steady beat of her heart and her breathing—all of it was soothing. The emotions with Gina were new for Jeremy, feelings he'd never experienced before with any woman. Gina was solace to him, and the knowledge of the power she held over him was a surprise.

He sensed her softening into him, melting into surrender. Things were going well, he thought. She was pliant under his lips and hands.

His body knew what it wanted. Oh, did it ever. He felt his cock respond, stretching out, growing long and hard—anticipating the moment her body would take him in. As much as he wanted to be inside her, he was remarkably in check. She controlled him. Jeremy needed her, but Georgina controlled his path to her. Right now, he drew strength from her.

Pressing his pelvis forward, he arched into her hip, finding the pressure of that hard bone meeting his hard cock to be so exquisite, he was afraid for a second he might embarrass them both by spilling all over the sheets.

"You feel so good," he murmured.

She nodded back. He was sure he felt her nod, but she didn't offer any words of her own.

*I want in you.* He wanted his mouth on her quim and her hand around his cock, or maybe her lips. That would have to wait though. She wasn't even close to being ready for that sort of thing yet, but the naughty idea of teaching her such delights was certainly worth contemplating and propelled him higher with desire.

Kissing her throat and collarbone, he nudged lower below the wide neckline of her gown.

"I want this off." He tugged with his teeth. "So I can see you now—see how beautiful you are. All of you. I want our skin touching." He moved his face to hover directly over hers, asking for her agreement and hoping like hell she said yes.

She answered stiffly, her voice flat, as if she were far, far away from him. "Whatever you want. I am not afraid of you. I—I want to please you."

*You should be afraid of me.* If Georgina knew what he really wanted to do to her, she'd probably leap up and run far and long, away from him.

Very slowly his hands went to the ties of her gown and loosened them. When he pushed it open, he could feel her trembling. She was stiff as a board. And so was he, but in a very different way from her.

By her words, she showed him she was willing, but he could tell the intimacy unnerved her. She was submitting to duty, he knew, and while it should relieve him, it did not. He didn't like it. He wanted more from her than just capitulation in the marriage bed.

"You please me, sweetheart, but I want you to let me please *you*."

He kissed over the tops of her breasts ever so slowly and softly, moving inch by inch across delicious skin as soft as down. He felt the pounding of her heart beneath his lips. Felt his own heart match the throb. Torn between desire and nurture, he struggled to temper his need.

Georgina seemed fretful. Skittish as a colt, wary of him getting close. *She knows what you're going to do. She knows, and she's afraid.*

"Relax," he told her, pulling away from her breasts to brush gentle kisses along her neck. "Just let me touch you—it'll feel nice."

He heard her expel a breath and felt her body ease a bit. God, he wanted to make this good for her—to bury the memories haunting her, to show her instead how he intended to cherish her.

"I promise you," he murmured through another kiss to her lips.

More kisses. Eons of kissing. Long, slow tangles of lips and tongues filled the minutes as he learned her. Soft featherings of breath along her sculpted collarbones, behind her dainty ears and up her slender throat before firmer presses paused him at the swell of a breast.

He pushed up from underneath and found one finally with his hand. He palmed the weight, learning the feel through the thin fabric of her gown. Passing over the hard bud of her nipple, he heard her breath come faster.

Suddenly she arched, thrusting her chest out. He didn't know if from fear or pleasure, and didn't really want to know. Not anymore. He was too far gone to think rationally.

He used her movement to pull the fabric down further, finally baring those magnificent mounds of sweet beauty to his hungry eyes. Suddenly the feast of gorgeous flesh was before him. And he was so starved. Creamy skin tipped with dusky rose centers called to him. He reached for one and thrilled in the sensation of incredible softness under his palm.

"Beautiful." He studied them in the lamplight.

She stayed very still.

"I have to—" he whispered before covering her nipple with his mouth. He swirled over it, feeling the bud harden into an even tighter peak under his laving tongue. It was pure glory.

Cupping both breasts, one for each hand, he held them secure, worshipping their soft fullness with his mouth. He moved between them, giving equal attention to both. He made love bites on the undersides, fully intending to look at his markings later and remember how it felt putting his sign on her. Oh yes, *his*.

She submitted to everything he did, and he was glad. This was a claim in every primal sense of the word. She was his woman. He had found her, wanted her, and won her. And now he was finally having her, claiming her. *My wife. Mine, mine, mine, mine, mine.*

And then Jeremy forgot about everything he'd told himself he wouldn't do.

The brush of her body was too tempting, the scent of her too delectable. He simply forgot himself, lost in the elixir of the senses swirling together, inciting him to reach out and take.

"Ginaaaa... You feel so good," he moaned. He was drunk. Drunk on her. Swimming in the river of sensations that washed over him, he drowned himself in the taste of her skin melting under his mouth. Jeremy was good and downright intoxicated to the point of no return, and quite pleased to be so.

The focus he'd held on her ability to tolerate his attentions fell away, quickly replaced by carnal appetites long subdued and the glory of indulging them.

"I—I need you!" His hands were everywhere all at once. Up under her gown, pressing on her belly, between her legs, squeezing that gorgeous bum of hers. Like he couldn't take his time to learn her, but needed to know everything all in an instant.

Ravenous. Propelled. Desperate. Jeremy was out of his blessed mind with desire and the urge to fuck.

Her rigid arms and legs weren't perceived at first. Neither the fisted hands, nor the stiff neck either. He didn't hear her whimpers or feel her shaking. He had one goal. And that was to get inside her and come.

When Jeremy rolled on top of her, the thrashing started in earnest, along with what his supremely aroused and very limited coherence finally understood as panic. Georgina bucked to get him off. She struggled to move out from underneath him.

Jeremy felt and heard her now.

Georgina's cries pierced though his fervor, the sound of her as loud as a cock crowing at dawn when it annoyingly interrupted right at the point of deepest slumber.

Everything illuminated all in an instant. His clouded awareness became as clear as fine crystal.

*Shit!*

# CHAPTER SIXTEEN

*Our doubt is our passion and our passion is our task.*
**—Henry James, "The Middle Years" (1893)**

Georgina couldn't breathe. Her impulse was a primitive one, directed wholly by instincts. Her thoughts revisited another time and remembered other words… *Keep fighting me. That's it, wildcat. Fight me while I fuck you…*

She had little conscious control over her response. The urge to flee was all she knew.

*"Stop! Please, just stop!"* Did she cry the words out loud or not? She had no idea.

He did stop though. He stopped everything he was doing. Stopped kissing her. Stopped touching her. He moved his body off her.

Bolting up from the bed, she scrambled to the corner, slamming her head back into the bedpost. It hurt, but more importantly served a purpose. The blow brought her out of the unbearable chasm of fear and into the present moment.

Covering her breasts, she drew her arms around them and hugged her knees, burying her chin at the top. It stabilized her, gave her a point of reference from which to gain bearings.

Jeremy lay beside her, rolled onto his back now, an arm draped over his eyes. He breathed heavily. His wide chest peeked beneath the cut of his dark-blue robe. She could see the hair that darkened his chest. He was naked under his robe. And aroused, too. She had felt him hard when he'd pressed against her hip. Now she could see it. Well, see evidence of it anyway, underneath the heavy blue silk. A solid ridge lying long on his belly. His manhood. Big. Enormous.

He wanted to have it inside her. But she knew all about that, didn't she? She'd been well schooled in knowing what a man did to a woman when he took her.

"Are you all right?" he asked.

"I—I am s–s–sorry for p–p–pushing you—"

"I meant your head. You hit your head."

"I—I am fine." *No, you're not fine. You're a wretch—a bad wife. You denied him. You pushed him away!*

He was quiet, still as a statue except for his breathing. She couldn't tell if he was angry with her or not. He should be angry. He deserved to be. She wasn't keeping to her end of their bargain was she? Heirs, babies—she'd promised.

Jeremy left the bed after a time. God, he was tall. His big body looming over her, tense and quiet, he seemed to be waiting for her to acknowledge him.

Georgina held on to her knees, afraid to move. She braved a glance up at her husband.

His expression unreadable, he broke the silence hovering in the space between them, as thick as drying mortar. "Good night, Georgina."

His voice sounded tight, but not harsh. He wasn't even going to make recriminations for her failure, and she realized he was taking his leave.

"Where are you going?" she blurted.

"To sleep in my chamber."

"I am sorry. Jeremy. I didn't mean what I did. Please don't leave."

He sighed. "I must. I am. You need—" he stopped himself and raked a hand through his hair. "We are both very tired from this long day of travel. Try to sleep now."

Then he walked out the door.

Tears flowed soundless for long minutes until sensibility returned eventually, and with it, mortification. Her husband had just walked out on their wedding night.

Unable to focus on the shame, she looked around the lovely room. The lady's chamber—her room. Done in pale blue and gold, the colors suited her, the dark woods in contrast with the lighter fabrics.

A stunning equine portrait of two horses standing along the coast hung opposite the bed. It was so unique. She'd never seen anything like it before and had to wonder about the artist. *It belongs to you now.* And then it hit her. She was now the mistress of all of this. *And you don't deserve any bit of it.*

She hadn't done anything to deserve what was now hers by right. *You're now his by right. He has the right to bed you whenever he wishes.* And he hadn't. *He wanted to though.*

Jeremy needed an heir for Hallborough and was doing what must be done to get one. And she'd agreed to it. He had not hurt her or done anything disrespecting. Some of what he'd done had felt…nice. He was her husband now. *You need to be a wife to him.*

Georgina got out of bed and poured water for washing. She cleansed her face of the salty tears and changed out of her rumpled nightdress. She brushed her hair for a long time and left it wavy and loose about her shoulders.

Squaring those same hair-draped shoulders, determination fortifying her, she left the elegant boudoir, lamp in hand, and made for the master's chamber.

Jeremy didn't know quite what he should do, being that he was frustrated and disappointed and, quite frankly, worried. *What if she always panics like that?*

First things first. He needed a drink. The scotch he threw back razed his throat in a fire that strangely served only to comfort as the heat burned all the way down.

What he did next, he really should have done before he'd gone to her. Maybe he might have been more in check and not frightened her. He figured it wouldn't take long considering the state of his cock and balls. His prediction was accurate. Once he set himself to task, it didn't take long at all. Prick in hand, Jeremy jerked himself as ably as any self-respecting gin whore could have done.

The release did help some, but not nearly enough. He crawled into his big, lonely bed after a quick wash and chewed on the dealings of the past hour some more. Not how he'd imagined it with her. And he had hours of imagining bedding Georgina under his belt.

Jeremy snorted in the dimness. What bridegroom tossed off alone in a chair on the wedding night? He did, apparently.

Now what? He flopped over onto his side. He wanted her. Both of them knew he was well within his rights to go back in there and have her. He could get her to submit. But would that be force? Or a husband exercising his marital rights?

Georgina felt badly. He knew she did, and her reactions were based on an understandable fear. She'd looked so distraught and ashamed with her knees tucked up under her chin. If he tried again, she'd probably yield, and most likely without much fuss. Once it was done, she would know what to expect and would see that there was nothing to fear, just like sleeping with him last night.

But he just couldn't be that way with her. He didn't want to force Georgina to accept him. He wanted her to *want* him.

Part of Jeremy was repulsed by her fear. By the idea of her equating *him* and his lovemaking with Strawnly and what he'd done to her. He didn't want a woman in his bed that feared him, or for that matter, thinking about the man she did fear.

Rubbing his chest, he willed the dull ache away. Jeremy knew shame for his selfishness. He must face that he'd been the one to push her into marriage. Georgina was candid with him right from the beginning. She'd said she didn't know if she could bear the intimacy. And he pressed her anyway because he wanted her so badly. He still wanted her.

Yet he was not without any hope at all. She had seemed genuinely sorry. *"I didn't mean what I did. Please don't leave."*

Jeremy would have liked to stay but knew it was an impossible notion. He simply couldn't have remained in bed with her and held himself back. He'd had no choice but to leave. He didn't trust himself not to take her. He'd find a way into that sweet cove of hers one way or another. What a goddamn debacle he'd made of this night. His cock to blame for all of it too. Literally.

The mattress didn't feel right, about as snug as a bed of gnarled rope. He flopped again, changing sides once more, not at all confident he'd ever find sleep tonight.

Jeremy closed his eyes and tried to get comfortable, determined to reach drowsiness, and acknowledged that he would just have to try again tomorrow in the wooing of his sweet but reluctant bride. Opening his eyes, he looked up at the ceiling and made a decision. He would give her some time to adjust to being married. He could do that for her. And it would be worth the wait because Georgina was worth it. Jeremy closed his eyes once more.

What beauty to be had in the male form. Sculpted muscle and

smooth swaths of golden skin stretched out before her. Greedily she stared at Jeremy, asleep in his bed, and as strange as the notion was, Georgina longed to have him over her so she could feel all that beautiful skin next to hers. Hopefully her overture here would be met with interest on his part.

She lifted the lamp to see him better. He slept partway on his side, his arm flung out, tousled hair feathering his cheeks and forehead. He looked younger to her in sleep.

Georgina liked his lips, the way they felt when they kissed. His bottom lip was much fuller than the top and more so even than was typical for a man. Even though Jeremy was all male, there was something womanly to his lips, and Georgina liked them all the more. They were soft, too. Maybe, if she was lucky, he'd want to kiss her again.

She set the lamp on the bedside table and lowered the flame. She turned back to look and froze. Jeremy's eyes glowed in the lamplight like blue glass and pierced right through her.

"What are you doing?"

"I want—I am to sleep with you, Jeremy."

"I don't think it is a good idea, Georgina, and you know why." His eyes swept over her body and he looked hard at her.

"Well, I do," she retorted. She fiddled with the belt of her robe, hoping she could still her shaking hands if she had something to hold on to.

"No. Please, I cannot keep from take—touching you." Jeremy breathed hard like he was holding himself back. "If you come into this bed, I won't stop this time. I will not be able to stop."

"I know." She finally got her robe untied. His eyes went to where the fabric belt fell away and then back up to her face.

"There's no turning back. Georgina, you'll get all of me. Are you ready for that?" The coverings slipped to his waist as he sat up. His long, ropy muscles tensed along the length of his body. No nightshirt on her husband. He was naked and gorgeous.

It was just as well, she thought. When Georgina changed out of her nightdress, she had chosen to put on her blue dressing gown instead, with one omission. She was just as naked underneath her robe as he was underneath his bed covers.

Georgina drew as close to the bed as she could and gave Jeremy her answer. Nodding, she opened her robe and let it fall.

Her husband froze for just a second before pulling her into his bed, and he mumbled something. It sounded rather along the lines of, "Thank God!"

She got her wish. Jeremy's beautiful skin was pressed against hers. The lick of desire lit up in her belly, and she recognized it for what it was the second she felt it—wantonness.

Underneath him, Georgina surrendered to his hands, mouth, lips, and tongue. Jeremy was gentle in the way he asserted himself with her. And it was fitting and proper because he was her husband and had rights and privileges to her now. He could do as he liked.

Surprised at herself for wanting more of what he was doing, and by how good he felt bearing down on her, his tongue moving in just the right fashion, soft but firm, she forced herself to let go and float in sensation.

"You taste sweet," he mumbled, flicking the soft roughness over her nipple, back and forth before covering the whole thing and pulling it up into his mouth.

Jeremy's mouth was softer than she remembered, for he'd shaved his face smooth. He usually wore a shadow of a beard, and she had felt the tickle of whiskers when he kissed her yesterday. The sensation of her flesh filling his mouth, of part of her body being inside of him was stirring. Pressing on the back of his head, Georgina brought his mouth harder against her.

"You liked that?" He lifted his head and moved up to her lips.

"Mmmmmm, yes," she panted back.

Jeremy's tongue speared into her mouth then—a portent of an invasion of firm flesh to fill another part of her soon. She knew what was coming, and strangely, she wanted it, from him. In this moment she knew no fear, only needed the completion of Jeremy—inside her? Georgina felt an aching need between her thighs.

Shocked at her own desires, she gave into the pleasure of his tongue sweeping deep in her mouth. She pushed her own tongue forward to tangle with his. The soft texture of their wet mouths coming together shot her core with a rush of wetness. There was a lot of heat and wetness between her legs. Clamping them tightly together provided little relief. She really just needed him closer.

"Please—" she begged without knowing what she asked for.

Jeremy felt her legs stiffen and heard her whispery plea. The urge to lose himself to abandon was great, but he held himself in check, for he would not scare her. Even if it killed him, he would not frighten her this time. That she was so willing to trust him again filled his heart. He wanted to show her tenderness and pleasure and remember forever that it was him who had given it.

Pulling back to see her, he wanted to soak in her image as she lay on the bed, for she was glorious in her skin. "Look at you..."

He greedily took in the magnificent breasts, tight and wet from his mouth, the sloping curve of hips framing a flat stomach that dipped down to a triangle of dark soft curls. Oh, how he wanted inside that part of her. That beautiful, mysterious, paradise of feminine splendor that was Georgina's alone. A place he could know but never fully understand because that was the beguiling thing about a woman's sex. The need to penetrate, to be in that part of her, would never grow dull. He would forever seek to put himself inside her depths, to be as close to her as he could get.

Slowly, he brought his hand down to her waist, over her navel, across to her hip, and inside to her thigh, tracing her shape. "Open for me, Gina. I want to see you and to know that you want this. Show me that you want...me."

He heard an exhale, as if she'd been holding her breath. Slowly she moved, and he watched those long shapely legs that he'd admired so well on that rainy day by the creek shift apart for him.

*Oh dear, God!* He gritted his teeth to hold back the orgasm that threatened to come barreling out the tip of his cock.

# CHAPTER SEVENTEEN

*The iron tongue of midnight hath told twelve;*
*Lovers to bed; 'tis almost fairy time.*

—William Shakespeare, *A Midsummer Night's Dream* (1595)

G eorgina couldn't believe what she was doing, but somehow didn't have much trepidation at following his request. Whatever he asked, or wanted from her, she could do. That he wanted her at all she found unbelievable. She watched Jeremy's face as she did his bidding. His jaw got very sharp and tight, like he was gritting his teeth.

"God, yesss. I want in you so badly I can hardly think," he said more to himself than to her.

He kept his eyes on her body and inhaled, his eyes looking very hungry. Breathing in, he blinked slowly as he sat back on his knees.

*Dear Lord!* Recalling his words just a moment ago, she could understand the sentiment. Now it was her turn to get the full view of him. If he thought she looked like a goddess, then he must certainly be the king of all the gods, for his body was stunning, erect and hard in all his male splendor. The muscles filled out his form just like a statue of marble from the ancient world.

Georgina felt herself inhale deeply at the sight of him bare. He was big. His proud sex jutted up and out, dark pink, stretched skin, a glossy drop at the very tip, and the twin weights below, high and tight.

*Now. It's happening now.*

She couldn't help tensing as he crawled up her body, settling himself between her thighs. His eyes tracked her the whole way. She adjusted her legs, accepting the weight and touch of his skin on her skin. He felt hot. So did she.

The time was now. Time to complete the vows she'd pledged earlier this day. To offer herself willingly—submit to her husband's demands—be a wife.

Fear still ruled her even though she was determined to do this. What if the memories came back again? What if he hurt her? What if she couldn't bear it? What if she panicked? What if he was disgusted by her?

He reached for the back of one knee, bending it slowly and locking it behind his hip, opening her up completely, and at the same time lowering his hips to hers, linking them together, pelvis to pelvis. Hot flesh to flesh. She couldn't help the whimper that escaped.

He whispered through light kisses, ever gentle and tender. "You're ready for this, Gina. You are. Don't ever be afraid of me. I won't hurt you."

When his sex kissed hers, Georgina felt a flash of alarm, and she braced herself.

He immediately held her face to him. "It's me, Jeremy," he whispered, pressing his lips to hers, caressing like she was made of the most fragile china, "making love to you."

"I know," she said, her breath beating against his lips.

He held himself still against her. "Trust me, beautiful. Let me show you how it can be."

The jolt at the solid contact of rock-hard, velvety muscle was impossible to hold back when it came. She started to shake, impassioned and nearly out of her mind when she felt the blunt head of him bump at her entrance. She closed her eyes.

Jeremy cradled her face in his hands, trapping her softly with his firm weight. "You feel good, sweetheart," he soothed. Kisses brushed over her cheeks and forehead. "Can you look at me?" he asked. "So I can see your eyes when I am inside you and we are that close."

"Jeremy..." She opened her eyes to him, willing herself to surrender to this intimacy with him. She couldn't do anything else really, or want anything different. Georgina needed him to do this. She truly did. This act, with him, right now, was the one thing that would obliterate the past which tormented her.

Jeremy let go her face, found her hands, and entwined their fingers together. He pressed forward.

She softened under his weight, and he kissed more deeply, forging his tongue farther into her mouth as he slid just a fraction inside. He kissed her over and over again, whispering, adoring. Telling her how beautiful she was and how she pleased him and how wonderful she felt. Through the kisses and words he continued to sink himself slowly inside her body until finally he was in all the way, velvety strength buried tight inside her.

"Is this all right?" he gasped.

"All—right," she panted on an exhaled breath.

The force of her inner muscles slowly surrounding him was dreamlike. He stopped and held still for a moment before moving with a firm, smooth stroke. He saw her eyes open wider as he withdrew and pushed back inside her slick sheath. In the same instant he whispered, "You're beautiful," and claimed her mouth again. "And you're mine now."

He shuddered with the awareness of what he was doing.

*Exquisite. She is exquisite, just as I knew she would be.*

The invasion into her body produced a little moan that he swallowed up with a kiss, the sound of her only sending him higher. He'd filled her up completely, utterly possessed her, brought them as physically close as was possible to be without any barrier between them.

He rarely did this without sheathing himself first. One of the first things a young man was taught were the evils of sexual disease, and that using prostitutes without precautions guaranteed a certain and permanent affliction. Jeremy had always been careful with his cock. He'd made sure to employ a French letter with courtesans, so the feeling of going bare inside her had him swimming in sensations he'd rarely known.

Seeing her eyes widen in what he hoped wasn't panic, he tried to tell her, "Gina, you know I—I must— It's like I have waited my whole life for this moment with you." He rambled the words, kissing along her neck, trying to slow himself down. "Tell me you are all right."

Her eyes flickered at him. "I—I am. Don't worry about me."

*I'll always worry about you.* "But you are everything right now," he whispered before recapturing her mouth, his tongue moving in the way that mimicked what he was doing down low.

He *had* dreamed of her like this for so long. He felt himself spiraling in all-encompassing, unrestrained desire for her.

Jeremy stroked another gentle length, watching her face. "It's good—so good with you," he croaked.

And then he started to move in earnest. His thrusts caused Georgina's head to roll in a rhythm over the pillow as he pushed back and forth, thinking all the time he could move within her forever. He wanted it to be forever. Her taut heat wrapped around him, her soft breathing showing response to his attentions, unlocked his heart all in an instant.

Jeremy felt emotional…different. This woman was precious,

and he needed her like he'd never needed anyone before. He reminded himself again to go carefully and gently, to teach her slowly.

She sighed into him, tensing against his strokes, finding a primal, rhythmic sway in cadence with his actions, her head arched back, eyes closed tight again.

Jeremy worked slowly but steadily, plundering her, claiming her, possessing her totally, and losing himself.

Thrusting a little faster, he judged her ability to tolerate his pace. "Look at me, Gina. I have to have your eyes on me!" He needed to see her eyes so he could judge how she was bearing it. The will to protect her from fear overrode most everything else.

Georgina opened her golden eyes again and showed him. He couldn't see fear exactly—more like incredulity. Her sweet surrender spurred him over the edge of a precipice, his balls going tense in anticipation of spilling his seed inside her, of sealing his hold on her, of making her his, irrevocably. Once that happened, their bond would be undeniably complete.

The passion engulfed Jeremy, and in good measure, the ardor that had been building and held back, since that rainy day he laid his eyes upon her, found its much desired liberation.

Pulsing above her, he gave in to the coiled tension. His cock got painfully harder, growing rigid before releasing a hot flood deep inside her.

"Ohhh, Gina! Gina…Gina…Gina…Gina," he chanted into her throat, his hands, still entwined with hers, pulled them up close to cradle her face, drawing her into a kind of embrace, their bodies still locked together.

Sating himself on the pleasure pangs that roared through him, he held on to her tightly. Sweet Christ, everything felt so different—this experience with her. Nothing would or could ever be the same for him again. This he knew without a shadow of a doubt.

It was happening. Right now he was inside her, and it did not hurt, nor was there any fear in the experience. Jeremy was passionate in the throes of his pleasure with her. Dominating, but tender, he demonstrated great desire and need as he moved. He was also a vocal lover, speaking all manner of things while he stroked into her—insensible whisperings, endearments, her name, the Lord's name, and an ever-present striving moan that showed her the mystery of a man's want for a woman's body.

Georgina felt every inch of him moving, and with each new pulse, the compressions gave way to willful feelings of desire, heretofore unknown. She let him take her. She wanted it. He was different right now. Jeremy was wild and unrestrained and abandoned and beautiful, utterly beautiful in his raging passion.

Eventually, it reached a point where she could sense a change in him. His breathing quickened, his shaft felt harder, and then he stiffened, his whole body becoming rigid over her. His head rocked, his lips pulled back to show clenched, white teeth that choked out her name, over and over. His eyes never left hers, looking fierce, emotional, pained even as he clutched her face close to his.

She felt his sex kick inside her as he held it for a time before slowing and then finally coming to a rest, his tension releasing into lax, languid limbs atop her. Georgina knew he had spilled his seed as he found his release. Then she felt a great deal more wetness. *Dear, God! That's how it will be with him.*

Wanting to give herself and be passionate in return seemed natural. This act, with him, was not unpleasant—far from it. Jeremy like this with her was meant to be. She'd felt how much he wanted her, and she would do this willingly for him because it was what he needed. There was no hurt or shame in what they'd just done. Oddly, she wanted more, but didn't really grasp what, exactly, "more" could be.

It took a long time for Jeremy's breathing to level out. Finally he moved off her. She knew a strange longing when he pulled himself out of her, felt the gush of his seed and her own slick fluids. The wet between her legs gave evidence of the most intimate union between a man and a woman. They were truly married now.

Jeremy kissed her forehead and brushed his thumb over her lips. "Tell me if you are well."

"Mmmmm," she assured, nodding against his hand that still held her face. "I am." After another moment of quiet, she asked the question she needed answered. "Jeremy, was it—was it—are you well? I mean, was it—did I do—"

He laughed at her. "You swell my heart with your sweet inquisition. And my answer can only be yes. You were utterly perfect." He kissed her once more. "Have no doubts about my pleasure when you are in my arms. In fact, that's where I must have you all night long." He adjusted her comfortably against him in anticipation of sleep. "Right here up against me." His hand smoothed over her curved hip and pulled her to him, fusing their lower halves.

Jeremy's words relieved her, for if she could have him next to her like this, she would feel safe and never worry. "And I wish to be."

The three glasses of wine must have finally taken effect when she drifted off because she opened her eyes sometime later. Jeremy was warm against her, his hand settled low at her breast. And he was something else, too. Hard. Georgina could feel the ridge of his shaft pressing into her hip, and oddly, she liked the idea that his body was affected to want her again.

"How are you feeling, Gina? Tell me. I must know," he whispered against her.

Georgina thought about the question before answering. "I feel much cherished by you, Jeremy."

Hearing her response must have been encouragement enough because he rolled atop her, starting the whole intimate act all over again.

She gasped in air at the thought. Thrilling, desirous feelings flooded her. *Yes! God, yes! Do it again!* There was no worry this time. Georgina knew she had nothing to fear from having Jeremy love her like this. The elation at such knowledge gave her a power she had not felt in a long, long time.

Jeremy moaned desperately. "I want you too much. I have needed you so badly, waited so long, and I cannot hold myself back from you—I can't—I'm sorry!"

Georgina pushed at him to get his attention, "Do not be sorry. No being sorry, ever! I wish this with you. Jeremy! Ahhh…never sorrrry!"

*She said it. She wants me.*

He took her again. Proving to himself he could be more gentle and controlled than he'd ever thought possible, Jeremy arrived at a blissful peace afterward. A peace such as he'd never known, content and relieved with their scents blending into the musky smells of sweat and their passion and her soft warmth folded against him.

"When I set out to bed, I want you in here with me so I can reach over and find you in the night. Every night, Gina. I want you next to me like this."

She sighed contentedly and nestled against him, her fingers brushing over his pectoral, caressing the same spot over and over. Jeremy had never known such depth of feeling in intimacy with another person. It was strange but wonderful. Now he was the one feeling cherished. God, it was such a good feeling!

Later still, their limbs entwined, it was an easy thing to find sleep together in this first night. The mere thought of Georgina anywhere but next to him seemed unthinkable.

He didn't make it through the whole night though. Watching his wife in her sleep, Jeremy was entranced. Dark golden hair mussed and swirling over the pillow framed her face, her neck, and the graceful hollows that smoothed into the cleavage of her breasts.

Those breasts of hers. He'd known they would be spectacular, but nothing had prepared him for the reality. They were a work of human art all on their own—creamy swells topped with dusky rose nipples that flowed out to her sides from the weight of gravity pulling on them. He could remember their taste, like pears. In the dim shadows, he could just make out the love-bites he'd sucked onto all that luscious skin.

God, she was an artist's dream. An artist that painted nudes, he thought wryly, remembering his shock when she'd dropped her robe. The best, happiest damn shock he'd ever known.

She looked peaceful right now, but he had to wonder how she really felt about the sex. Did she submit out of duty only? Had it been pleasurable at all?

After that first part, when she came to him for a second try, she hadn't seemed frightened or upset. Hadn't cried or resisted him. Hell, she'd even asked him if he'd found the experience to be satisfactory, melting his heart in the process.

She might be a gentle person, but she was brave. If he understood one thing about his wife, it was that she had the heart of a lioness.

The sudden insight into what kind of mother Gina would be caused him to smile in the dark. He had made the right choice in her, for sure. This he knew without a doubt.

Jeremy also knew he hadn't done his best work tonight, and he felt bad about that. At one point though, he thought he sensed her thrusting against him, seeking to take him deeper. He *would* do better for her next time. He would show her pleasure if it killed him. Jeremy realized his desire had simply overtaken him and he'd become lost in the need to release before he could stop himself.

It had been challenging to hold back the urge to fuck with abandon. But he'd done that at least. Jeremy understood that Gina was incapable of tolerating such treatment from him. And even though he knew regret that he wouldn't be able to have that experience with her, the need to protect her and be a gentle lover was overriding. Gina's well-being was more important than how he preferred to fuck.

The thought of that depraved beast ravaging her, shattering her innocence, stealing her peace, was too awful to imagine and keep his wits. One thing was certain though, when the time was right, and the opportunity presented, that foul bastard would be dispatched straight to hell, and Jeremy would enjoy doing it.

*No question at all.*

# CHAPTER EIGHTEEN

*Trip no further, pretty sweeting;*
*Journeys end in lovers meeting…*

—**William Shakespeare,** *Twelfth Night* **(1601)**

G eorgina woke alone in the very early hours just before dawn. She knew he was gone because the delicious warmth of his body was missing against her skin. She couldn't smell him either. His unique scent was already familiar to her and comforting.

The feeling of abandonment threatened to overwhelm and the urge to cry rushed up her throat, followed quickly by disgust at herself. She was sick of crying. It seemed like that was all she did around him. It *was* time to grow up and stop behaving like a child. She blinked in the dark.

He'd left though, and that didn't make it any easier, especially after he'd told her he wanted to sleep with her the whole night. She wanted his arms back around her, protecting her, caressing her. In Jeremy's arms she felt very safe. Where was he? Why did he leave the bed? She tried to hold down the nasty, clinging doubt.

Remembering back to earlier, she'd called upon calm and serenity to cloak her as she prepared to do her duty to her good husband. She knew Jeremy cared for her by the way he spoke to her and treated her. She also knew he was gentle and kind, telling herself she could get through it, for him.

But what a revelation! The marriage bed was nothing like what she had imagined. She'd found him to be a careful lover, tender and sweet. When he'd put himself inside her, she had wanted it. In fact, every part of the experience had been welcome.

She felt empowered to be able to give him pleasure. Even though she knew it was a wife's obligation, it had been wonderful to grant fulfillment to him. Was he disappointed because she wasn't a virgin? she wondered. Where could he have gone? Should she go looking for him?

She sat up in the bed, pulling the blanket along to cover her bare skin. "Jeremy?" she called out softly.

"Sorry for waking you, sweetheart." His voice returned to her from across the room. He was kneeling naked beside the fireplace. "The fire was low and needed stirring. I can't have my bride awakening to a cold room on her first night at Hallborough."

"Oh…" Relief flooded her. He hadn't left her after all. She propped herself onto her side, taking in his splendid form, backlit from the flames. He was the epitome of male beauty, she thought, watching him boldly, feeling no small amount of pride and appreciation for the rippled chest, sculpted arms, and muscular legs. It felt a reward to know he was now *her* husband.

Standing slowly, he walked toward her, comfortable in his nudity, his heavy sex swelling before her eyes. Jeremy was a large man all over, his burgeoning shaft no exception.

"I thought you had left to sleep…elsewhere." Her voice came out more tremulous than she would have liked.

"I told you I'd sleep next to you, that I'd want you close so I could reach out and find you," he responded firmly.

She nodded back at him.

"Do you want me to sleep elsewhere, Gina?" She could sense a hint of frustration in his tone.

"No!" She reached out a hand, urging him to come to her.

"What do you see when you look at me right now?"

"I—I see that you are…beautiful. To me you are a beautiful man, and I think you are wanting me again."

"You're right about that, my Gina. I have to be honest. You deserve as much. If I get back into bed, with you looking at me like you are right now, I cannot help—" He put his hand on his sex and stroked it. "I want to be inside you, as deep as I can go. I want that badly, but not if I frighten you."

*Dear Christ!* His frank words sent a thrill straight to her core. She wanted him. Shaking her head, she insisted, "You're good— good for me, never frightening. Come back to bed." She lifted the covers, exposing her own nakedness.

He made a sound, a cry of sorts, before veritably leaping into the bed, his strong arms enfolding, drawing her breasts tightly against the hard, pulsing muscles of his chest. His skin was chilled though, from being up tending the fire, exposed and bare.

"You're cold," she murmured into his shoulder.

"You're warm," he countered. "So warm and soft and beautiful." He kissed her deeply, plundering her mouth with his tongue. The softness and the firm pressure penetrating her mouth made her anticipate what he would do next. His hands sought hers determinedly, entwining their fingers level with her head.

She liked when he trapped her hands like that, but couldn't fathom why she liked it. She just relished the feel of him taking charge of her body, holding her secure. Thinking was unnecessary, unwanted even. This was all about feeling and sensation and the friction of skin touching skin.

He mounted her, urging her legs apart with his knees, his sex seeking hers, instinctive in finding the way. Very wet and ready to take him in, she bent her own knees this time, loving the weight of him settling on her.

"Warm me up then," he breathed as he thrust himself deep and slow.

"Ahhh…"

Something seemed to spur him. Maybe it was the cry she made, but he was freer, more abandoned in his movements this time. He stroked with more force.

"You're tight." He began to moan in that surging way, punctuating an exhale with each thrust.

Georgina loved the sound of him when he moved in and out. It made her feel powerful to know that taking him into her body felt very good to him. She didn't know much about male physiology, especially when it came to sex, but it didn't take brilliance to understand that the sounds Jeremy was making meant he liked what they were doing.

Bearing down on him, she squeezed her inner muscles around his shaft and the onslaught of his strokes.

"God, yes! Keep squeezing me. Don't stop! Gina!"

The plunging sex barreled on, his lips dropping to her breasts where he drew her nipples into his mouth, suckling deeply, first one and then the other. It was ravishment, pure and simple. And being ravished by Jeremy was nothing less than divine. Georgina could only describe the sensation as a hunger. The sliding back and forth got her moving against him. She felt the soft slap of testes bumping her with every stroke. He fit perfectly inside her, and she wanted him to keep moving forcefully like he was. Using her inner muscles to squeeze tight around him some more, she heard him rasp out strained words. "I'm going to—"

As soon as he spoke, he released one of her hands and moved his palm down between them. Long, purposeful fingers glided over and into her soaked core as he continued to pump hard against it. "Come with me, Gina. Come with me, please!"

Something was happening to her. His movements, his words, and now the stroking to her slick nub forced a building roar to come erupting through her body. Intense convulsions consumed her so that she couldn't help but cry out. Jeremy seemed to be cresting the final surge of his own release, growing rigid as he shot his seed on a hard thrust and filled her up. All she could do was cling to him and ride the wave of satisfaction that pulsed through every part of her. She melded into his body, letting the senses take her over.

Eventually awareness returned, and she was brought to the realization that both had stopped moving and were flat on their backs, side by side. Panting together for a long time, unable to do anything other than breathe.

She reacted first. "I—I—" Unable to stop the tears, she brought her hand up to her mouth and wept, the emotion of the experience all consuming.

Jeremy spoke stiffly. "I was too rough. I scared you, didn't I?"

"Nooo." She shuddered, looking over at him.

"You can tell me, Gina. I know I'm a beast when I fuck—umm when I took you just then—I'm sorry!" He looked totally miserable and unsure of himself. "Shall I go anyway? I can sleep in another—"

"It's not you or how you did it! Jeremy, please don't leave me here—" she wailed, knowing she sounded hysterical and pitiful and couldn't blame him one jot for wanting to get away.

"What's wrong then? Why are you upset?" He loomed over her now, frowning.

Georgina attempted a calm response hoping it might soothe him. "Something happened to me. I never felt anythi—"

"You came," he interrupted. "You got an orgasm, a release, a rush of pleasure that overtook you. Am I right? Please say I'm right!" His eyes entreated as his voice sounded hopeful.

She nodded. "Jeremy, it felt good. Wickedly good." The need for air into her lungs was still great. Even now she still gulped in air as she came down from the heady peak. "I had no idea such—"

He kissed her hard, interrupting again. "That's what you're

supposed to feel, what I want you to feel! Wickedly good, every time!"

"Truly?"

"I don't lie. Truly." He began showering kisses over her cheeks, kissing away the tear streaks. "You please me so much, Gina, and giving you pleasure in this makes it all the more perfect." His expression changed then. He looked rueful now.

"What is it, Jeremy? You are frowning at me again."

"I'm afraid I won't ever get enough of you. I am a randy lout. I'll want you like this all the time. Gina, I know I will."

"I don't mind," she whispered against his lips, "and you're no lout. Can you make that happen again? What you did that felt so nice? Next time?"

She felt those same lips stretch into a smile at her request, and then a most emphatic "yes" was whispered against her mouth.

# CHAPTER NINETEEN

*Beauty is the lover's gift.*

—William Congreve, *The Way of the World* (1700)

G ood morning, Mrs. Greymont." Georgina opened her eyes to Jeremy's grinning and rather smug face above her.

"What are you doing?"

"Watching you wake," he said naughtily, "a most mesmerizing sight."

"Why?" Indulging in a satisfying stretch, Georgina became aware of her lack of clothing and the newness of being in bed with a man. A very masculine and amorous man.

"Well, imagine my surprise this morning to find a gorgeous woman, naked in my bed. Wherever did she come from? I wondered. And what should I do with her?"

His silliness forced a true laugh from her. She giggled, playing along. "Maybe I am lost. You should send me on my way, I think, and by the by, my memories of you are quite clouded. I don't remember much. Your name, sir?"

"You don't remember? Tsk, tsk, we cannot have that," he purred, arching a brow and looking so very devilishly handsome in his mock displeasure. "And you are going nowhere!" Reaching her waist, he tickled quickly. "Do you remember now?"

Shrieking laughter was the only response she could give him.

"I like you here in my bed, especially the naked part!" He raised both brows rakishly. He was a rake. A very sweet and lovely rake. And he was hers now.

"Your name?" She managed to ask through bubbled laughter while attempting to block his tickling. "You neglected to tell me your name, sir!"

He loomed over her lips, hovering close. "I am Mr. Greymont, besotted husband of Mrs. Greymont, a most beauteous woman who must be ravished properly, and most urgently I might add."

"Ah, really? Is this something Mrs. Greymont should expect to happen often? Ravishment?"

"I should say, yes. In fact, I *know* she should resign herself to it."

"And why is that?" she quipped.

"Because Mr. Greymont cannot keep his hands off her! He's only a lowly man for God's sake." His hand started roving purposefully over her hip and the swell of her bottom, just to prove his point. "He cannot help himself."

"Mmm, they are lovely hands, and he does such wonderful things with them."

"He is skilled with other parts besides hands," he reminded knowingly, his voice dropping to a husky burr as his blue eyes deepened in color. He wanted to have her again. This she was certain of. The previous night's instruction had taught her that much at least.

"Ah, yes." Heat flooded her lower parts at his naughty words. She knew what was coming. It felt good to be touched and caressed and kissed. Desired.

He pressed forward, his stiff shaft to her core and his hot mouth to her breasts. The heat of their bodies coming together, ignited an incendiary fire with only one way to extinguish.

"And to think we worried you'd be unable to bear this," he murmured, tracing a finger over the curve of a breast.

"I find myself completely and utterly happy for all my misunderstandings." Gina rolled on top of him and grinned. "It's a good thing to be wrong sometimes."

"I am so relieved you're not afraid of me—of this. I never want to hurt or frighten you."

"I know that."

Jeremy reached around the small of her back with his hands and pressed downward, smoothing over her lush hips and gripping both sides while grinding another erection up from beneath. His near-constant state of hardness around her was another surprise.

He couldn't help any of it. Biology simply took over, his cock heating up, lengthening, wanting to penetrate into her clutching depths. If she was close, his body sought what it needed, wanted, and craved.

"I could touch your body forever. Every part of you is delicious and so very fine..." he whispered up at her.

She stared down at him, focusing in on his lips. Impulsively, he told her, "Kiss me."

Gina's lips parted before dropping down to join his. He could see the white of her teeth as her mouth opened. The soft brush of her tongue pushing out and into him was another jolt to the raging thing between his hips. She swirled around his tongue and over his teeth and then sucked on his bottom lip, just the way he'd done to her last night. His bride was a fast learner. Jeremy let her explore with him, thrilled with her gentle attempts at discovery.

"Your lips are softer now that you've shaved, but I like your scruffy beard shadow as well. Makes you look rugged and mysterious."

"Do you?"

"Oh yes."

"And here I thought I should please you by being all smooth and civilized for you at our wedding."

"Civilized or rugged, you please me."

"What a lucky, lucky man am I!" he told her, and believing every word.

She just looked down at him, a half-smile on her face, her topaz eyes warming him, making his heart swell with possessiveness and something else. Love? How was such sentiment even possible for him? Jeremy had lived for years, detached and unemotional in his dealings with scores of women. And now? Not anymore. With Gina he felt nothing *but* attached and emotional, wanting only to show her how very important she was to him. How could he have transformed so completely and so quickly? Jeremy didn't even miss all the empty, rough sex he'd had before. It was nothing to him now. Not after last night. But the intimacy with Gina had sure meant something. He could only describe making love with her as special and precious. Jeremy realized that sex with a person he cared for made it fulfilling, and this was a completely new experience to him.

"What would you like to do today?" he blurted.

Her eyes flickered as she looked away shyly.

"Tell me."

She tried to move off, but he snagged his hands onto her bottom to keep her securely on top of him. "Are you shy now?" he whispered. He tickled her side a little. "After last night?" He rolled them over so he now had her trapped below him. Nuzzling her neck and lower to her breasts, he licked slow circles around the centers until she arched into his tongue, an erotic moan tumbling out of her. The sound that came from her throat so dripped of sex he felt himself punch out a hard erection on her thigh. *What a surprise!*

"Don't be shy with me, Gina. You need only ask," he purred, sure she wanted more from him, more of his cock, more orgasms. "I can make you find heaven again." He ground his hips downward. "Do you want me to teach you…other ways we can be together?"

Jeremy could do all of that for her and would be happy to be of service. In fact, the idea of leaving the bed, leaving her body right now was an unbearable notion.

"Maybe later?"

"What?" Did he hear correctly? Did she say "later" to the sex?

"I—I thought I'd have a bath…and maybe some tea?" She lifted her lashes, her eyes hopeful.

He felt his cock wither, and the guilt took over from there. "Shit! Aw, pardon the language. Of course! You must need some privacy, and food, for God's sake!" His shoulders fell. "Gina, I am a beast, and I apologize. I don't know anything about being married. I'm an insensible lout who can't keep away from you for a—" He shut off the lunatic babbling coming from his mouth and leapt off of her and out of the bed. He grabbed his robe and shoved his body into it.

His back was to her. Gina was still lying like a goddess in that bed, and he was afraid to turn around and see her face. Afraid of what she must think of him. What a "prize" she had won. Lucky her! A rutting ape for a husband who could think of nothing but sticking his cock into her while she suffered of hunger and thirst. And with a past like hers! God! A knife would be a useful tool right about now…for slicing off his traitorous balls.

"Jeremy?" Her voice called to him, soft and gentle.

"Hmmm?" Still with his back to her. Still afraid to look.

"Turn around and look at me." Her voice was firm.

He obeyed, but he didn't want to. He turned his neck and looked over his shoulder, wishing instead he could run out the door and board a ship bound for the nearest penal colony.

The sight that met his eyes was lovely though. Gina had sat up in the bed and now leaned against the headboard. The sheet was pulled over her splendid breasts, flattening them somewhat, and held in place with her arm. Dark-blonde waves settled over her shoulders, and her lips were all puffy from being kissed for hours.

She was the epitome of sensual beauty. A woman fresh from a night of slippery sex and numbing pleasure, looking well ridden and fulfilled but still as alluring as if she were an untouched maiden. And she was smiling at him. And crooking her finger. And calling him over to her!

Again, he obeyed, some small part of his brain shocked at how easily she commanded him, but knowing he couldn't or wouldn't do anything else. He stopped at the edge of the bed, awaiting whatever she had for him.

Gina patted the mattress next to her, still smiling that unruffled grin of hers that he recognized as her signature expression.

He sat down carefully, praying he could maintain some self-control in spite of being so close to her very soft and very naked body. He folded his hands tightly in his lap. "I am ashamed—"

"You should not be," she interrupted, pressing two fingers to his lips.

"But I've not seen to you as I should." He spoke right through her fingers. "I've kept you here in this bed, giving you no time for yourself—"

She pressed a little harder with her fingers. He blinked at her and kept right on speaking. "You have to tell me! Gina, I'm an imbecile. I don't know anything about—"

She kissed him on the lips to shut him up. And thank Christ she did. Who knows how many other sins he might have confessed.

"I disagree with you, Mr. Greymont. I have it on good authority that my husband knows many things. So he is definitely not an imbecile." She peppered each statement with short kisses.

"He has been nothing but sweet and gentle and caring of me," she said firmly, "but now, I think the time has come to leave the bed and have our breakfast, and then I'd like a tour of my beautiful new home."

He nodded stupidly before finding his voice. "And you shall have your wish, my sweetheart. Again, I apologize for being so ravenous with you, but I know it's inevitable whenever you are near. From the moment I saw you in that rainstorm and smelled your scent." He tilted toward her neck and inhaled. "Is that eglantine you use? I love the way you smell."

She smiled some more at him. "Eglantine with a hint of orange. It's what my mother wore and reminds me of her. I'm glad you like it, Jeremy, and no more apologizing for being as—as a husband wishes to be with a wife. I'm happy that you want me, and I don't mind that you are…ravenous…" Her voice trailed off, that adorable shyness creeping in again.

He leaned in for a soft kiss and then looked down to where the sheet covered her breasts. "You are a beautiful woman. I love to look at you, and I'll never get enough." He inserted a finger under the edge of the sheet. "I'm greedy." His finger dipped lower. "I always want more." His finger tugged at the sheet. "Will you grant your ravenous husband one last peek, my sweet wife?"

She bit her lip adorably and got a saucy glint in her eye before lowering the sheet, giving him a full view of those luscious breasts he so admired.

He had to catch his breath at the sight. Hair spilling over bare shoulders framed the soft flesh smattered with the marks made by his mouth in the night. The dusky centers budded at the tips from his bold gaze.

"Splendor," he breathed. It was all he could say, really. He didn't want to talk. He just wanted to look.

Because she was so beautiful and because she was so giving and accepting of him, he couldn't respond, couldn't speak words, or be coherent in any meaningful way without embarrassing them both. The best thing he could do for Gina right now was to give her the privacy she had so gracefully requested.

He stood and crossed his palms over his heart, bowed his head, and told her he would meet her in the breakfast room.

As he pondered his good fortune in gaining a wife such as her, Jeremy knew. He knew it with certainty because the feeling of leaving her behind was so acute. He knew it because he wondered how many minutes he'd have to wait before he could be with her again. He knew it because he'd never felt anything even remotely close to this before. He knew what it was. Love. He loved her.

# CHAPTER TWENTY

*O Love, O fire! Once he drew*
*With one long kiss my whole soul through*
*My lips, as sunlight drinketh dew.*

**—Alfred, Lord Tennyson, "Fatima" (1832)**

Georgina watched Jeremy stalk out of the room. His distress at misunderstanding her request was charming. The look on his face! He'd been afraid to confront her after he'd leapt out of bed, the poor man. His response surprised her.

In fact, the whole of their wedding night had been astonishing to her. Her perceptions and then the reality coming together from such opposite extremes and ending in the most wonderful disclosure. Being with him, making love, the closeness, the intimacy, was glorious. And something never to be feared again. Nothing had prepared her for *wanting* the sex. And she had. Last night she had been wanton in his arms. Another flush overtook her as visions of what they'd done clouded her thoughts.

She was a wife now. She had duties and responsibilities to her husband, the foremost being to give Jeremy the heir he needed. She had been willing to do as such when her agreement to wed him was given, but never in her wildest dreams had she believed she would desire the actions necessary to get her with his child.

She drew her hand over her belly and thought about what was inside her. His seed. A great deal of it she supposed from how wet she felt and the number of times he had shuddered into her.

She remembered how wild and unbound he looked each time he'd done it. How he stared into her and seemed to need the contact of their eyes meeting in that most all-embracing moment. Perhaps they had started a baby already? She hoped so. But regardless, whenever they came, she hoped his resemblance would be born in them. Boy, girl, rascal, or angel, Jeremy's babies would be beautiful.

A knock at the door interrupted her musings. The small, dark-haired maid, Jane, who'd assisted her last night bobbed into the room. "Good morning, Mrs. Greymont. Mrs. Richards has sent me to attend you. How may I serve you this day, madam?"

Georgina felt the thrill of Jane's address, first as "Mrs. Greymont" and then as "madam," and had to make an effort to keep her composure. It was hard to picture herself as a Mrs. or a madam, but there it was. The monikers were her due now.

"Thank you, Jane. I believe I would like to start with a hot bath," she said bravely, eyeing the bed for her dressing gown. Where was it? She had used it to cover up when she'd gone to the water closet in the night... *Oh, right!* She blushed, recalling how Jeremy had delighted in "unwrapping" her, as he put it, when she had returned to the bed. God knows where the garment ended up.

Jane speedily came to her rescue, sweeping the blue silk up from somewhere and holding it open for Georgina while discreetly turning her head.

Bless her, Georgina thought.

"There's some morning tea for you just through those doors into the adjoining sitting room. The master insisted you get it straight away." Jane pointed. "If you'd like to go in there and have it now, I'll just prepare the bath for you."

Bless him, Georgina thought.

Having arrived into a steaming bath, Georgina washed her body and thought she might need to pinch herself. Two days. Everything had turned in just the past two days. Two days ago she cared little of life, having nothing to live for or look forward to, feeling broken and useless and a burden.

But then Jeremy came for her. He'd changed the whole landscape. He had walked right back into her world and told her that he wanted her and that he wouldn't take "no" for an answer. He'd taken her out of the hell in which she had been trapped and offered to her a life. A real life. A life she wanted. And something worth fighting for.

Sitting in the warm water, she also realized how much she had changed in those same two days. She had gone from being a frightened little mouse that had to be convinced to accept an honorable man, to a very awakened and aware woman of just how blessed she was in her husband. There was no denying it. She had won a rare prize with Jeremy. And she would hold on to him with everything she had.

"Success! I have found the breakfast room. I wasn't confident I'd make my way here. Thankfully Mrs. Richards happened by and directed me. I hope I haven't made you wait a very long time."

Jeremy jumped up and helped to seat her at her place. He leaned in at her neck with his soft lips and nuzzled right below her ear. "I assure you the wait was very worth it. You look superb. That green is excellent on you."

"Thank you." She looked him over, appreciating his dark-blue waistcoat over a fine white shirt. He wore his clothes *very* well. "You look quite well rigged-out yourself."

"I have been quite productive actually. I wrote a letter to the grandparents and shared the happy news of you." He smiled and his blue eyes turned smoky. "Can't wait for the reply I'll be getting." He winked at her. "The sun is out. And since the day is dry, I thought we might have a walk after we get you fed. I could show you the grounds, and then we can take to the sea path and bring a blanket for sitting on the sand."

"Sounds perfect, Jeremy."

"Now for some food. What's appealing to you, eggs, bacon, porridge, toast, a bun? Cook is wickedly skilled, and eggs are a particular specialty of hers. You must try some of everything." He took up her plate to serve her, and in its place he set down a velvet black box.

"What is this?" She picked up the box.

"A gift, for you. Open it."

She lifted the lid to reveal a pair of pearl drop earrings set with diamonds. "Jeremy, these are outstanding! So lovely and elegant." She reached out to clasp his hand.

He took her hand to his lips and kissed. "I am pleased you like them. I think they'll go well with your mother's pearls, don't you?"

"I do. They are so beautiful and unique in design. Thank you for such a precious gift. You are spoiling me." She locked on to his eyes. "I feel as if I'm in a dream and you—all of this—cannot be real, cannot be happening to—"

"It's real." He nodded his head and took her chin in his hand. "*You* are what are beautiful and unique. Last night, with you, was the precious gift, and like those pearls, rare and treasured, but far above all other things."

They held each other's eyes for the longest time. When Jeremy finally spoke, the words were important, and precious, and valued above all other words. And what made them even dearer was that they were the same words she needed to say to him.

"Georgina, you hold my whole heart now. You know that,

don't you? You make everything bright and good. I want to experience joy together and learn every secret part of you." He leaned in to kiss her lips. "My dearest lover—my only lover."

His declaration thrilled her, but she knew that last part couldn't be true. Jeremy had been with women before, as sure as the sun rose in the east and set in the west.

"I see your puzzled look, sweetheart. I think you don't believe me."

"Well, it's just that—you must have—there've been women you have—" she said haltingly, biting her bottom lip. Thinking of Jeremy with other women was not something she wished to ponder.

"I speak the truth, Georgina. I am many things, and several of my traits are less than desirable. But one thing I am not is a liar. I've had women before, yes, but never a lover."

"No?" she asked, hardly able to contain the joy she felt at knowing her husband might actually have deep feelings for her.

"Not before you, my Gina. Not even close."

"Oh, Jeremy, you fill my heart until it overflows." She cupped his cheek.

He spoke solemnly. "I have never known the deepness of emotion you cause in me, and it even frightens me a little, but still, I find I must ask the question."

"What question?"

"Will you be my lover then?"

She laughed at him before answering. "A little late to ask me, I think, but yes, Jeremy, I am honored to be your lover." Leaning forward, she kissed his beautiful lips and knew great contentment in having the right to do so.

"Thank Christ!" He breathed out a sigh as if he'd been holding his breath, waiting on her answer. "It's settled then, sweetheart. We shall be the happiest of lovers together."

# CHAPTER TWENTY~ONE

*Love seeketh not itself to please,*
*Nor for itself hath any care;*
*But for another gives it ease,*
*And builds a Heaven in Hell's despair.*

—William Blake, *Songs of Experience* (1794)

What a difference a week could make in a lonely man's life. He now had a wife, a lover, companionship, intimacy, hope, comfort...more loving than he'd ever known. A future to look forward to.

The autumn sun warmed the sand and the blanket upon which they reclined. The sound of the swirling surf singing in his ears, Georgina's fingers trailing through his hair, her lap pillowing his head, Jeremy thought the moment couldn't be more perfect.

He watched her as she looked out to sea. The elegant cheekbones that swept back to her hairline, the oval face, the rosy lips, the amber eyes, and the glinting hair all captivated him. And she was his to adore and protect.

In the past week, he had taken her around to every part of Hallborough Park and proudly introduced her to the staff and the tenants. He felt ten feet tall every time he announced her as "Mrs. Greymont," and would bet that everyone who had known him before was no doubt sniggering behind his back at what a sap he was and the fact that he had a ridiculous grin stuck eternally on his face. He did not care. He was a man in love.

Jeremy had a wife. A most splendid wife. A wife who was caring and kind and generous, who welcomed him into her arms at night and into her body. A wife who smiled at him and kissed him and by all accounts appeared to love him back, as remarkable as that seemed. The empty void that had been his heart was filling up.

His grandparents had speedily sent their congratulations, thrilled at his news. They extended an invitation for a visit to their London home and hoped the newlyweds would come as soon as they wished for Town.

But he wouldn't bring her yet. Town would have to wait. Jeremy was not willing to take the risk of Pellton and that monstrosity of a nephew of his crossing paths with Georgina. She seemed at peace with the memories of her assault, but he couldn't take the chance that a meeting might trigger something. The bordello guard, Luc, had reported to him that Pellton and Strawnly were still in London, so for now he'd keep her safe at Hallborough. And he'd gotten no word from Paulson that Marguerite had called in for her passage to Calais either. Jeremy really hoped she would take him up on his offer. He had many hopes about a lot of things.

Why hadn't he courted Georgina sooner? Just a few months earlier and he could have prevented—

"Why are you grimacing?"

"What?" He looked up to see her lovely eyes trained on him, her head tilted slightly. His eyes trailed to the scar on her left cheekbone.

"I saw you grimace. You looked so peaceful at first, and then your forehead got all wrinkly and you frowned. Rather dreadful really," she teased. "Made me take a second glance!"

"It's nothing." He reached for her hand and brought it to his lips to kiss.

"Tell me, Jeremy," she entreated, looking much more serious this time, her jaw clenching a little.

He hated to tell her, but thing was, he didn't lie. He always told the truth because he abhorred what lies wrought. Lying led to disaster and ruin and betrayal. There was no good in it. And also he knew Georgina wouldn't let it go. As much as he adored her, there was a stubbornness in his wife that commanded respect.

He worded his response carefully. "I was wishing I had gone to court you sooner—about six months sooner. If I had done so, you never would have been...hurt. Would that I might have kept you from such a thing."

She kept on stroking his hair and spoke softly. "There is no use in regretful thoughts, for we cannot undo the deed nor turn back time." Her voice had an empty tone to it.

"I know. I just wish you were free of it, somehow."

"Jeremy, if it helps you to know that I don't remember the act—actual attack, then there is that."

"You don't?"

She shook her head. "I thought you knew. It caused some frustration with my family, especially Papa, because I could tell them so little—"

He knew he shouldn't and wanted to cut out his tongue the instant the question left his lips, but out it came anyway. "What *do* you remember?"

Her hand stilled on his head just slightly, but he felt the pause clearly before she recovered and continued on with the soft fingering through his hair.

"Dear God, Gina, please forgive me for asking you—I don't know what came over me. I apologize—"

She interrupted, her voice steady and smooth. "I remember he wore a red coat, and he was drunk. I could smell it on him. I remember his voice was cruel and he spoke nasty things that terrified me. I thought that he enjoyed my fear and that I fought him. But mostly all I remember is the fear. It's just a black wall of fear right in front of me, and when I turn to avoid it, the wall moves to stand before me again."

"I am so sorry, Gina."

"The worst part is that my father is ashamed of me for what happened."

"That is an offensive notion to me. You were the victim in all of it. Surely your father knows that. And if he does not, then perhaps I should tell him!" Jeremy's chest hurt. Listening to his sweet Georgina speak with such dignity about someone so evil made him nearly snap in two, he was so tense. He wanted that fucking piece of shit, Strawnly, in front of him, and he with a sharp knife—a large one—so he could slice and peel off his skin, slowly, inch by agonizing inch. He'd start with the bastard's defiling cock.

She shook her head before she spoke. "But you are helping me to forget, my dearest lover. Each day that passes with you loving me so sweetly, I feel it less." She smiled down at him.

Her kind words killed the tension in him, just like that. "Well then, I shall have to be an even sweeter lover to you than I have been thus far," he declared and popped up off her lap. "Starting right now!" He put his lips to hers—

—and nearly had an apoplexy! Loud barking thundered in his ears, the smell of wet dog met his nose, and the spray of sand hit him in the back.

"What the hell?" He jerked his head around to meet the very large, very shaggy, and very enthusiastic greeting of Brutus, the wolfhound.

"You have a friend I have not met, Jeremy!"

"Indeed," he muttered. He helped her to her feet and did the introductions. "Gina, may I introduce my neighbor, Brutus. Brutus, my bride, Georgina." He wagged his finger at the hound. "That's Mrs. Greymont to you, and no jumping, or salivating, or any other ungentlemanly conduct out of you, young man!"

The great beast sat promptly and whined, cocking his head.

"Oh, Jeremy, he's magnificent!" She reached out to stroke the giant dog. "Who does he belong to?"

"The Rourkes, my neighbors." He scanned the beach. "Ah, here they come now. They must be out for a stroll like us."

Georgina looked to the couple walking toward them. Another wolfhound accompanied the pair, keeping sedately to their side. The woman was stunning with her dark hair and perfect skin. The man was also darkly handsome and tall, with noble features, sharply edged and serious.

"Brutus! Come!" the man commanded. "Sorry for the intrusion. He is an utter scallywag!" He called to Jeremy and Georgina as they crossed the distance on the hard sand.

"He is that, Rourke, but my wife seems to be taken with him regardless," Jeremy countered.

The woman's face alighted in a beaming smile and so did the man's. "Greymont, did you just say, 'your wife'? We've only just arrived back to the country and must've missed hearing the pronouncement. Congratulations are in order, my friend, if that is the case!"

"Indeed I did," Jeremy returned, smiling at Georgina and again providing introductions for the second time in just as many minutes.

Georgina found Darius and Marianne Rourke a charming pair. She liked their dogs, too. The rascally Brutus and the elegant Cleo were gorgeous, and huge, Irish wolfhounds. The Rourkes insisted on having them to dinner at Stonewell Court, seemingly thrilled to meet the woman who had ended Jeremy's stint as a bachelor. And Georgina looked forward to knowing them as well. It would be a good thing to socialize as a married couple for the first time.

"I would love to accompany you, Georgina. The best modiste is Madame Trulier, and she has excellent taste. She can fit you out with everything you need." Marianne smiled kindly.

"A French modiste?" Georgina remarked. "Are her designs very scandalous?" She blushed at her new friend.

"Yes!" Marianne told her with a giggle. "But your husband will love them. Darius certainly enjoys her efforts!"

They laughed together, and Marianne put her hands protectively over her belly. Georgina realized she was pregnant. "Congratulations," she offered, directing her eyes at Marianne's small swell.

"Thank you. By April, the wait will be over. So you see, I have a valid reason for visiting Madame Trulier myself. Nothing much is fitting me anymore," she said ruefully.

"Jeremy told me you were recently wed."

"Yes. We married in June."

Georgina froze. June… That month was probably not a time she would ever feel happy about even if she lived to be an old woman. June had been the end of innocence for her. The end of her old life.

"Are you well, Georgina? You look like you've seen a ghost." Marianne seemed genuinely concerned and had no idea how apt her metaphor really was. "Let me get you some refreshment," she urged.

She saw Jeremy's head turn her way. Even though he and Darius were engaged in conversation across the room, he was attuned to her, able to pick up on her reflection into the treacherous past. Jeremy was ever watchful over her. And that was just another reason to love him so much.

Georgina turned her full attention to Marianne and smiled.

"Oh, I am fine, really. Thank you for your kindness. I can't tell you how pleasant it is to be in your company." She shook off the melancholy forcefully. No way would she allow it to penetrate her happiness in the present.

"My husband also tells me that you like to sketch." Georgina steered the topic. "I do also. I'd love to see what you've done, Marianne."

"Yes, please. Let me show you to my studio. The view of the sea is lovely from up there. The stars will be shining over the ocean tonight."

When they descended the stairs a half hour later, both husbands awaited their wives at the bottom.

"We wondered where you'd got to," Darius remarked, stepping up to assist Marianne down the final steps, his solicitousness of her very apparent. That Darius Rourke treasured his beautiful wife was no secret, that and the fact he had no qualms about demonstrating it publicly either.

"I took Georgina up to my studio," Marianne told him. "She liked the view very much. She said it reminded her of a painting of a seascape she'd always admired, at her home, growing up."

"How marvelous for you two ladies to enjoy the same pastime. I hope you and Marianne can come together to sketch. I'd love for her to have some company, Mrs. Greymont," Darius said.

"I shall look forward to just that, Mr. Rourke," Georgina told him.

Jeremy looked up at her. She could see hunger in his eyes, like he was thinking about striping her naked before he devoured her. He reached for her as she neared the last step, latching onto her arm and pulling her in tight to his side. It felt nice to be fitted up against him, his tall frame warm and firm, seeking her, wanting her close to him. God, what a good feeling.

# CHAPTER TWENTY~TWO

*He is the portion of loveliness*
*Which once he made more lovely.*

—Percy Bysshe Shelley, *Adonais* (1821)

He hit the door hard with his stick, leaving a dent in the wood. The uninspired butler who let him in looked liked he'd just swallowed a mouthful of turned wine.

"My lord," Bowles greeted with a pinched expression, as if doing his job were an extreme effort. God how he'd love for Bowles to get run over by an ale wagon. The simpering man was privy to far too much, damning knowledge of activities which wouldn't sit well with society if they ever got out. But murdering Bowles wasn't quite appealing either, or in his repertoire of tricks, not yet at least, he thought.

"Bowles, bring my nephew down to me at once!"

"Mr. Strawnly left instructions not to be disturbed this evening, Lord Pellton," Bowles replied haughtily. "He has a...guest."

"I don't give a maiden queen's first fuck what he said, you cod-faced dard. Get my *heir* down here to greet me with the respect due or you can leave this house for the gutter, starting tonight!"

"Yes, sir," Bowles chirped, already out of the room, a decided urgency to his step as he left to retrieve his master.

Pellton waited impatiently for his reluctant host to present himself. Pulling out the newspaper, he read the notice again, feeling himself grow hot with rage. *How dare he take that which was meant for—*

"Uncle. This is a pleasant surprise," his nephew drawled at him from the drawing room doorway.

The boy was a bit touched in the head, but knew his place. Simon would have to do as an heir if he couldn't manage a legitimate son. He'd followed orders thus far, even though it had all turned to a stewing vat of liquid shit. *Damn Greymont to hell!* "Have you seen the announcements?"

Simon stared blankly back.

"*The Times*, you fool! Have you seen it in the paper?"

"No. It's a lot of blithering rubbish of no interest to me," Simon whined.

"God help us!" he yelled, shaking his head. "It's of great interest to me, as it should be to you! That cocky bastard, Greymont, has married Georgina Russell! Already done. More than a week ago!" He stabbed a finger at the announcement on the news page.

Simon narrowed his eyes and came toward him. He snatched the paper and scanned the section. "That presumptuous prick!" he shouted, flinging the paper down. "She was to be for us!"

Pellton took some solace in the apparent disappointment Simon showed at the loss of such a prize. At least the boy had a partially functioning brain. Hell, he'd even gotten to fuck her sweet cunt. "Aye. The operative term is 'was,' but not anymore. She's Mrs. Greymont now and off the marriage market. He's no doubt stashed her in the country where he can keep an eye on her."

"That is downright tragic, Uncle. She was delectable beyond words, and I was looking forward playing with her again. She is a rare combination, that one. Lots of fight left in her."

"As you've reminded me more times than I care to hear," Pellton retorted. "I am feeling very bereft at the moment, Simon. Let us go out and drown our losses in some shared quim. What do you say, son?"

"An excellent plan, Uncle, but...we needn't leave this house for it."

Pellton felt his cock tingle as the blood rushed in. "Who do you have upstairs?" he asked.

"I believe she claimed her name to be Ella, or Emma, something like that." He shrugged. "I snatched her off the street early this morning. She's not of our class of course, but unridden before today."

Incredible. Simon had more guile than he ever thought possible. "You snatched a virgin off the London streets this morning?"

"Yes. A lush berry ready to be plucked. She begged me to let her go. Said her father would pay coin for her safe return. But I figure he couldn't have much capital being a tradesman."

"What trade? He might have more than you think?"

"Oh, a lowly tanner or some such dirty business. I don't care for the tainted money. I told her the pink slit between her legs would suit me far better."

"Mmmm. And she is amenable to ménage?"

"Amenable? Who would ask her opinion? I won't. Will you ask her, Uncle?"

Pellton's cock was fully hard now, and he no longer cared about anything but fucking away his anger at losing Georgina Russell to that rake, Greymont. He swept out his arm to Simon. "After you, Nephew. Please introduce me to Ella, or is it Emma? I can't wait to meet her—um, I mean, *fuck* her."

The carriage ride home was a short one. Sitting opposite each other, Georgina could sense tension in Jeremy. The perfect gentleman, but also like a wolf about to pounce. His eyes looked positively feral, gleaming at her in the dark.

"Did you enjoy the evening?" Jeremy asked her.

"Very much. The Rourkes are lovely, and I look forward to more pleasant times together."

They rocked slowly from the sway of the coach along the road.

"Jeremy, what were you thinking about when we came down the stairs from Marianne's studio?"

"What?" She saw his legs flex, and he shifted in his seat.

"You looked at me profoundly, and I want to know what you were thinking just then."

His eyes stabbed her. "I was thinking of how gorgeous you looked coming down to me, and how you would be tonight when I'm buried deep inside you."

Dear Christ, she nearly choked. His direct talk had an immediate, visceral effect. She clamped her thighs together to try to relieve the wet heat that suddenly pounded between them. A moan slipped out from between her lips of its own free will, and despite the chill of the night air, sweat broke out between her breasts and on her neck.

Yes. She had guessed right. A vision of Jeremy looming over, thrusting into her wildly, eyes all abandoned, flashed in her head. The rawness of it made her completely and utterly wanton for him. He incited a part of her she never knew existed but, now that she did know, shocked her to her core. The air suddenly seemed sucked out of the coach, and she gulped a breath, and then another.

Somehow she formed the words to speak. "What—what do you want?"

He didn't pause even a second. "I want you to—"

But then the coach pulled to an abrupt stop, cutting off his reply. A rap on the door sounded, and then it opened. Jeremy got up and exited first, giving his hand to assist her out.

In they walked to the house, where their coats were given to the butler. Up the stairs to the second floor, west wing, he escorted her. They moved fast. The end of the hall suite was their destination. He opened the door for them. She entered. He closed the door with a firm push and faced her, and finished the question she had asked him in the coach.

"—come into *my* bedroom tonight. Wear nothing apart from your dressing gown. I'll be waiting."

He bowed, turned on his boot heel, and left her standing alone in her bedroom. Georgina heard the door to the master's chamber open and then shut, and then she heard no more.

The need to sit down was paramount, before her legs gave out and she ended up in a heap on the rug. He had her so worked up she was shaking. She didn't sit long though. Moving to the sideboard, she poured a hearty portion of wine, of which no time was wasted in knocking back. As soon as the spirits were sucked down, she rang for Jane.

Georgina felt her every sense heightened as she crept toward the door to the master's chamber. The cold brass of the handle stung as she turned it. She pushed forward.

The room was dimly lit, lamps on low beside the massive bed, a good fire going in the hearth. The room smelled of him—spicy cloves and his unique manly scent. *Delicious.*

"Slide the bolt behind you." His voice reached across the room.

She pushed the metal firmly and slid it home with a grating click. The snap and pop of the fire was the only sound, if she didn't count her escalating need for air.

"Walk out to where I can see you and you can see me and stop."

She did as he asked and had no trouble stopping because the sight of him would have done that for her anyway.

He lay naked on the bed. Acres of golden skin over smooth, ropy muscles stretched out languidly, his upper body propped up by pillows. The stark, packed muscles low on his chest drew her eyes lower down his body to his— *Oh, sweet Jesus!* His cock. She watched it twitch above his hips as he saw her eyes so focused on it. Stiff already, his shaft grew tauter, moving, filling, rising up to lift a fraction off his belly. God! He looked like a beautiful, ancient, pagan idol. More animal than human—

"Open your robe and let it drop."

Her nipples were already tight before the cool air hit them. The sound of her robe hitting the floor made a soft swish. She couldn't hold back the shiver.

"Come to me, and walk slowly," he told her.

Careful steps brought her closer to her male animal. A beast who looked at her with ravenous hunger, like he was concentrating very hard on keeping still, waiting, yearning, anticipating the instant when he would pounce and take her underneath him, cover her with his greater weight, press her down and open her legs, mount her, and pierce her, thrusting deep and—

"Crawl up here and sit on me."

"Oh." She started to shake. Her whole body becoming affected by the vibrations as they took hold.

"Mmmmm, all is well," he soothed. "Take my hand and come up here to me. I will help you."

She took the hand he offered, and somehow she moved, propelling forward and up, her long legs folding over his hips, her wet core coming to a rest directly atop the steel ridge of his velvet-skinned shaft. A shudder of exquisite pleasure shot down her belly, like a tiny version of the orgasms he'd given her.

He gave her a moment to settle. A slow smile spread on his mouth, and they stared at one another's faces until he broke the silence. "You are so beautiful to me, right now, like this."

He stroked a hand up her leg and looked down at it. "Your legs are so finely made. I saw them that day in the rain."

"You saw my legs?" she asked.

He nodded wickedly. "Oh yes, I saw. You took off your stockings to cross the creek and then had to put them back on again. I watched the whole delicious show. Thought my heart might give out from the beauty of you."

"How shocking and devious on your part."

"Are you angry, my sweet Gina?"

"No. If our situations had been reversed, I probably would have done the same. So, did you skulk behind a tree and stay quiet so I wouldn't know?"

He slid his other hand up the other leg. "Exactly, my darling. Your perfect limbs stunned me silent anyway. I just had to keep still and not move." He closed his eyes for a moment as if he was remembering the scene from that day. "You are beautiful," he hummed.

"So are you. I think, have always thought, that you are a beautiful man."

His hands came up to her shoulders and then to her neck and the base of her head, cradling her to his lips. Mouths met in a seeking rush to fuse together. He thrust his tongue deep into her, sweeping in a wide circle, searing over every plane of her mouth. When he pulled back, he sucked her tongue as far as he could pull it until his lips popped off with a wet draw. And then he delved back in for more.

Movement became as necessary as breathing. She couldn't help the slow grinding her hips fell into as he plundered her mouth with his tongue.

Wide palms left her head and slipped down to cup her breasts. His thumbs and forefingers met to pinch the centers, drawing them into even tighter bundles. The glory of it brought forth a deep moan and a steep arch to her back. She needed to get her body closer—

"I meant what I said. Before… I want in you," he breathed, his mouth now at her neck. His teeth came onto her skin and bit gently.

"Yesssss, please," she begged.

Jeremy pushed her backward, his hands supporting her shoulder blades as he laid her far down onto the mattress so her head was now near the foot of the bed.

She was aware of him changing positions, transferring to his knees and opening her legs, bending her knees, splaying her wide for mounting, but that wasn't what he did. Instead, he did something much different. Something so shocking and so unexpected she would have frozen in mortification, that was, until she felt it.

Oh dear God in heaven and the angels! Was that his mouth on her nether parts? Lips to lips, tongue to quim, soft to soft. *Sweet unimaginable bliss…* Oh God, she was going to die from the exquisite pleasure. Georgina was going to die and love every lick and swirl, every sucking draw, and every penetration of his tongue inside her as she moved toward death. He'd told her he wanted in her, and he was, thank Christ! *Please let it go on forever—*

He started with long, slow licks, like she was a cat he petted. Each pass over her slit opened the folds a little more until her swollen nub was revealed itself for special attention. He covered it with his lips and drew it in a suck that slammed her hips right up off the bed as she ground against the sweet torture.

When he entered her with his tongue as far as he could get it, she could feel his nose pressing hard above. He cupped her bottom to lift her closer. Mouth, tongue, and lips worked together to ravish her sex, holding her captive, a slave to the sensations that drove her toward incineration.

The orgasm was so powerful, she cried out. No, it was more of a shout, but she couldn't help it in the slightest because another one followed so quickly on its heels. The pleasure gripped her, shot her body to a place where she shattered apart, completely blown, no skeleton left inside her skin to keep her from becoming liquid.

Ensnared in the gratification of pleasuring her, Jeremy felt the contractions of her orgasm on his tongue. That, and the taste of her honey down his throat and the sounds she was making, flipped a switch in him. He knew he was crossing into dangerous territory— a place he'd sworn he wouldn't go with her.

But he loved Gina. He wouldn't hurt her. *Goddamnit!* The need to break free of all this restraint was just so overpowering he couldn't—stop. He just couldn't hold back what he was going to do—

He twisted up so fast, and before he even knew what he'd done, he had both of her wrists gripped firmly in one hand. His other palm supported his weight. He penetrated her convulsing core, and the fucking started. *Yes...oh, yes!* Glorious, demanding, animalistic fucking. The kind that was all about carnality and, in its crushing dominance, pretty much blotted out every other paradigm he held to. His mouth found its way to her neck, latched on, and bit. None too gently.

He worked her wickedly fast, and if his sexed-up mind could even deduce that he should hold back for fear of scaring her, at least he didn't last long.

A minute or so of fierce pumping and he was ejaculating and moaning into her throat, thrusting slower but getting his seed worked up in her good and deep. Somehow in his befogged brain, his male awareness told him this was imperative. *Get it up inside!*

When at last he stilled, it was more of a collapse than anything.

He wasn't even sure if he might have lost consciousness, and for how long. The first thing he felt were Gina's wrists coming away from his now-slackened grip. That jolted him into wakefulness real quick. He pushed up on his palms and looked down at her. *Oh no! No—no—no—no—no!*

Her eyes were closed, and the streak of a tear tracked from each. On her neck was a huge love bite, the delicate skin marking quickly from the voracious nursing he'd done.

"What have I done? Gina. Oh, fuck…goddamn! Forgive me…"

Her eyes snapped open. She looked stricken, just absolutely devastated, pinned underneath him, his cock still halfway stiff, buried to his balls. Shallow breaths moved her beautiful breasts up and down.

"No, Jeremy…" she told him.

# CHAPTER TWENTY~THREE

*The mind is its own place, and in itself*
*Can make a heaven of hell, a hell of heaven.*

—John Milton, *Paradise Lost* (1667)

T he sight of her husband leaping off her and out of the room was not what Georgina was expecting.

"No! I am well, truly! Wait! Jeremy, wait!" She called after him, but he didn't even slow, like he didn't even hear her.

She did not get up immediately because she couldn't. Her body was sapped after that session with him on the bed. *Hell's bells!* Her blood hummed from what he'd done to her in a very good and very wonderful way.

Georgina realized he was horrified by how he'd taken her, but she wasn't. His desire was apparent, and if he needed her fierce like that sometimes, then she wanted to give it to him. For her to comfort and serve him was her duty, her *right* as a wife! She felt the tingle of anger.

As she waited for him to come back, her irritation grew. Jeremy needed to get over this worry about treating her like a fragile bloom. She thought she'd explained it clearly to him enough times! He didn't frighten her and never had. His loving her body was certainly glorious, and from the first time, a heady surprise, but never hurtful or frightening.

An hour passed. The room next door was quiet. She heard no sounds apart from the fire dying in the grate.

Where was he? Where would he go? Frustration mounting, she made a decision, left the warm bed that smelled of him, and returned to her rooms.

Quickly donning a gown and robe, Georgina went to her dressing table to arrange her hair into some semblance of normal. Frowning, she tilted her neck at the mirror. There was a large mark—ah, it was a love bite. He'd made it when he'd suckled, no, bit at her neck.

She shivered at the remembrance. The pain of the bite had made for sweeter pleasure, and she longed to feel it again. His face had looked so tragic when he'd stirred above her after his fiery release. Realizing that seeing the mark he'd made would probably upset him more, she wisely arranged her hair to one side and covered it up.

Tonight was cold. She found a green shawl, wrapped it around her, and left her rooms in search of her much loved, but very misguided husband.

After Georgina explored all of the usual places, Jeremy stubbornly remained absent. His study, the library, billiard room, and guest bedrooms were all searched, and he was not in any of them.

Mrs. Richards came to her rescue though. The woman appeared in the hall, silent as a cat, when Georgina stepped into it after checking in a guest suite.

"Oh Lord! You startled me," Georgina gasped, bringing her hand to her throat.

"Good evening, madam," the housekeeper replied smoothly, with not a trace of surprise that anything was out of order with the mistress of the house skulking about in her nightclothes by candlelight. "Such cold in the air. It is good you have covered up well," she said, eying Georgina's shawl. "That is a lovely shawl you have, madam."

"Thank you, Mrs. Richards." Georgina looked straight into the housekeeper's intelligent eyes.

"It will warm you, should you choose to look at the portraits."

"Portraits?"

"Yes, madam. I should imagine it is *very* cold in the portrait gallery tonight." She bade Georgina a graceful leave and glided away.

*Bless that woman.* Mrs. Richards was a definite jewel, Georgina thought. It was a good thing to have an ally. She made her way to the gallery on the second floor, wondering what she would say to him.

Jeremy brooded. Her scent clung to him all over and just served to remind him. How could he have lost control like that? The look of her, the tears—

Damn it all to hell, what must she think of him? How could he ever repair the damage he'd done? She wouldn't love him now. She would probably be afraid of him. God, it would kill him if she cringed away from him in fear.

He stared up into the eyes of the enigmatic woman in the portrait, hoping she could impart some wisdom. Jeremy must be such a disappointment to her, and it was ironic, too, after all this time, all these years of telling himself he'd never be like his father, yet here he was stepping right into the role—

"You must be very cold with only that robe covering you."

He snapped his head around, in disbelief that she'd come after him. Gina looked as gorgeous as ever, wrapped in a green shawl he'd never seen her wear. Green was her color—definitely. She wore it splendidly.

"Coldhearted, yes, I know."

"No. You are never that. And I should not have had to come searching for you like this!" She sounded angry more than frightened, he thought. "Mrs. Richards must think—God I don't know what she thinks now!" she sputtered, stamping her foot. "No doubt we are providing good gossip for the servants."

Yes, she was definitely angry, and looking down fiercely as she stood over him, her cheeks pink, eyes sparking, arms folded, and more beautiful than ever. And she wasn't done speaking her piece either.

"Why are Mr. and Mrs. Greymont flittering about the house in their nightclothes, and in the dead of night? *Well, I don't know. It is very unseemly though! Maybe they're having a spat.* I heard the master stormed from their chamber with the mistress calling out to him to stay with her. *Well, I heard the new mistress searched all over the house for an hour before she found him sitting alone in the portrait gallery!* My God, the master must be truly dicked in the nob to be sittin' in there. He's going to freeze his arse off!"

Listening to her mock tirade between the servants was good medicine. The short laugh slipped out of him before he could pull it back. She was so witty and beautiful and brave and... everything.

"You speak cant magnificently."

"Well, Tom is my brother. You know then I learned from the master."

"Indeed you have done." Jeremy chuckled despite the circumstances.

"Does that laugh mean you're ready to come back to bed now?" she asked.

"How could you even want me back there with you?"

"Because it is where you belong. And...we are the happiest of lovers, remember?"

His breath punched out in a gush. He hadn't realized he was holding it in. "Still?"

"I am certain of the fact."

"After that—after I was so rough in bedding you? How can it be, Gina?"

She set down her candle on the floor and deliberately plopped onto his lap. She wrapped her arms around him and rested her head on his chest. God, she felt and smelled divine, her hair just under his nose. He folded his hands together over her hip to secure her, the lovely warmth of her melting his cold dread instantly. Miracles of miracles, she wasn't disgusted or afraid of him!

"My feelings for you will not be denied. I am right where I want to be, next to you. And I know you have never hurt me or scared me or made me frightened of anything you've done, ever."

"But I saw your face! You had tears, and you looked stricken, and I marked your neck all up! I am so sorry—"

She put her fingers over his mouth again. "You misinterpreted what you saw." She stroked his lips softly, the pads of her fingers following the curves. "Jeremy, I did have some tears and I may have looked stricken to you, but it was not from fear, rather the shattering pleasure—"

"Truly?" he cut in.

She nodded slowly. "Truly. I was in disbelief from what we'd done, and you took those signs to mean I'd been frightened and you tore off before I could explain."

He took her face in both of his hands and just held it for a moment. "I adore you. And I only want to show you, but I made a bloody mess of it. Gina, I know I let my self-control slip tonight, and I fell into behavior I swore I'd never show to you."

"You don't want to be like that with me?"

"No."

"But what if I want you to be—" She frowned at him. "Well, I suppose it is forgivable to let your self-control slip when in the throes of what…we did tonight." He could tell she blushed even though the light was too dim to see it. "I know I had no self-control when it was happening to me." She whispered the rest to him. "You should know that I—I liked it—the whole thing—and I hope we do it again sometime." She kept her head down when she was done.

*Can this be happening? Can she be real?* Jeremy was in utter shock at what she was saying to him. Could his beautiful Gina, traumatic experience and all, be telling him she liked what he'd done to her? Not offended by the hard fucking? Because that was what it'd been. He loved her, yes, but he'd fucked her all the same. But as impossible as he thought it to be, it seemed she didn't have a problem with the rough ride he'd just given her.

He met foreheads with her and whispered back, "Are you real?"

"Yes." She made a soft sound, halfway between a laugh and a sigh.

He had to shake his head in disbelief, rocking their heads together. "You amaze me and I don't deserve you, but still I count myself among the luckiest of men."

She snuggled down against his chest, and he gripped her a little tighter. "Do you feel better now?" She spoke at his throat.

"Much better." He kissed the top of her head.

"Better enough to come back to bed? 'Tis like ice in here."

"God, yes! For I think my arse is truly frozen to this marble bench I was stupid enough to sit on."

She laughed at him and slipped off his lap. "Come on then. I promise to warm you."

"Hmmm, I cannot wait to be privy to your methods." He leaned in behind her to whisper at her ear, his mind running rampant at the idea of what they'd do to find warmth together. "You're exceptionally skilled at warming me."

"Thank you for the compliment, lover." Georgina bent down to retrieve her candle from the floor, and as the flame was lifted, it illuminated the painting behind it. Her soft gasp caught his attention.

"Who is that, Jeremy?"

He put his eyes on the painting again. "It is my mother, Clarissa."

"She was lovely, your mother. I can see you, in her. Your eyes are the same."

"Gina, when you look at her, how do you find her countenance?" he asked.

Georgina observed carefully in the candlelight before answering him. "Well, she is beautiful but composed in a way that seems…well, almost sad to me. She does not look happy, I think. How did you lose her?"

"I was ten when I lost my parents, well, mostly just her. My father was always a distant parent, literally and figuratively. He left in my tenth year, and it killed her. Truly it did, for after he left, she died of a broken heart."

# CHAPTER TWENTY~FOUR

*Now let it work; mischief, thou are afoot...*
—William Shakespeare, *Julius Caesar* (1599)

Georgina looked up at the painting. In the daylight, the nuances of color were exceptional. The light brown hair and blue eyes so emotive of Jeremy. The son definitely took after the mother.

Clarissa Greymont, nee Bleddington, had been blessed with beauty, but not in love. She married a cad. Henri Greymont was a poor husband and even worse father. Jeremy had shared the sad tale when she'd asked about his parents.

Henri married Clarissa, the only child of Jeremy's maternal grandparents, Sir Rodney and Lady Bleddington. Clarissa loved Henri. Henri loved her money even more. Jeremy was a product of the very first years of the marriage, when they'd actually lived together.

Henri spent the majority of his time philandering and racking up debts. Clarissa spent the majority of her time pining for her husband and welcoming him home with open arms, that is, whenever he deigned to return to it.

But Henri finally killed even that eternal optimism. When there was no more money to extract from her, Henri left England with an actress he'd taken up with. He wrote, saying he wanted a divorce. That was the final nail in Clarissa's coffin. She lost the will to live and simply faded out of life. Within six months, she was dead. And even in her death, she granted Henri Greymont's last request of her—an irrevocable dissolution of their marriage.

Yes, she was right to look sad in the portrait, Georgina thought. Clarissa Greymont was a tragic woman with a heartrending past. Yet, selfishly, Georgina could not regret the union, for without it, Jeremy would not be. He wouldn't be in her life. He would never have found her, saved her, given her a life.

Turning abruptly away from those melancholy, blue eyes, she left the gallery for other pursuits, thinking about how lucky she was. She *had* married well. Jeremy was nothing like his father. He would never treat his wife and children in such a way…

Jeremy returned from the day's business. The dark, rolling sky, ominous above him, foretold of impending rain. He quickened his pace, thinking of Gina and what she might be doing. The tremor between his legs inspired thoughts of what he'd like to be doing with her. Yes, with the day so ugly, outdoor pursuits were not an option. How timely, he thought. What better way to pass the afternoon than in a warm, cozy bed—naked of course—and making love to his wife.

Pulling up to the house, he handed off his horse to a groom and took the steps two at a time. He figured the faster he found her, the sooner he could be inside her. With all the sex they'd been having, he should have been able to focus on something else. But no, not really the case. The more he had her, the more he needed her, and not always just for the sex. He just needed *her*. Needed to be with her, spend time in her company, be near her.

Handing over his overcoat and gloves, he inquired of the butler, "Clarke, where can I find Mrs. Greymont?" He smiled, thinking how much he loved saying "Mrs. Greymont."

"Madam is in with Mrs. Richards, sir." Nothing much ruffled Clarke. He was as somber as they come. His voice was all muted dignity and calm.

"Thank you, Clarke."

A few minutes later, Jeremy popped his head into the housekeeping office after a short preemptory knock. There she was, head bent, furrowed brow, all concentration as she reviewed accounts with Richards. It made him all the prouder of her, seeing how she stepped up to her new role as mistress by learning the workings of Hallborough. So diligent in her efforts.

God, how she aroused him! Just seeing Gina now made his cock ache to be inside her. He wanted to stride over and sweep her into a deep kiss, and then carry her upstairs to bed, where he'd see her clothes removed slowly, and one garment at a time, until she was gloriously naked. Gina liked him directing her, taking comfort in his mastery at pleasuring her. And pleasure her he would. He'd lay her out on the bed and kiss every inch of skin. He wanted his tongue on her breasts, inside her quim, anywhere, everywhere. He needed to taste her honey again—

"Jeremy?" She smiled up at him, inquiring with a gentle look.

*Caught again...thinking with your prick.*

"Oh, hello. Sorry for interrupting you at your work. Just wanted to let you know I've returned. Made it inside before the rain."

Christ, he was rambling like an idiot, and his cock was throbbing like a bass drum in a soldier band. He wondered if they could hear it. Thank heavens his jacket covered him. He was stiff enough to work as a coat hook for the damn thing in case he decided to take it off in any case.

"Um, come find me when you are done? Yes? I'll be in my

study."

Flustered, he shut the door and got the hell out of there as fast as his feet could take him, the ache in his kecks subsiding only a little. He needed a drink.

The scotch soothed him some. Seated at his desk, he worked through some correspondence that had accumulated, hoping the time could pass quickly before Gina came to him. He was still halfway hard when the knock at the door came. His cock punched against the fabric. She was just behind that door. Relief at last! Maybe they could play in here, with the door locked of course. Perhaps, just possibly, she might want to try a new game...called fellatio. Jeremy's mind went rampant with the possibilities of fantasies he only dreamed about with her, but so far had not attempted. He was taking a slow path with Gina, and felt that when the time was right, they would know.

He arranged himself in the chair, leaned back, spread his thighs, cupped himself, and slapped a very naughty, very randy look on his face. "Come!" he sang at the knock.

The sight of the burly Mr. Mills, his steward, coming through the door, killed the throb in his prick, that and the pain of slamming his knee into the desk as he jerked upright. A ripe curse greeted the steward who entered hesitantly after that salute, peering around the door to see if there was someone else already in the room with his master.

"No, just me, Mills. What can I do for you?" Recovering his poise, Jeremy gave in with resignation and just in time to be snagged into a discussion about some troubles with the tenants.

When Gina did step in some three quarters of an hour later, he was still tangled in pressing estate business. Both men stood to acknowledge her. She greeted Mr. Mills and tilted her head.

He felt like moaning, she looked so delectable. He smiled longingly and flashed a wink instead. "I'll find you as soon as I'm done here. Where will you be?"

"The library...I shall be in the library." She showed what he interpreted as a smoky glance in his direction and let herself out.

The snail's pace of the business with Mills was near to making him scream. He needed to get the hell out of here and into bed with his wife! Still, it was another half hour before he could get rid of the tenacious man. At the moment, Mills might be as unwelcome as a stiff prick in church, but he was a damn fine steward and Jeremy was not stupid enough to offend him.

Jeremy flew to the library. She wasn't there. He called her name. No answer. Frustration took hold. He spun out and into the hall. He hadn't taken more than a few steps, and there she was. She had just turned the corner and faced in his direction.

As soon as Gina saw him, she stopped. They both did. Standing there in the hallway, gazes locked upon each other, something very sensual passed between them, so strong he imagined he could smell the scent of arousal in the air. The moment ruled them, taking over, making this encounter into something all about naked skin and bodies coming together.

Jeremy knew what she was going to do the split second before she did it. He wanted her to—so badly.

She did it.

*Yes, oh yes...this is going to be fantastic!*

Georgina felt wicked desire fill her soul and knew what she had to do. Didn't know why, but just knew she had to. It would drive him wild. So she turned and ran from him. She ran as fast as her legs could go.

Down the hall, up a staircase, another hallway, more stairs, she kept going. Jeremy chased after her, his boots pounding under the size of him. Each thud of his boot drove up her excitement to the point where she was without conscious intent as she fled. This was pure animal reaction, and thoughts of what her lovely beast would do once he got his hands on her made her shudder.

Georgina didn't even know what these rooms were. She was in a narrow hallway of the east wing's third floor. This was a part of the house she'd never been before. Flinging open three doors in a row, she picked the one on the right and dashed inside. It was some kind of storage room, with trunks and crates and odd furniture stacked about.

Ducking behind a wardrobe, she wedged herself between it and the wall. Her heart beat so heavy beneath her breast, she figured the sound couldn't possibly be silent. It was probably rather like a beacon, calling him straight to her location.

She waited. No more loud boots thumping on the floor. He was taking quiet steps now.

"Gina," he called, his voice dripping with sarcasm. "I'm going to catch you…soon. And you know what I'm going to do when I find you? I'm thinking about it right now, what I'm going to do to you."

She heard a few more soft steps. "You are so clever to open those doors, trying to throw me off like that. But I know you're in *this* room, Gina."

*How do you know I'm in this room?*

"I can scent you. I love your scent—fragrant eglantine with a hint of orange. So delicate, yet powerful enough to make me hard for you just from smelling it." More soft steps sounded just to her right. "I'm hard right now, Gina, so damn hard my cock aches. It wants in you."

*Oh dear Lord.*

He walked past the wardrobe and toward the left corner of the room. "Where are you hiding my dear, naughty, sweetheart?" he crooned. "It won't be long now, Gina, before I catch you, and you know what's going to happen then…"

If she crept out from her place, she thought she could just slip out the door by running behind him with his back turned. Georgina heard the rustling of boxes being slid about and took her window of opportunity. She bolted for the door.

Georgina didn't make it far. Powerful hands latched on to her shoulders and dragged her against him. She screamed and a hand clamped over her mouth, cutting the sound off. His lips came to her ear. "No screaming, sweetheart. The servants…"

She nodded against his hand.

"Good girl," he whispered, removing his hand from her mouth and dragging it down over her neck and throat to cup her breast. His mouth stayed at her neck, and his tongue flicked out to swirl just below her ear. His other hand moved to her hip and pulled her back as he ground his erection into the cleft of her bottom.

She panted against him, grateful he could hold her up. It was wonderful to be captured. She pressed herself into him, arching her back and her neck, giving in to the coiled anticipation.

"Do you like being chased?" He teased her breast.

"Yes."

"Do you like being caught?" He swirled his tongue in her ear before biting the lobe.

"Yes!"

"Do feel how hard I am for you?" He ground into her again.

"Yesss!"

"Well then, I know just what you need!" He turned her, hefted her over his shoulder, clamped on to her legs, and started walking. Fast. "And you're going to like it," he promised.

Oh yes, she *was* going to like it and could hardly wait, she was so aroused by his questions, his touches, all of him. Jeremy carried her down to the end of the hall and turned left, descended some stairs, purposeful in his steps until he met his destination. He stopped, opened the door with one hand, and brought them into a bedroom.

"Put me down, now," she told him, wriggling against his grip.

"I'm going to put you down," he declared, "right where I want you, on this bed, so I can get all over you—and up in you."

The moan that escaped her throat seemed to spur him. He'd never moved so fast, dropping her on the bed and securing the door latch. Turning to face her, he leaned against the door and pulled off his boots. The massive ridge in his trousers told her all she needed to know about his intentions. He pounced.

The weight of him covering her was heaven. He had his hand up her skirt and his tongue in her mouth before she could suck in a breath. Two long fingers sank into her core as his thumb stroked her, rubbing in a sweet, slick, wet circle.

She thrust against his hand, rotating her hips, lost to the building, raw tension. Higher and higher he drew her along until she was barely clinging to the edge, ready to plunge into the abyss of shearing pleasure. As she writhed against his hand, she was vaguely aware that he watched her. His head drew back, and he stared at her, into her.

"Look at me. I want to see you coming. Don't close your eyes, Gina."

She kept her eyes on him, but her hand shot out to rub down the iron length of his cock, something she had never done. He had touched her plenty, but she had never been bold enough to touch him there. He jerked when her hand made contact, and his eyes rolled back.

"Yes! Touch me! I want your hand on my cock!" he ground out.

Emboldened by his command, she grappled with the buttons on the flap of his kecks, springing him free. Her fingers closed around the stiff length by feel. She couldn't see what she was doing, but he seemed to be very pleased by her efforts.

"Ah, like that. Stroke up and down. Feels so damn good!"

She kept her eyes on his, working her fist around his cock, learning the feel of the skin sliding over hard muscle underneath its satin sheath. The circling of his thumb and the penetration of his fingers had her about ready to fly. "Jeremy! I can't wait—I want you insi—"

He angled himself, thrust powerfully, and gave her what she wanted. Long, sliding, intense pulls, back and forth, bumping the wall of her womb with each deep pulse.

"Like this?" he asked, his breathing going into the predictable wheeze she knew well.

"Just like that!"

She gave him everything she had, meeting each stroke, thrust for thrust. She dug into his back with her fingernails, wishing she was touching skin instead of his shirt. The explosion, when it came, was shattering. They came together. She cried out, caring little if she was heard or if she was too wanton. In this moment, with him, abandon consumed her and she could know nothing else.

Jeremy caressed her neck with his lips. Gina shifted against his nuzzling, coming awake from their ragged romp like a languid, sleepy kitten. After that first blinding release, they'd gotten good and naked and gone again, collapsing into needed sleep together when it was done.

Burrowed in the blankets with her warm curves fitted to his body like a snug-fitting glove was illuminating. He could feel a glow infusing him with love and feelings of possessiveness he'd never believed possible. Having her reach out, touching and demanding of him during their encounter had been like a lightning strike. Igniting in him something he'd never known with a woman. She excited and soothed him at the same time. Made him feel reckless and cautious both at once. She stirred him up and smoothed out his rough edges. She completed him in so many ways—made him feel like a real man, a husband, a grown-up. She was all-powerful.

"That was the most memorable romp of hide-and-seek I've ever had." Jeremy kissed her lips gently. "When can we do it again?"

Gina smiled at him. "I liked it, too." She blushed beautifully, her shyness taking over.

"I love that you get shy, but there's no need." He tickled her a little at the ribs. "I like you wanton and shameless."

"You do?" Her eyes widened at him.

"Oh yes! In fact, I love for you to be so. You have my wholehearted approval to behave as wanton and brazen as you like, whenever you wish." He whispered, "I hope it's all the time."

"That won't be difficult," she said ruefully. "All you have to do is pass me a look like the one you did in the hallway, and I'll bolt."

"I'll remember you said that."

"What is this room, Jeremy?" She snuggled into his side, facing him and looking out at the walls.

"Can't you tell?"

"Was this yours?"

He nodded.

She sat up and took in the furniture and the juvenile décor. "Yes. I can see that it was a boy's room." She smiled, wrinkling her nose at him. "You slept right here on this bed?"

"I did." He pulled her possessively back down to the mattress, his hands sweeping over breasts and hips, his knee splitting her thighs so he could settle in between. "But never enjoyed myself as much as I did today—or had such a delightful companion to share it with."

Hell, he was hard for her again, his cock straining for her, pulsing on the flat between their stomachs.

"I'll never think of this bed in the same way, I'm afraid," he told her, emphasizing with a notable thrust downward.

"I should hope not!" She giggled and melted under him. He

loved that she was so willing to take him in, to be with him like this—

The rattle at the door handle froze them both. Then a sharp rapping. "What's going on in there? Open up and show yourselves!" The gruff voice of Mr. Clarke rang through the walls.

Underneath him, Gina gasped and slapped a hand over her mouth, her eyes flaring.

Jeremy just grinned at her and called out, "That won't be happening, Clarke. All is well and need not concern you."

Mr. Clarke choked a reply through the door. "Oh! Apologies, sir, I had no idea—"

"And, Clarke?" Jeremy interrupted.

"Yes, sir?" Clarke's voice trembled.

"Tell Richards that Mrs. Greymont and I will have dinner served in our rooms this evening. And have them ready a bath. That is all."

"It will be done, sir." The butler's footsteps could be clearly heard, moving out quickly, nearly running in his bid to flee the scene of certain mortification for him.

"That poor man. Jeremy, I hope he recovers from his fright and makes his way safely to Mrs. Richards. He sounded about to have an apoplexy."

"Aw, old Clarke will be completely restored back to his stiff self the next time we see him. Besides, I'm just making sure we provide ample gossip for the servants. I consider it my duty as master. They're probably bored as hell and will appreciate the diversion."

"So wicked…" She clucked at him.

"Always." He winked at her. "Now where was I?" He thrust again, this time finding his mark, entering her in one glorious, slick slide. "Oh, I remember. I wish for the wanton Gina to rematerialize. I *know* I've not had enough of her quite yet."

# CHAPTER TWENTY~FIVE

*When her loose gown from her shoulders did fall,*
*And she me caught in her arms long and small;*
*Therewithall sweetly did me kiss...*

**—Thomas Wyatt, "They Flee From Me" (1557)**

The shared bath had been lovely and even more enjoyable because they washed each other, slippery soap and fragrant bath oils making the washing, or pleasuring, unlike any bath either had ever had opportunity to experience, but would surely want for repetition.

Both had worked up quite an appetite from all that chasing about and resultant love-making, so the dinner set out before them in their private sitting room, dressed in *dishabille,* was equally lovely. Cook might have served boiled tripe, and they probably wouldn't have noticed.

"We should do this more often," Jeremy remarked, dashing in a dark brown silk, his hair still damp and matching in hue because of it.

"Track around the house and shock the servants?" Georgina quipped.

"You are such a wit, my sweetheart. I love the verbal wrestling"—he paused and gave a sly grin—"almost as much as the more physical variety. But no, I was referring to having dinner in our rooms and knowing that you are naked under that blue robe you fill out so prettily." He nodded toward her breasts, a wicked smile curving his mouth.

She laughed at herself and felt a blush take over. "I should have realized since you seem so bent on feeding me."

For the past minutes, Jeremy had insisted on cutting up her meat and placing bites in her mouth.

"Oh, no." She shook her head at the offered morsel of lamb. "I am positively stuffed. I can't take any more!"

"Just this one last bite?" His eyes grew hooded. "Please?"

"Why?"

He swallowed deep, his throat flexing just above the cut of his robe. God, he was delicious to look at. "I want—I love to watch—when you open your mouth…"

The heat thrown from him was searing, and she knew exactly why he wanted to watch her mouth opening. He was thinking about something else going into her mouth.

In all honesty, she had pondered it before this. When he'd pleasured her with his tongue, she had been shocked at first, but the gratification had been so exquisite her shock had evaporated quickly. He had mentioned before that there were other ways for them to be together, and she had to assume that if he could use his mouth on her, then she could do the same to him.

"All right, one last bite." She humored him and parted her lips, lifting her chin a fraction. Accepting the piece, she chewed slowly, keeping her eyes on him the whole time. When it was down, she licked her lips and told him, "I know why—the reason you want to watch me."

The breath left him in a hiss. "Why?"

She didn't waver. She'd started them down this path, and she was going to finish it. "You're thinking about if it was your cock in my mouth instead of that piece of meat."

A whimper escaped him, and his face flooded in a deep red blush.

"I have shocked you. You blush."

His eyes darkened but stayed on her.

"But I am right, aren't I? That's what you were thinking, wasn't it, Jeremy?"

He gave a single nod and said "yes," but no sound came out of him, as if he had truly lost his voice.

She knew he'd tell her the truth, for he did not lie. Feeling suddenly bold, she drew on that knowledge, imagining how he would feel under her tongue. "If you want me to, I will."

His eyes bulged in response.

"Do you want my mouth on your cock?" He kept staring. "Jeremy?"

He looked about as tight as a bowstring and his voice had a bit of a waver, but his answer came to her emphatically clear. "Dear God, yessss."

Jeremy was in shock—a good kind of shock. His fantasy was about to come true. His body strained as she stood up from her seat and moved over to him, her mouth set with determination. She was really going to do it. And it even looked like she wanted to. He didn't know how or why he could be so blessed, but this was one offering he wasn't going to decline.

He turned his chair out from the table, taking in her unusual boldness and finding her more alluring than ever.

Gina stopped before him, in all her loveliness, and stared down. "You'll have to tell me what you like."

Her voice was beautiful, just like her. He loved the way she pronounced certain naughty words with perfect elocution. *"Do you want my mouth on your cock?"*

He gave one sharp shake of his head to clear it before he came under his robe. *Now that would be a downright tragedy!*

"I can do that," he whispered back.

She knelt on the rug and brought her hands to his thighs. His whole body jerked at the contact and her eyes flashed to his in question.

"Go—go ahead. I—I want you to." He could barely get the words out. *If you stop now I will die.*

Her hands moved up his robe and took hold of the belt. Christ, he was burning hot for her. He watched her face as she untied the sash, pushing open the two halves to reveal his jutting erection, straight up, rock hard, and waiting for heaven to enfold him.

"Now open up your robe so I can see you when you do it," he said more decisively.

She got a little smile and slowly pulled the tie to her wrapper. The two halves of the robe stayed in place. The sound of the swish of the silk felt like it brushed along the whole length of him, but it was just erotic sound serving to increase the anticipation.

Gina looked up at him. No guile, just frank innocence waiting for him to tell her what to do.

"Show me. Show me your beautiful breasts."

Her long fingers drifted to the lapels and drew the blue silk apart, like the parting of the sea—a miracle performed by an otherworldly deity. She was the deity, or looked like she could be, all creamy flowing flesh and pink nipples bared for his pleasure.

"Put your hand around it like you did before and take the tip in your mou—" He lost the rest on a hiss as she quickly followed his directions.

Her lips closed around the head and her tongue swirled at the base. Taking him in deep, she sucked, quickly finding a compatible rhythm between the stroking of her hand and the suction of her mouth. Her thumb found the vein that ran up underneath him and rubbed back and forth. She did all that, and he soared.

The erotic view of her working on him, taking his cock in and out, just about made him come in the first minute alone. Those luscious pink lips closing in with each suck, and the sounds, helped to crank him higher. He wasn't going to last long—seeing her mouth full of him. The suck and pull ratcheted his body until he was ready to burst—

"I'm going to come!" He tried to withdraw, but she just drew him right back in. It was clear who was in charge, and he wasn't going to argue, being past the point of no return anyway. But he desperately needed to see her—

"Your eyes…please… Look at me!" he begged.

Those amber eyes lifted up. He reached down and cupped both sides of her face. Holding her steady, he thrust to the back of her throat and erupted.

The roar that came forth shook his whole body all the way to his heart, and he held on to her, and loved her, their eyes meeting in deep communion as he spilled in a hot rush.

"Love…you," he mouthed, shuddering. He saw her eyes smile back at him and felt her swallow. He nearly wept.

She finally pulled back and sat on her knees. That signature half-smile of hers in place, her hand came up to wipe her mouth. He just stared at her in amazement. Couldn't believe what she had just given him and with such generosity.

"I know."

His heart just cracked right open—not from hurt, but from love. Pure, unadulterated, and precious. He rubbed the top of his chest and told her, "You own me, Gina, and I don't want it any other way." He pulled her up from kneeling and brought her to his lap, cradling her in his arms. "When I see you, I can't look away. When we are apart, I feel you on my skin. I can taste you on my tongue. I smell your scent and I am so utterly and blissfully lost in you."

Gina nestled in under his chin. "So, you liked it? I want to do it again, sometime."

She was feeling shy once more. He could tell by her voice. That was the thing about Gina, what made her so captivating and alluring. She could be boldly sensual one minute, modestly restrained the next, and she was real like that. There was nothing false in her behavior.

"Well, I can be very accommodating, I assure you. Any time you wish to repeat that particular performance, you just let me know." He held her a little tighter, unwilling to leave the moment but needing to be close with her. "Bed, now. I need to hold you."

Settling into bed with her, he was struck with how easy it had been to get used to having her for a sleeping companion. The idea of sleeping alone now, apart from his wife, was a horrifying prospect. He had subsisted on such a lonely life before Gina. He just hadn't realized how empty and uninspiring it had been.

His three decades had been lived without a great deal of pride thus far, but he wanted to change that. He wanted purpose and honor to shape his life from now on.

As his senses took in the essence of Gina pulled in heavenly close and soft against him, he knew all of those good feelings and inspirations and ideas he had rolling around in his head now were only there because of her.

If having dinner set out in their room had been an inspiration, then the idea of breakfast followed shortly and became the rule. They both enjoyed regular breakfasts in their suite most days, unless, of course, they had church or company.

Jeremy asked from behind his newspaper, "What are your plans today, sweetheart?"

"Marianne is taking me to the modiste. Madame Trulier, I believe is her name."

He peeked over his newspaper at her, his eyes lighting sinfully. "Ah, well, I want lots of green and plenty of French underthings and *dishabille* gowns. I'd love to see you in some of those colored silk—" He stopped himself, cleared his throat, and ducked back behind the newspaper.

"You are very knowledgeable, Jeremy." She had seen his awareness of his mistake and how he'd shut his mouth right down. A spark of irritation took hold, or maybe something a little stronger than that. She waited for him to say something, but he stayed quiet. "Anything else? Other requests?" she asked him, her voice carrying a sharp bite across the table.

The paper lowered, and a gentle but inquisitive mask appeared. "Ah, no. You have such lovely taste, sweetheart. I know you'll make perfect selections." He smiled and reached to cover her hand. "Surprise me."

When his hand touched hers, she stiffened. She couldn't help feeling insanely jealous. Of course, all those women in his past! He was friends with her brother Tom, for Christ's sake, and she knew her brother took his pleasures in Town like probably most gentlemen did. What did she expect? That a man of his age had lived like a monk? Somehow she knew Jeremy had never lived like a monk and no doubt had sampled more than a few.

Her breath got heavy, and she felt the sting of tears at her eyes. She couldn't hold it back, and the question fell out of her mouth anyway. "How many women?" She clapped a hand over to shut herself up the second the words were spoken.

He winced, and his eyes looked pained.

"It is a lot, isn't it?"

"Gina, they don't matter." He squeezed her hand and swallowed.

She was compelled to know, like a demon sitting on her shoulder telling her to ask the next question even though she knew the answer would hurt terribly. "How many? More than ten?"

He nodded weakly.

"More than fifty?" God, the pain in her chest hurt!

Another single nod.

"More than a hundred?" She looked down at her chest, sure she'd see a gaping wound and lots of blood.

This time he closed his eyes and his head fell when he nodded. "I don't really know. I've never counted."

"You've been with more than a hundred women?" she wailed, knowing she sounded like a hysterical fool.

For a moment, all Georgina knew was a kind of jealous madness. She wanted to find those women and rip out their hair and scratch at their eyes. Jeremy was *her* man, and she had no intention of sharing him now or ever. Best to make that clear to him right now! Taking in a calming breath, she opened her mouth to say her piece, but he beat her to it.

"You have every right to be disgusted with me. I was never a saint, Gina. Not even close. I was—I was empty inside until you. I never felt anything when I was with others. It was merely a need for release."

She nodded her head, gulping for air, trying to push down the jealousy and accept that she couldn't hold him to his past, to a time before her.

He had more to say though. "It is well that you are upset with me. I want you to be so because it was bad behavior on my part and I deserve your repulsion. But you must hear me now. This is critical information. No matter how many women I've had before, there is only one woman I will ever be with now. I don't miss a thing about that life I lived before, and I'll never go back to it. I only want you. The most beautiful and perfect woman I have ever known. You. My first and only lover."

"It is a good thing, Jeremy Greymont, because I will not share you! Not ever!" Close to breaking down, she drew deep breaths, willing herself back to the rational.

Jeremy got up from his seat and came to her, drawing her up against his chest. He took her face in his hands and spoke close. "And you'll never have to. You're all I want. You're all I need. You are everything."

The quiet lasted a long time, nothing but soft breathing between them. Finally she spoke. "I've learned something I didn't know before," she whispered, taking in his words and opening her heart to trust.

"What is that?"

"Loving can hurt, too."

"True. So very true, my Gina."

She looked up at her husband. "But it's worth it. If we can be together in the end, then it's worth it."

The letter arrived that very afternoon. Jeremy realized his error as soon as the sender's address was revealed. *Mdm. T. Blufette, 26 Oxley Court, Covent Garden, London.*

He did not welcome the missive. This was not good news. He didn't want any connection with his old life. And coming on the heels of his disclosure this morning at breakfast! God help him if Gina knew the abbess of a popular bordello wanted an audience with him. His wife had a bit of a jealous streak, he'd discovered, and wouldn't take to it well. Jeremy had his failings but wasn't stupid enough to risk his marital harmony on a brothel madam.

And what could Therese Blufette possibly want from him? He'd forgotten his promise to meet with her the night he'd talked to Marguerite and Luc. After discovering the true identity of Gina's rapist, his one and only thought had been to get to her as soon as possible and secure her safety. He had put Madame Therese Blufette out of his mind without a second thought. He read the letter.

*Dear Mr. Greymont,*

*It is with deep regret that I write this. I so hoped we could have talked that night you were in London, but we did not, and alas I am afraid, sir, that I can no longer be patient. Time is of the essence now.*

*All I can say in this letter is that the matter at hand is in regards to your family. Our meeting must be in person. The Velvet Swan will do.*

*Please come to me in London at your earliest convenience.*

*Therese Blufette*

Jeremy was dumbfounded. Not what he was expecting in a letter, although very intriguing. What "family" did she mean? He didn't have much family. His mother had been an only child like him.

It must be family from his father's side. There was some family he'd never known, and of French citizenry. Madame Blufette was French.

He knew his father had died around ten years ago, somewhere in his native France. Jeremy didn't even know exactly when and where, for they had never seen each other again after the day he'd left when Jeremy was just a young boy. A notification of death had come through a solicitor, and there was no property to inherit that Jeremy was aware of. The miserable matter of Henri Greymont had finally been laid to rest, literally.

And Jeremy did not care to know or have anything of Henri Greymont's either. The man had walked out of his life more than two decades ago, and Jeremy felt nothing. As far as he was concerned, his "father" was Sir Rodney, the man who had raised him from a boy and been his guide into adulthood, his grandfather.

The only part of his real father that he had to show he'd ever existed was his name—Greymont, French in origin but styled with proper English pronunciation, that being a hard *T* rather than silent.

Making his decision, he wrote a brief but terse decline to Therese Blufette. He explained he was recently wed and could not leave his new bride unattended and that he really had no interest in anything to do with family he'd never known and was unlikely to ever know. He wished her well and expressed his hope that she would honor his request to remain uninvolved.

Setting the letter on the tray for posting, he was interrupted by shouting and commotion coming from the front of the house. He went to the window and saw Mills giving terse direction to the stable hands, a look of immediacy on his face, his hands waving wildly. Jeremy knew something was very wrong, Mills was cool and reserved all the time.

Racing out to the front steps, he was greeted with words that were never welcome. "Bad fire, sir! Rawles's cottage. Their boy's been burned. I fear the worst."

His gut twisted as he sprang into action, directing all available hands and equipment to the scene of the disaster. He called for his horse and headed out with Mills, grateful that Gina was occupied with Marianne Rourke on a shopping excursion.

He smelled the acrid smoke before he sighted it, bracing himself for the dreadful prospect of the loss of a young life. This would no doubt be a very long day.

# CHAPTER TWENTY~SIX

*A shudder in the loins engenders there*
*The broken wall, the burning roof and tower*
*And Agamemnon dead.*

—W.B. Yeats, "Leda and the Swan" (1928)

Georgina arrived home to a solemn and nearly empty house. Mrs. Richards provided details on the fire and discussed what arrangements would be needed for the Rawles family. Burns were deadly more often than not, and everyone was well aware of the likely outcome. They could only pray for the boy.

All on her own and in gloomy spirits, Georgina ate a light dinner then retired to her chambers. She had a bath and unpacked the things she had brought home from Madame Trulier's.

Many dresses and gowns had been ordered, but a few items she had been able to take with her today. Among them, two silk nightdresses, more like chemises really, very French, very alluring, and sleeveless. One in green and one in yellow. That French modiste knew a thing or two about dressing a woman to incite her husband, Georgina realized. She thought Jeremy would like them and had made the selections with him in mind, the whole time remembering how he'd hated admitting his very experienced past to her this morning. Yes, he'd hated telling her, but the fact remained that he did tell her. He told the truth, painful as it was for them both. His honesty was one of the traits she admired in Jeremy. When a person was honest, she knew where she stood and could count on trusting them at their word. Jeremy said he only wanted her, and she believed him. He insisted that his old life was well in the past, behind him forever. And she believed that, too. Georgina had mulled his disclosures over enough times during the day, and she was ready to put it away for good.

She wrote a long letter to her brother and a short one to her father before getting into bed. A headache had plagued her for the last hour, and with Jeremy still gone, she figured sleep was the best thing she could do for herself. She hoped he was well, wherever he was, and that he would have some good news to report about the burned little boy.

Lying alone in the big bed, she lay awake for a time. When she did finally sleep, it was a restless slumber, awash in images, dreams, and terrors her subconscious mind had buried away for a long time…

Jeremy went straight to his study and poured a double scotch. It was the only thing for him right now. The fire's devastation had been pretty complete, right down to taking the life of the Rawles's youngest son. The boy had gone into the burning cottage to retrieve his puppy and had been lost when a falling beam had struck him. Ironically, the dog had not even been inside.

He looked down at his empty glass and refilled it. The auburn liquid burned his throat, but he hardly felt it.

*Sweet Jesus!* The looks on their faces had just crushed him inside. How would they bear the loss? He'd seen how Mrs. Rawles had reached out to touch the blackened skin of her child and how her husband had held her back, his eyes utterly empty, as dead as little Tim Rawles's young life. The father had loved his son. He grieved for his boy.

The two older children had just stood, so stoic in their pain and probable guilt for not keeping their brother safely back from the fire.

Time to top his glass again.

Yes, destruction had come for the Rawles family tonight and had triumphed brutally. What a horrifying waste, he thought, as he kept communion with the bottle until he'd emptied the damn thing.

There were some other reasons for the drinking as well. The way Gina had stared at him this morning. Her shock at the number of women he'd had. It was exceptionally painful because Gina was the only one who had ever thought of him as an honorable man. She was always going on about how he was such a gentleman and so considerate. He'd bet his ballocks she didn't think so now.

And then that goddamned letter from Therese Blufette and the dredging of memories he wanted no part of. His father hadn't loved him or his mother. Henri Greymont was a selfish bastard who had walked right out of their lives without a backward glance. His father had let them go.

Staggering up to bed, he felt positively wrecked. There was only one thing that could fill part of the gaping wound he had right now. Or only one person. His Gina could heal his heart. She made everything good and happy and right. If he could just hold her, and maybe kiss her, and touch her, and—

"Where is my beautiful Gina? Gina? There you are. You are so soft and smell so sweet. I need you…"

Georgina was brought to wakefulness by insistent hands and warm breath smelling strongly of scotch. "Jeremy? Are you foxed?" she mumbled, trying to make sense of him.

"Mmm, yes. Foxed and desirous of a fuck!" He undid his kecks and pushed them down, his erection high and hard. "See? My prick always leads the way straight to you, my sweetheart!"

Georgina gasped at the coarse words and the sight of him naked with his cock looking to devour her. He never spoke to her like that. She had never seen him drunk before either.

Jeremy grasped a handful of her new gown and shoved it up, took a palm up her inner thigh, and spread her wide, obviously intent upon carrying out his spoken wish, drunk or not.

"Ahhh, you feel so good, Gina. So warm and lovely in the bed. When I am away from you, I can think of nothing but the next time I'll be able to have you underneath me." He whispered the rest. "It's all I think about most of the time—your lovely cunny and my cock getting into it."

His eyes widened like he was trying to focus. She was touched by the impression that something was wrong with him, but even so, he did not hesitate to complete his mission. He gripped under her hips firmly.

Georgina couldn't believe what she was seeing and hearing and feeling. Especially when he flipped her over and gripped her bum, his hands sweeping over the cheeks.

"You have the most gorgeous arse...just sublime," he murmured, while covering her, his urgent heat pressing hard between the folds at her core.

He had never taken her from this position before, mounting from behind. Unease filled her, but she told herself that everything was all right. It was just Jeremy, too much drink and feeling passionate. The feeling of unease only grew stronger. The words, sounds, and smells bored into her subconscious, bringing up the memory of something evil as each second passed.

Jeremy's grip on her hips was hard, forceful even, positioning her to accept him whether she wanted it or not. She was trapped in his embrace, unable to shift away or pull herself down.

Georgina panicked. All in a moment, the scene returned, and it wasn't Jeremy mounting her. It was *him*. She remembered that day—in all its gruesome clarity. What he had said and done to her, and how it felt when he violated her body. He had done it like this... *Do you like my cock, wildcat? You like it, don't you? We've got hours and hours. I've fucked that sweet cunt of yours, and now I'll do the same to your pretty— You're a special, special girl. You get it all, wildcat.*

"No! No don't—please!" She resisted his invasion, bucking below Jeremy to get him off. Her hands flailed back to push him away.

She was strong, but not as strong as Jeremy. He had no trouble sinking his cock deep. So deep, she felt the soft slap of testicles as he reached his limit. The thick muscle plowed easily into the furrow of her body, his big hands framing her hips steady as he thrust forward over and over, his pace nearly frantic.

Hitting back with her hands, she pawed and scratched at him, her panic overriding every other thought. "Noooo! Stop! Nooooooo!" She began to cry her pleas in earnest, no longer aware of who was doing what to whom.

Jeremy was vaguely perceptive that she thrashed against him. The sound of her agonized weeping pierced through his inebriated fog just enough to register. The alcohol dulled her blows anyway—he barely felt them. He stilled his thrusting for a moment, his cock still buried in her delicious heat, and loomed over her, trying to make sense of the situation.

"What?"

She continued to weep and push her hands back.

"Gina?" He bent down to kiss her cheek, but she flinched her head away, so his lips landed on the back of her neck instead. Realization dawned.

*I am scaring her.*

"You are afraid? No, no, no, no, nooooo!"

A chill iced through him. He moved out of her and rolled her onto her back once more, holding her face, forcing her to look him in the eyes.

He saw only terror in hers.

"No! No, my sweet Gina. You are not afraid of *me*. It's Jeremy! Your lover who adores you."

Sobriety claimed him immediately. He continued to hold her face, but the look of terror stayed there, biting back at him. When he finally released her, she cringed away, scooting to the far edge, up against the headboard. The look of shame and distress on her face before she covered up with her hands, killed him, just ripped right into him like a broadsword cleaving him apart.

"Jeremy?" she wailed.

"Oh, dear God. I've scared you. I've scared you to death. Oh, Gina, I'm so sorry. Sweetheart. Sorry. I've terrified you." More weeping met his ears as he kept babbling the same thing over and over.

Jeremy reached out and touched her leg, feeling so very helpless. Gina flinched from the contact. She actually flinched at his touch, and he instantly knew the need to be sick.

Some of that scotch was going to come up! Now! He lurched from the bed and made it to the water closet just in time to heave his guts out. A second wave of retching and then a third passed before there was nothing left down there but roiling guts.

A gentle hand landed on his shoulder and then a cool, wet cloth was proffered. Dazed at first, he took the cloth anyway and pressed it to his face, heaved himself up from the floor, and told her, "I hate that I've frightened you. I don't ever want to hurt you, but I know I will. I'll hurt and scare you over and over again because I am a beast when I fu—"

She stood there beautiful in a yellow shift, looking like a goddess but unable to meet his eyes. She hugged her arms and stared at the floor, her chin propped on crossed arms.

He shook his head back and forth. "I'm not fit for you, Gina."

"Jeremy," she whispered, "no."

He sighed heavily, feeling utterly lost. "I'm going to go."

Silence.

He moved toward the door, not sure how his feet were managing to take him there, his heart aching at the thought of leaving her behind.

Jeremy's declaration to sleep apart from her was motivation enough. It careened Georgina back to the here and now. This was her husband, not some criminal rapist. Jeremy—her lover. And it was really the shock of remembering that paralyzed her, not what Jeremy had just done to her in their bed. Georgina had never recalled the details until now—

"No!" she cried. "I can't be alone here, Jeremy!" She grabbed his arm to stay him. "I don't want you to go. I'm sorry I panicked. For the first time, I—I remembered things about—about what happened that day," she panted, hurrying to get the words out. Swallowing hard, she attempted a calm tone. "Please stay with me. I know that it's you. Not—not him. And you did not hurt me."

Jeremy seemed shocked by her request. He hung his head. "Yes, I did! I saw your face, how you looked at me. You were terrified of me." He scrubbed his hands over his face. "I'll only frighten you again."

"You won't." She shook her head emphatically.

"I will, Gina. I will frighten you again because I cannot help the way I am when I want to fu—when I want to make love to you.

Which is whenever I'm near you." He looked into her eyes helplessly. "You incite me. I always want you, but it was wrong of me to demand this from you, to expect you to put up with—"

"And I want you, Jeremy. It's not you when we make love that frightens me. Something tonight sparked a memory. You took me by surprise, awakening me from sleep like that." She tried to explain without losing her composure. "You came to me from...behind...and I smelled the drink on you, and you said you wanted to 'fuck' me, and for a moment it was reminiscent of—of him." She heard Jeremy gasp, not knowing if it was from disgust or remorse, but forged ahead anyway. "He said that, and he was drunk, and he—he—he did it like that."

It got deathly quiet in the room. Jeremy was frozen stiff before her, his face a mask of remorse as he took in her description of that time, on that day in June, with the monster who had ruined her. And as bad as that day was and the fear she known then, it felt worse right now telling him about it. What if Jeremy didn't want her anymore, couldn't be with her because of what he now knew? Fresh panic hit her—the panic of losing him.

"I did not remember everything until just now!" She dropped to the floor, putting her head at his feet. "I am so, so sorry, Jeremy, my husband. I panicked and knew not where I was or with whom. I lost my mind for a moment."

He slumped down to meet her on the floor, pulled her head onto his lap, and stroked her hair. After a while, he spoke, "I scare you half to death, and yet you apologize to me? I should be begging your pardon for my beastly actions. I am so ashamed." He gently held her face to look up at him. "Can you ever forgive me?"

"Yes! A thousand times, yes! If you don't go and you stay with me."

He did stay, but the mood was somber. Both of them nursed their own regrets in the dark, their misgivings like a blanket that did not give much warmth or comfort. Georgina felt the change between them. Jeremy had doubts about her now. She remembered everything that had been done to her…now. And the worst part of all? Jeremy knew it.

# CHAPTER TWENTY~SEVEN

*In thy green lap was Nature's darling laid.*
—Thomas Gray, *The Progress of Poesy* (1757)

The funeral for little Timothy Rawles was held on a dismal November day, the reality of loss and grief leaching into the wet soil along with the tears shed by many. They had seen to relocating the family to new lodgings and replacement of necessities, but there was no replacing a child, was there?

After the funeral party broke, Georgina lingered back by the gravesite. Jeremy was in conversation with some of the men when she noticed a child, standing behind a tree, head bowed, shoulders trembling as she wept. She approached the girl and saw that a shepherd pup was tied to the tree next to her.

"That's a lovely dog you have." Georgina spoke softly so as not to startle the child.

"My mum says he must go as she cannot bear to see him anymore." She sniffed.

"Is he the reason your brother went into the fire?" Georgina asked, her heart breaking for this poor, grieving child.

The girl nodded. "But it wasn't his fault. He's a good pup, and the fire scared him, too. I brought him here to say good-bye…for Tim—" She broke down then, her small body crumpling forward with sobs.

Georgina knelt and took the child into her arms, the small, thin little body quivering as she wept. "It is a lovely gesture to bring him here. I am sure Tim is very happy about you doing that."

"Is Tim an angel now? In heaven?" the girl murmured into Georgina's shoulder.

"He is, and has not a care or a worry, nor will he ever have again." She smoothed over the girls chestnut curls. "What's your name, child?"

"Mariah," she snuffled.

Georgina took out her handkerchief and wiped Mariah's cheeks. "I am Mrs. Greymont, and I am happy to meet such a brave and loving sister as you were to your brother. I'm sure he's very proud, looking down on you from heaven."

"Thank you, madam." Mariah looked at her in wonderment. Then she bent to throw her arms around the pup, who had sat quietly patient the whole time they'd been talking. "Good-bye," she whispered into the soft brown fur.

"What will you do with him?" Georgina asked.

"I have to leave him here. Someone might want him. He's very good and smart. Tim and me, we taught him to sit and stay, and he doesn't bark hardly at all, and he never does his business indoors." She bowed her head and stroked her pet. "I'll miss him."

"What do you call him?"

"Frisk. Tim named him that because he frisks about."

Georgina bent to pet the adorable dog, who nuzzled right over, stuck his nose in her hand, and looked up at her with round sable-colored eyes. She made her decision. "I could take him for you."

"You would?" Mariah smiled with a child's optimism.

"Yes, I would. Frisk can live with me, and you are welcome to come and visit him whenever you wish. He can still be your dog, too. I'm sure Frisk would miss you as well, Mariah."

"Oh, thank you, madam. You are a good lady. I'll try to come."
Mariah curtsied and made her way back to her parents.

Georgina untied the rope from the tree and bent down to stroke
Frisk again when Jeremy's voice came to her from behind. "So,
you've got yourself a dog, Mrs. Greymont."

She spun around in surprise. "How much did you hear?"

"Enough. I heard enough to puzzle it out." He smiled wistfully.
"And the girl was right. You are a good lady."

"Oh, Jeremy," she whispered, putting her arm through his. "Let
us go home now." Suddenly feeling very overwhelmed by all the
sorrow of the occasion, she was grateful to have her husband for
support and strength. She held on to him tightly as they left the
little graveyard, which had just increased its innocent souls by one
on this cold and cheerless day.

Jeremy figured there must be something to the saying
"misfortune never comes singly" because here was yet another
horror staring him in the face. The letter in his hand was chilling
and spurred him into action. He had no choice. The time of
indecision was over, and vengeance would no longer be denied.
Retribution was coming for Simon Strawnly. Jeremy was going
after the bastard.

*Greymont,*

*You don't know me, but I know your wife. Know her in every
sense of the word. I was annoyed to hear you snatched her away
for your own pleasures. She takes a cock real well, doesn't she?
I'll never forget how sweet she felt when I shagged her till she
bled. Or maybe that was her virgin blood. All the crying and
fighting just made everything that much sweeter. Does she fight*

*you?*

*You took my plaything, and I'm not pleased. Uncle would have married her if you hadn't come along, and by the way, he's still heated you put a gun to him. Now that whore from the bordello, the blonde one that looks like her, will have to do. She's not as good though—not much fight in her. She mentioned you...that whore, Marguerite. Said you asked about us. Said you gave her money to leave England. Now why would you do that, Greymont? Could it be you wish to protect your bride's reputation? I'm thinking that must be it. Lucky for you there is a way to accomplish this goal. It will require capital though. Shouldn't be a trouble for you. Come three days hence:* 44 Peake Street, Knightsbridge, *and await direction.*

*Ahead of you,*
*S.S.*

The urge to kill boiled inside his body. Jeremy was not a violent person by nature, but this letter had changed that facet of his character. With buried rage simmering, he forced a calm presentation on the front, knowing he had to find Gina and tell her he was leaving immediately for London. And another of his character traits was about to take a hard blow as well. He was going to have to lie like hell to her.

"But why must I stay with the Rourkes?" Georgina pleaded. "Can I not go with you?"

"No, sweetheart. This is urgent, dreadful business—lives are at stake. There is no time for anything social, I'm afraid. Not this trip." He smiled a little and stroked her cheek.

"I don't care about parties. I just want to be with you."

"And I hate to leave you here, but I'd be in negotiations all day and we'd have no time together anyway," he said firmly. "No—it's best for you to stay. I've spoken with Darius, and he said Marianne is thrilled to have your company. You can sketch and go to the shops together, take Frisk along—"

She shook her head at him.

"Gina, you will indulge me in this." He gripped her arms. "I—I cannot leave you alone here, unprotected." His voice lowered to a hard whisper. "I just can't. Not after what happened to you."

She froze. There it was again. Her shame thrown back in her face. Now Jeremy was doing it. Would she ever be free? Free of the hold it had on the both of them?

Georgina gave in because it seemed so important to him, but she spoke stiffly. "All right, Jeremy. I'll go stay with the Rourkes, as it obviously pleases you."

He kissed her cheek. "You are a good wife. Thank you, sweetheart, it eases my heart knowing you will be safe."

She stayed stiff when he touched her, but had to ask him, "When will you go?"

"Today. As soon as I can be ready."

"Oh, well, I'd better leave you to it then. You must have much to do."

Georgina stepped back, and Jeremy didn't stop her. She wished he would've. She wished he'd take her in his arms and kiss her wildly and tell her he couldn't be parted from her and to go pack her things because she was coming with him. But that wasn't happening, was it? From the look of him, she'd say he was eager to get on the road, and that felt like a stab to the heart. She would miss him, but it seemed he couldn't wait to get away.

"I'll come find you when it's time to bid farewell so we can have a few minutes alone before I go." He smiled again, but she could see it didn't reach to his eyes.

"As you wish, Jeremy." She bowed her head.

Georgina let herself out of his study with her dignity intact. She hadn't cried at least. And he was being kind and solicitous of her, considering the pressure he was under. It would only be for a few days, she reminded herself. So why then did she feel such a foreboding, like Jeremy was slipping away from her in parts?

# CHAPTER TWENTY~EIGHT

*...Murder's out of tune,*
*And sweet revenge grows harsh.*

**—William Shakespeare,** *Othello* **(1602)**

The trip to London gave Jeremy plenty of time to think. Leaving Gina on the steps of Hallborough had been agony. She had stayed on the landing, her willowy shape still discernable when he turned Samson and looked back as he left the grounds of Hallborough.

Their parting had not been as he'd wished. She was hurt, he knew, at being left behind, but he couldn't have her in Town, not where Strawnly or Pellton might see her. No telling what could happen. It was far too dangerous a risk, and she was too precious to him for risks of any kind to even be considered.

This past week had been a bloody nightmare, a vile weed that just kept spreading. First the boy's tragic death, then the drunken ravishment that resulted in making her cringe from him like he was some monster, and now this!

Jeremy wasn't too worried about Strawnly's extortion attempt though. He had other plans for that shit-bastard, and money wouldn't be needed where he was going.

Riding Samson reminded him of the time he'd ridden with

Gina. It was the day he'd come to Oakfield, the day he'd first seen her again. She had allowed him to lift her up and steady her on Samson's back, offering herself to trust him.

And that was a curious thing about her. For all that life had done her wrong, she wasn't hardened by it. She was a generous person by nature. And she trusted him even when she shouldn't.

He missed his Gina already. Missed making love with her. Missed having her shoulder tucked under his chin while they slept. Missed her scent up in his nose.

He pictured her beautiful body, of how her breasts puddled to the side when she was on her back. He thought of the small birthmark on her left hipbone and how he liked to trace over it with his tongue. He thought about how glorious it was to be covered deep inside her heat, of wanting the sensations to go on forever, but knowing he'd die if he didn't spill, thus bringing that encounter to a sweet kind of death.

They hadn't made love together since that night she'd recalled the details of her attack, and the loss made him melancholy. And it worried him, too, now that she remembered everything. In a way, not knowing the specifics had been easier for her. He hated to think of Gina suffering anew as she dredged up exactly what had been done to her. He couldn't even bear to think about the specifics what she'd suffered. He didn't want those images sullying the beautiful thoughts of her he carried around in his head.

And that last time he'd taken her, drunk and out of his mind? Hell, he'd wanted to gut himself when she shrank from him in fear. In that instant, in her view, she'd seen him as her rapist. He shuddered in the leather saddle and rubbed the middle of his chest.

Jeremy was determined to make it up to her. As soon as this "problem" was resolved, they could begin enjoying perfectly lovely, mundane days filled with baby-making and whatever the hell else struck their fancies. They had a life to get started, and he vowed no single person or any other obstacle was going to get in the way.

At their farewell, he'd promised they would make plans for a trip to Town at Christmastide, as soon as he returned from this "urgent business." Thank heavens she hadn't inquired too far into the details of that imaginative fabrication. He felt guilty for lying to her, but he deemed that the justification served the means when it came to protecting her.

Looking over the dull autumn landscape, his eyes confirmed what his nose had detected earlier. London could be scented long before it could be seen, and even in the stench it looked lovely, the lights of the outskirts twinkled like glow flies hovering on the heath.

Two hours more and Jeremy was seated in a hired hackney. He'd ensconced Samson at the first London stable they'd come upon with instructions, and plenty of coin, to insure his horse was rewarded for getting him to Town so swiftly. He hoped Samson was contentedly enjoying a bag of oats right about now, for the lovely beast truly deserved it.

Jeremy rapped on the window to signal the driver. A few moments later the hack pulled up to the prearranged stop. From the opposite side of the road, Jeremy took in the surroundings of number forty-four, Peake Street. He perused and sized it up from all angles. He needed to know everything he could about his enemy before he struck. That's why he'd come three days early. His knuckles rapped again to indicate it was time to move on.

The next stop was as familiar to him as the previous had been unfamiliar. He knew every inch of it. His grandfather's townhouse in Grosvenor Square was situated on a corner, very smart, bright white with black trim. A servant admitted him from the back entrance, stealthily quiet and under shadow in the dark alley. Other than the occupants inside, who awaited him and would keep his secret, he didn't want anyone to know that Jeremy Greymont had arrived in Town. Not yet at least.

The wet drizzle prevented a walk along the shore, so Georgina opted to return to Hallborough for the day. The discomforts of pregnancy had Marianne resting anyway, and Georgina wanted to check on any correspondence that had arrived while she'd been gone. The note she left for Marianne promised her return by dinnertime.

She smiled down at Frisk, leaning into her on the carriage seat. He was just as good and smart as Mariah Rawles had praised him to be, and she didn't have a single regret about taking him. He would grow into a magnificent dog when he reached his full size, and no doubt be an excellent companion for her. She stroked the soft waves of warm umber fur and thought about Jeremy.

The past three days at Stonewell with the Rourkes had been all right and she'd done her best to quell her growing unease, but self-doubt was definitely getting the upper hand. Jeremy had seemed so different the day he'd left for London. Granted, the time leading up to his departure had been awful with the death of the Rawles boy and then her memories returning of the attack. With his business in crisis—something about one of the ships fallen into piracy—she wondered if he'd had time even to write yet.

How could she have cringed from him like that? She cursed herself, wishing she could take that one night back. Jeremy had been aghast. She'd seen the stricken look on his face. Her fear had bewildered him until she told him why.

And that telling of the reason had been the very worst of all. Even though he had said he didn't care about her past, she knew that he did care. It bothered him that another man had taken her, and she worried about what would happen now between them. Was he disgusted? Or was he wary because he figured she couldn't bear his touch when he wanted her in that wildly passionate, desperate way of his?

Georgina didn't know exactly what Jeremy was feeling, but she did know they hadn't made love since that night. He'd slept in the same bed with her, but he hadn't reached for her under the covers like he usually did, telling her how much he needed her and how beautiful she felt to him, the declarations of a lover. And this had her greatly worried.

Mrs. Richards brought all of the correspondence and a cup of tea to her desk in the library. With Frisk at her feet, she sorted through everything. There was no letter from Jeremy, but one missive caught her eye. It stood out starkly from the rest. The hand was rough, readable but unrefined, with no address of origin. Something compelled her to open it. The essence of urgency screamed from the folded paper for some reason. It was short, but very telling.

*They have Marguerite. Madame Therese begs you to come, as do I.*

*Luc*

Georgina let the note slip from her hand, her fingers losing their grip. She watched it flutter gently down to the desktop. The parchment, the black ink scrawl, contrasted harshly with the mahogany table.

Who was Marguerite? Madame Therese? Luc? Who were these people, and why had she never heard Jeremy speak of them? Unease settled in her belly. It came on her instantly, the second she read the words, like a flash of lightning. One minute she was assured. The next she thought her breakfast might come up. She brought her hand to her mouth and willed the bile back down, just standing there, clutching the side of the table and forcing her stomach to calm.

It didn't take Georgina long to decide what to do next. She left the library with the letter and went directly to Jeremy's study, Frisk close at her heels.

The search through his correspondence bore fruit about ten minutes later when she found a letter from someone named Therese Blufette. In it, she asked Jeremy pointedly to come to London, saying it must be in person and at her place of business, an establishment with the unusual name of *The Velvet Swan.* Comparing the two missives, she deduced that *Therese Blufette* from the letter in his study and *Madame Therese* in the note from Luc were one and the same person. It wasn't too much of a stretch to figure this was most likely the reason Jeremy had left so abruptly for London.

Her Jeremy had gone to meet a woman, and this Luc person wanted him to come because of…Marguerite? And he hadn't said anything to her. She froze, her mind struggling to accept that which surely was the truth. Jeremy had lied.

"Why did he lie to me, Frisk? Why would my Jeremy do that?" she murmured down to the dog. He sat patiently, blinking his attentive eyes back up to her.

She thought she knew. And it crushed her. Maybe he'd gone back to be with other women—women who could bear his touch and wouldn't flinch away in panic like she had done. This Marguerite, whoever she was, worried her, too. Was she someone Jeremy cared about? A past dalliance? Might he want to go back with her again? The very idea crushed her heart to bits.

That last time, when she'd recalled her attacker, Jeremy had been horrified that she was frightened of him in that moment. Jeremy didn't like her afraid or scared—ever. This had always been an issue between them. He hated for her to fear the sex, or worse, fear him. And Georgina was always having to remind him that he didn't scare her.

Then the unthinkable happened. She remembered. Everything. And for a few moments she *was* scared, but losing Jeremy scared her more. Much, much more.

Georgina remembered the panic she'd felt when he'd said he was going to sleep in another bedroom. She had willingly begged him to stay with her, and would do it again in a heartbeat.

Jeremy was a considerate husband. He probably didn't want to make demands on her anymore because he believed his attentions would cause her to remember her attacker.

But that wasn't true, and never would be. She loved Jeremy and wanted to be with him, wanted him to love her with his body, in the manner he needed from her. No matter what.

"Come, Frisk! We must pack." Feeling possessive and suddenly jealous, she knew the urge to fight. She was his wife, for God's sake! And she would not let her husband go like this. If she must follow Jeremy to London and make him understand, then so be it.

# CHAPTER TWENTY~NINE

*Mine is the most plotting heart in the world.*

—Samuel Richardson, *Clarissa* (1747)

**M**arguerite's somewhere, Greymont. They're keeping her somewhere in this city, and God only knows what's being done to her!"

"Easy, mate, we're going to get her back, and you'll have your chance to go at Strawnly, as soon as your woman is safe." Jeremy's attempt to soothe the frantic Luc was only marginally successful. The man was a mess over Marguerite's abduction. The big guard's affection for her went far beyond a working relationship, as Jeremy had discovered. The two of them had been planning to leave England together when Strawnly managed to get her.

Two days ago, when Jeremy had summoned Luc to his grandfather's townhouse, Luc was surprised at how fast Jeremy had been able to get to London. Apparently Jeremy wasn't the only person being extorted for money by Strawnly. Gina's reputation as well as Marguerite's safe return to Madame Therese both carried a price.

Strawnly was in trouble though. Serious trouble. His

predilections for brutalizing young women had won out over his humanity long ago, that was, if he'd ever had any to begin with. Strawnly had raped before, and it wasn't difficult to locate other fathers and brothers who wanted justice for their loved ones. That, and the fact that Strawnly was looking for a way out of England, provided the perfect opportunity to make things right.

"All we have to do is let him walk into the trap. Think, Luc! If we jump him now, he won't get on that ship. You want him on that ship and Marguerite safe, back with you," Jeremy reminded the anxious Luc. "Therese will be here any minute. As soon as she hands over the money, he's going to take off for the docks and we'll go get her. This won't work if Strawnly doesn't get on that ship!" With victory so close, Jeremy didn't want to lose their advantage.

"I know. I just can't bear to think of him hurting her—" Luc scrubbed his face and dropped his head. "I love her. I want to be with her."

Jeremy clapped him on the shoulder. "And you will be with her. I'm going to see to it."

Jeremy remembered back to last night's negotiation with Strawnly. It had been Luc who'd restrained Jeremy then...

...At number forty-four, Peake Street a boy waited outside in the moonlight. The waif leaned against the building, eager to capitalize on any opportunity that might be extended.

"Lookin' for Greymont. That you, mister?" the urchin asked Luc. Luc poked out his thumb at Jeremy and kept silent.

Jeremy took the missive and passed the boy a coin. He read the note and then looked at the boy again. "Do you know the man who wrote this?"

Clever green eyes snapped to attention. "Aye, sir."

Jeremy held up a pound note. "The location where he's keeping a working girl, French and blonde, hazel eyes, called Marguerite, and this will be yours. Find her by tomorrow, and I'll make it double this."

"You'll have it, sir. I'm on the job right now. If anyone will do, Danny can. Where canna I find you?"

Jeremy told him and watched the boy lope off into the twisting streets, silent as the faint mist which clouded the night.

Strawnly's instructions brought Luc and Jeremy to a seedy pub on the outskirts of London. The sour smells of fermenting ale and the accumulated grime of unwashed bodies assaulted the senses, but seemed fitting considering who had summoned them here.

They found a dark corner and waited. Jeremy passed on the drink, or more precisely, the mug it was served in. Typhoid fever came to mind, and he felt the sudden urge to find soap and water for washing.

The cur came slinking up and sat across from the table. Dark hair hung in dank strings from an average-looking face. He wasn't ugly, but his bones made for sharp features. His eyes were what made him evil. So dark brown they almost looked devoid of color, but it wasn't the lack of pigment. It was the absence of humanity that made Jeremy recoil. Strawnly was an animal—vicious— soulless—and it didn't take knowledge of the irrefutable facts to recognize this. His inhumanity was as visible as filth on a white shirt. He just provided further proof of it the second he opened his mouth.

"So this is the bastard who took my plaything away from me," he said, giving Jeremy a full stare, his eyes flicking over his fine clothes, sizing him up, no doubt.

Jeremy felt the blood in his temples pounding through his veins as the muscles in his face tightened, his own humanity in full question right now.

This degenerate lump of unrepentant flesh had dared to put his hands on Gina, stolen her innocence from her, hurt and beat and savaged her. Jeremy knew the desire to kill. Bloodlust, pure and simple, was what it was. To kill this *evil* sitting before him would bring no sting of conscience. A goddamn public service to England is what he'd be doing!

"Took? You pile of shit, I married her. She is my wife!"

Strawnly flicked his tongue out and swiped both corners of his mouth with it, looking just like a lizard, his dead eyes going back in between Jeremy and Luc before settling on the guard. "My new dolly doesn't quite compare though. Her tits are smaller." He looked to Jeremy again. "Now, your wife…mmmmm…her titties are simply magnific—"

Jeremy lunged so fast Strawnly jerked backward and hit his head on the wall behind him. Luc held Jeremy back as he spat out his response in a lethal rasp. "You'll shut your fucking mouth before you see so much as a farthing. Don't speak of her again, or I might lose my temper and kill you right here in public, consequences be damned."

"So volatile, Greymont," Strawnly grumbled and then shrugged him off. "About my instructions, have that cunt abbess bring it to the same place as before." He wagged a finger at them. "She comes alone though, tomorrow night—the money *and* safe passage. There's a ship out of this pissing rain and doldrums island at midnight tomorrow, and I'm going to be on it."

"Good for you," Jeremy said. "And Marguerite?"

Strawnly rolled his eyes. "God, why do you care so much? She's just three holes for my cock. That's all any female is good—"

Jeremy lunged again, his face so close to Strawnly he could smell his fetid breath and nearly gagged. "Where is she, you degenerate animal?"

"Easy now. We don't want to cause a scene," Strawnly drawled. "For some reason, that whore is important, and it works out all the better for me anyway. If you must have her back, it'll cost you a little more. Another thousand would be sufficient, I think, and providing you keep to your end of our bargain, I'll tell where she's been keeping. After that, gentlemen, I'll be gone from here, and you'll never see me again." Strawnly looked confident.

*That part of it is definitely true, you soulless bastard…*

Now Jeremy and Luc waited in the building across the street, hidden and undetected. Nightfall would come, and soon after that, Therese Blufette would arrive to deliver the money. Strawnly would take it and board his ship. Marguerite would be retrieved. And then? Well, nature would take its course, as was right and proper…

Georgina had not been to London in more than two years, and never had she travelled alone. Well, not precisely alone. Apart from the driver, Ned, there was her maid, Jane, and then at the last minute she'd decided to bring Frisk as well. The group of four was hardly an impressive sight. A person unknown to them would be pressed to deduce who was in charge of their expedition.

Getting off from Hallborough had been a challenge, but she had done it. The staff there had not yet seen signs of her stubbornness before today. Mr. Mills and then Mrs. Richards were intent upon trying to dissuade her, but she'd simply ignored them. A quick explanation to the Rourkes was sent off, a coach ordered, her bags packed, and Ned told to drive them to London. And to her surprise, all of that was done.

The trip in to Town had proved easy enough, and dusk was beginning to transform the hues of the landscape as they pulled up to what was to be the first destination on the itinerary—number twenty-six, Oxley Street, Covent Garden.

Ned was nervous, fumbling with the retractable steps, before assisting her out of the coach. He looked up at the fashionable house sporting a red door and then back at her. "Madam, are you sure this is where I must take you? I don't think Mr. Greymont would approve—"

"Thank you, Ned. Your loyalty is noted." She cut him off imperiously. "This is indeed where you must take me."

Ned dipped his head in deference and asked, "Shall I escort you inside?"

She shook her head. "Please await me here and stay with Jane. I hope I'll not be a long time."

Lifting the ornate, swan-headed knocker, she gave it a good smack, thinking that red was an unusual color to paint a door. A thin man answered, she assumed the butler of the house. "We are closed for business this evening," he informed her.

Closed for business? What kind of business did they do here? she wondered. It looked like a private residence to her. She blinked at him, standing her ground.

He raised a brow. Finally, he asked, "May I help you?"

"I have come to call upon Madame Blufette," she said firmly, lifting her chin.

The man's face changed into one of dismissal. "Madame is not receiving tonight. She has a previous engagement and will be going out shortly."

Georgina felt frustration. "Please, I only need a few moments of her time."

"Sorry. That will not be possible, Miss…err—"

"Greymont. Tell Madame Blufette that *Mrs.* Greymont came to call." She felt the waver in her voice but held on to her composure, determined to keep to her goal. She was going to get to the bottom of the mystery somehow. The mystery of this Madame Blufette and why she wanted to meet with her husband! The butler's eyes seemed to widen at the mention of her name, but then he bowed and shut the door in her face.

Georgina fumed as she went back to the coach. Ned leapt ahead to help her in, seemingly thrilled she was not getting inside that house.

"Are we on to Sir Rodney's townhouse then?" Ned inquired hopefully.

"Not yet!" she snapped. "I want to wait here for a while."

Ned went back up to the driver's seat, and she glared out the window of the coach, keeping her eyes fixed on the glossy red door. Jane gave a weak smile, and Frisk crawled over to Georgina, putting his paw on her lap. Her hand went to his neck instinctively, her fingers drawing through the luxuriant fur over and over again as they waited.

A hired hackney pulled up to the front of the house, and then some ten minutes later, a woman in a dark cloak slowly descended the steps. She had a black velvet bag and a leather packet with her.

Georgina flew out of her coach and walked right up to the woman. "Are you Therese Blufette?"

The woman turned her head and lifted her eyes up to Georgina, who topped her by about six inches. "*Mon Dieu!*" she gasped, and then whispered something indistinct that sounded as if she said, "like Marguerite."

"What's that? And why are you sending letters to my husband and asking him to come to you?" Georgina demanded of the older woman. Yes, Therese Blufette was much older than Georgina had assumed. She was probably late in her fourth decade and, although had the bearing and form of a considerable French beauty, did not look at all well. Her complexion was sallow, her brown eyes dull, her movements deliberate and stiff as if suffering from an affliction. The only colorful part of her was the deep red chestnut of her hair.

"Mrs. Greymont?" she asked gently.

"Yes." Georgina braced herself, afraid to hear what this woman might tell her.

"I am an acquaintance of your husband's, nothing more. I know him to be an honorable man, honest and loyal. And I offer my congratulations on your marriage, Mrs. Greymont. I wish you all the best of life. I hope you will be very happy together."

The sincerity with which she spoke was disarming. Therese Blufette did not give the impression of a woman out to seduce her husband. "But why do you send this letter and ask him to come to you?" Georgina waved the letter in her hand.

Madame Blufette eyed her intently, her voice full off emotion. "I am trying to make things right—before it is too late." She looked up at the sky and the position of the full moon, and then her awaiting hackney. "Mrs. Greymont, I have to be somewhere right now. It is imperative that I go immediately. Perhaps you can call tomorrow..." She trailed off and turned away.

Georgina watched the hack pull onto the street and snapped into action. She wanted answers now! Tomorrow was too long to wait. Shouting up to Ned, she knew she was not behaving as the lady she was brought up to be, but didn't give a tinker's damn right now. "Ned, follow that hack and don't lose it, whatever you do!"

# CHAPTER THIRTY

Anxious and tense, Jeremy watched through the window from across the street. Therese had just been admitted into the house only a minute before. He wanted this god-awful exchange over with and Strawnly on his way to the docks, just as he'd designed. Everything was in place, and he could taste victory in the back of his throat. Almost. He had to remain unseen for just a little while longer.

And then, like a curtain being drawn at a theater, the scene changed. To one of abject horror. His heart denied what his eyes were seeing. Something was wrong with his legs, too. He couldn't move them fast enough to get to her. Wrenching out of the building, he burst onto the street, maddeningly mute, struggling to warn her before it was too late. Fate did not help him in this though. He was not quick enough. He got to the road just as his Gina, his precious Gina, was admitted into the same house Therese had just entered. The train of her blue cloak disappeared as the door shut behind her. Strawnly was behind that door. *Nooooooooooo!*

* * * *

A rather dour and unkempt servant admitted Georgina after she gave her name and demanded to see Madame Blufette. He mugged an irreverent sneer, shrugged, and told her to follow him. His attitude gave her some hesitation. What was she really doing here in a strange house, chasing after a woman she did not know? But it was too late now, she thought. She was already in, and trepidation or no, she was determined to get some answers.

Just before she stepped into the parlor, Georgina heard their voices. The name "Marguerite" was thrown out. Madame Blufette was conversing with a man. A man who sounded angry. A man owning a voice she had heard before. Her neck tightened as the hair stood up, like she was being stabbed by a needle straight through to the bone, and she knew paralyzing fear. Dear God, what had she done by coming here?

Her error was a grave one, she knew, but it was far too late to correct it, for her presence was made known by the manservant right then. "Mrs. Greymont," he announced.

*The one.* A man in a red coat, bearing evil eyes, snapped his neck in her direction and lost his speech, so shocked he was to see her in his house. She turned to run, but he caught her easily, his arms like a vise around her ribs, pulling her back into his body.

"What a surprise," he panted, his mouth at her neck, and then one of his hands gripping fiercely around her throat. "Ohhhhh, I've missed you." He shuddered, clearly undone at his good fortune in snaring her. She felt his erection pressing against her hip. He ground against her. "You smell just as I remember. Will you feel the same, too, I wonder…when I fuck you again?"

It was him! Just like before, only this time she had walked right in freely—a witless fly into his spider's web.

Madame Therese protested to him from across the room. "Mr.

Strawnly, let her go!"

"Shut up, cunt!" he snarled at Therese. "Don't interrupt my reunion with my lover."

"No! I'd rather die than be touched by you!" Georgina screamed, twisting in his grip. Her warrior instincts kicked in, and she fought him with every bit of her strength, but he held the advantage over her as he tightened his fingers around her throat and squeezed off her breath. No air to breathe. Her head felt like it was going to explode, and then the colors of the room started to dim to darkness. On the brink of unconsciousness, she stopped struggling, and he loosened his grip.

"That's it," he purred as she gulped in deep breaths. He slapped her face hard and then a second time. "Take some air, wildcat. I want you strong, for when we fuck." His eyes widened in the euphoria of madness.

The slaps hurt and her throat ached, but nothing was as awful as the searing regret she knew for her folly.

"Right now, we've got to get gone, my special little whore. Later you can fight me. I want you to…then. God, it's going to be good!" He pulled out a knife from somewhere and laid the blade up against her throat. "So you must behave yourself for me right now—"

A thunderous pounding at the door got everyone's attention. "Ginaaaaaaaa! Strawnly, I know she's in there with you! Let her go!"

Jeremy? That was Jeremy shouting on the other side of the door! Jeremy was here, too! *What in the hell?* "Jere—" Her scream was cut off by the filthy hand of her attacker, clamped tightly over her mouth, the knife pressing a bit harder into her skin with his other hand. Georgina's thoughts leaped erratically, and she was nearly unable to comprehend her situation. Where she was, who she was with, what was being discussed. His name was Strawnly, apparently, and Jeremy *knew* him. How could this be even possible?

Strawnly yelled through the door. "Greymont, you're not supposed to be here. You're breaking the rules of our little agreement."

"You have my wife in there!" Jeremy yelled back, his voice low and harsh.

"Ahhh, but she came to me."

"Let her go, Strawnly. If she is harmed, you'll hang, you know that!"

"Not if I get out of this hellhole of a country." The negotiation stopped, both men seeming to weigh their options.

Jeremy spoke up, more calmly now. "Strawnly, no attempt will be made to stop your departure if you send her out, unharmed. There's a hack here to take you wherever you want to go."

"I don't trust you, Greymont. How do I know you won't have a gun on me, like you did to Uncle? No, here's how it's going to work. You step back, to the other side of the street. I'll send my man out to spot you first. If you're not far back, I will kill her. There's a knife on her throat right now. You push me, I cut her!"

"I'm going back right now. Do not hurt her!" Jeremy returned through the door.

And then nothing, no sounds coming from the other side of the door at all.

*Oh dear God, Jeremy, what have I done?*

Jeremy was in hell. Truly. Strawnly had Gina in his grip right now with a knife at her neck. *No, goddamnit!* Keep your wits, he told himself. Be strong, for her. Just get her to safety and worry about the rest later. Nothing else was of consequence in this world but Gina's safe return.

A slight, weasel-faced man stepped out on the landing and

made eye contact with him. Jeremy nodded and held his hands out to show he had no gun, and then pointed to the hack which was still parked in front. The man went back inside. He saw Luc emerge from the building they'd been hiding in. "Stay back, Luc. No telling what he'll do to her if he sees you." Luc nodded and slunk back into shadows.

The door opened, and Gina was pushed out first, Strawnly clenching her from behind and a glinting knife, indeed, stretched across her throat. Her eyes were wide with terror, bouncing about as she tried to find him in the moonlight.

"Gina," he shouted, and her eyes found him and locked on, rolling back in their sockets with relief. He started toward her.

Strawnly moved quickly toward the hack, pushing Gina ahead of him. The driver looked worried, bolting up in the seat, holding out his palms.

"Sit your arse down, driver!" Strawnly screeched.

"It's all right," Jeremy told the driver. "You'll take him wherever he wants to go so he doesn't hurt her. I'll pay. Here." Jeremy passed up a pound note to the nervous driver, who accepted it with a shaking hand.

"Stand back, Greymont. That's close enough!"

Not nearly close enough was more like it. The malevolent snake still had Gina, and there was a good ten feet between them. Jeremy held his breath and waited. He stared at his beautiful wife in the clutches of a vile beast who had a fucking knife on her neck!

"Gina…I'm going to get you. Everything will be all right." He nodded, sucking in a gasp, and then he focused on Strawnly. "Let her come to me. You have everything you want, Strawnly. Release her and go." He held out his arms out to Gina.

"Oh, Jeremy, I'm so sorry," Gina whispered.

"It's all right, sweetheart. I'm going to get you," he told her.

Strawnly grinned evilly. "This is touching, really, you two," he mocked. "But she feels good, Greymont. I've missed her." He snaked out his tongue and licked her cheek.

Gina cringed and clamped her eyes shut.

"Suddenly, I feel the need for a companion on my trip abroad." He leaned into Gina's ear. "What do you say, little puss? Shall you come with me? I promise to fuck better than him."

"Nooooo," Gina sobbed, succumbing to panic. She struggled, realizing he intended to take her, until he pressed the knife in a little farther, her skin rising up on either side of the blade from the pressure.

"Gina, be still, sweetheart! You'll be all right." Jeremy held on to his composure, the instinctive part of his brain taking over, understanding that rash action on his part would only serve to get her throat slashed.

"Don't do this, Strawnly. It's madness to try and abduct her. Let her walk away." He spoke in a dead calm to the demented Strawnly, attempting to impart some reason through the fog of insanity the man was cloaked in. "If you want ransom, take me instead and let my wife free."

"Ah, but, Greymont, it's not you I wish to fuck."

"Strawnly, that definitely won't be happ—" In the next moment, the street urchin, Danny, came around the corner. He treaded silently, walking slowly up behind at Strawnly's shoulder. Jeremy met Danny's eyes, and Strawnly sensed the change.

Strawnly turned back to find Danny, and the intrusion unsettled the balance of power just enough to give advantage. "Be gone, boy. This has naught to do with you!" Strawnly barked. He must have loosened his grip on Gina when he turned because she took the opening to struggle anew, twisting back from the knife.

Opportunity must strike when the moment is right, and though Frisk was not a human, he seized his opportunity just as astutely as if he were one, choosing just the best instant to serve his mistress. He shot out in a furious ball of flying fur and sank his adolescent canines deep into the back of Strawnly's calf.

Strawnly cursed, buckling at the knee. To fight off Frisk, he had to let his hands go, and Gina dropped to the ground as she fell from his grip.

Danny jumped into the fray, wrenching Gina out of the mess, and Jeremy lunged for Strawnly. He was not completely conscious of what he did. A burning sting kicked him in the ribs, but he ignored it. Strawnly's neck felt real good underneath his hands as he squeezed. In a mindless rage, killing this monster was all Jeremy could care about. "This is for what you did to her," he gritted out.

Strawnly still had his knife though, and with the strength of the truly mad, he lifted it to strike at Jeremy's head. Jeremy ducked to the side in the last second, saving his skull, but the blade of the knife went into his shoulder. White hot pain razed down through to his muscle. Cursing, he lost his grip on Strawnly's neck.

Jeremy sank to the ground and clutched his shoulder, watching as Strawnly scrambled back toward the hack, kicking his leg out in vicious jerks. Frisk came away, flew about five feet, and landed with a yelp at Jeremy's knees.

"Go!" Strawnly screamed at the driver, flashing the bloody knife. The driver didn't need further motivation. The hack engaged the second the whip was cracked over the horse's flank. Away it clattered, somewhere into the dark London streets, its depraved passenger escaping the retribution he was most definitely due.

Strawnly's madness revealed only more certain from the cackling laugh that punctured out of the hack, its evil rumble causing all who heard it to shudder. The vile noise violated the very air of an otherwise lovely, moonlit night.

# CHAPTER THIRTY~ONE

*None are so desolate but something dear,*
*Dearer than self, possesses or possessed*
*A thought, and claims the homage of a tear.*

—Lord Byron, *Childe Harold's Pilgrimage* (1812)

The Hallborough coach was full to bursting, probably never having had quite such an assemblage before. Jeremy, Georgina, Jane, Therese, and the valiant Frisk were contained within, while Danny and Luc rode pillion with Ned. They were en route to collect one more, as Danny directed Ned to the place where Marguerite had been kept against her will for four days. Or at least this was the gist of what Georgina was able to make out. Georgina had spoken very little, couldn't really indulge in conversation quite yet, the shock of what had just happened still ruling her.

Jeremy was also quiet but held her tight to his right side, his grip fierce for a man who'd just been stabbed in the left shoulder. She could feel the deep breathing moving his chest and the thump of his heart, so very grateful his wound was not life-threatening. His head turned away from his injury and rested on top of her head.

The coach pulled to a stop. Jeremy disengaged from her and

stepped out. "Do not get out of this coach for any reason. Stay. In. Here." His voice was harsh, angry in a way she'd never heard in him before. "Do you understand me?" he rasped, his eyes narrowed, his frown just as hard as his voice.

"Yes," she choked out, vowing she'd never disobey him again as long as she lived.

"Let's go get her," he said to Luc and Danny, the three of them taking to the back entrance.

Therese looked at Georgina sadly. "The world can be so cruel sometimes, but you should try to find the good wherever you can. Your husband loves you, Mrs. Greymont."

"And I love him." Georgina nodded, a sob escaping from deep in her chest. Frisk crawled into her lap, as if sensing her pain. She buried her face in his warm fur and shuddered to think where she might be right now if not for him.

"Thank you, Frisk, for saving me," she whispered. She turned to Jane and asked, "How did he—"

"He was frantic to go to you, Mrs. Greymont. The whole time, he scratched at the door like a wild thing. I popped the latch, and out he went."

The sounds of the men returning, low and hushed, interrupted the conversation. "We're going to need the room in here so I can hold her," Luc said, his deep voice tremulous.

"Jane, will you ride outside with Ned?" Jeremy asked her, his voice low and clipped.

"Of course, Mr. Greymont."

Jane got out, and the massive Luc took her place on the seat, cradling in his arms a battered, but lovely, blonde woman wrapped in a blanket. Her neck and face were bruised and her lip bloodied. Her eyes were closed, but it was clear she was awake and utterly terrorized. *Just like when Tom found me.*

"*Mon Dieu,*" Therese gasped, "what have they done to you, *chéri?*" She put her hand to Marguerite's cheek, and the woman flinched back in a whimper, terrified of even that gentle touch.

Georgina didn't need an explanation. She had lived this very nightmare herself. She knew exactly where Marguerite's mind was, the terror, the shame, the agony of remembering, and the unbearable intimacy of touch.

"Don't touch her," she blurted. Jeremy and Therese turned to stare at her. Luc kept his eyes on Marguerite.

"She cannot bear it just yet. It hurts, in her mind. Just talk to her. She'll hear you. Tell her she's safe and that you're going to take care of her, and tell her—tell her it's not her fault—" Georgina lowered her voice to a whisper. "That's all she needs right now."

Jeremy squeezed her with his good arm and leaned against her. His anger from before seemed to have fallen away, and she was grateful. She thought his skin felt cold to her though. His weight was heavy, but she didn't mind in the slightest. Having him safe beside her was all she wished for right now. Quiet enveloped the passengers, except for Luc, who murmured soft whisperings to Marguerite in French, his love for her apparent in any language.

When the coach stopped again, Therese got up stiffly. Luc carried Marguerite out and then turned back to Jeremy. "I'll make sure." There was steely determination in his eyes.

"You know where to find me," Jeremy told him and then leaned heavily back against Georgina again, as if he could barely hold himself up. He stomped his foot on the floor of the coach, and Ned pulled out for the final jag to the townhouse in Grosvenor Square.

Now that they were alone, she reached out to him. "Jeremy, I am so sorry for everything I've done. I shouldn't have come, but that letter arrived and—"

"Shhh," he hushed her. "It's my fault. I should have told you why I came here. I lied to you...wanted to protect you from him...from gossip...from being hurt again. Love you...so much…"

Something was terribly wrong. He wasn't talking right, and he was so very cold. When she put her hand on his chest, he winced. Her hand came away wet, the cool night air chilling it instantly. As she held her palm up, a shaft of light from a streetlamp lit up the coach. It was a deep, dark red. Blood!

She pulled open his jacket frantically and saw his white shirt was soaked underneath his waistcoat.

"Jeremy! Oh, no, no, no, God, you're bleeding so badly!"

Screaming out the window to Ned, she told him to get them to the closest hospital. The coach swayed in a deep turn, their speed increasing quickly. Frisk hunkered down in the corner.

Jeremy moaned from the force of motion, and she used the momentum to push him flat on his back on the seat. Opening his waistcoat and then his shirt, she found the stab wound, right between his lower ribs on his left side. She bunched up the loose fabric of his shirt and pressed firmly onto the bleeding cut, while kneeling on the floor of the coach.

"Don't you die, Jeremy. You stay with me, now. I need you to fight to live!" She begged him, tears streaming down her face. The thought of losing him was too frightening to contemplate. "I love you…and I can't live without you, Jeremy! Please don't die!" She wept, her hands trying to keep the blood from vacating his body by force of will. "Please, please, please, my Jeremy, my lover, stay with me!"

His eyes flickered open. He spoke softly, his lips barely moving. She leaned forward to hear him above the din of wheels flying over the cobblestone streets. His eyes looked at her with love in them.

"Gina… You…were…the best thing to ever happen…in my life. I hope you have our child inside you…right now. …Don't want you to be…alone… You'll be such a good mother…so strong…and brave. Love…you…both…always…"

And then he closed his eyes. Those beautiful, deep blue eyes of his curtained off, and he spoke no more.

Georgina kept the pressure on his wound and prayed. Prayed like she had never prayed before in the entirety of her life. If there was anything she could offer, any wall of fire or earthly hell she could have walked through in order to save him, she would have done it, and done it with her whole heart.

*Death was not so bad, he thought. It is peaceful, and calm here, like a sanctuary. An angel spoke to him. She smelled of fragrant eglantine. He liked the scent. He could not see the angel, but he could smell her and hear her. She had a lovely voice and spoke the sweetest words.*

*She told him he couldn't stay with her though.*

*"You must go back... There are those who need you. You have much yet to do. And she who loves you will help. This is not your destiny...today. Love well, my son."*

His hand felt peculiar, all tingly and numb. Something was pressing on it. Jeremy cracked open an eye. Dark blonde hair hovered over the general direction of his deadened hand. He flexed it and she shifted, removing the pressure. He sensed the blood go rushing into empty veins.

Blood... There had been a lot of blood. He remembered blood and Gina frantic and begging. He remembered other details, too. Like Gina in the arms of a madman. The fight. Recovering Marguerite, the state of her a vivid rendering of what Gina had once suffered—

*Don't think of it!*

Some things were better left buried, he thought. He had Gina safe now, and he was alive. Given a second chance it seemed. Jeremy vowed not to waste it.

That dream had seemed so real. *"Love well, my son."* Those were her parting words. *"My son..."* Could it be? He tried to remember all of her words.

His hand, now restored to normal sensitivity, reached out and touched the silky hair. Jeremy buried his fingers in the golden softness and combed through a loose portion, reveling in the simple gift and cherishing the moment.

He felt her stiffen and continued with his finger-combing. "Jeremy?" Gina breathed his name. The most beautiful sound in the world. He knew she was awake, but she kept her head down. Then she stopped breathing.

"You're stuck with me a bit longer, sweetheart. Death, it seems, is not willing to have me just yet."

Gina whipped her head around so fast, his hand fell away. "Thank the heavenly angels," she blurted, gripping his palm and showering it with kisses.

"You have no idea," he murmured. He smiled at her and noted she looked bone-weary, dark circles under her eyes, a bruise on her left cheek, a small pressure cut at her throat, and very pale, but still the most beautiful vision he'd ever seen or imagined to see.

"I prayed so hard. I was so afraid of losing you—" She lost her words as the sobbing took hold. "Couldn't—live—without you—" She hiccupped.

He cupped her face with his one hand. "Nor I without you, my sweetheart." He brushed his thumb over her unmarred cheekbone. "Your face is the most beautiful sight I've ever seen, but you look like hell, love."

Her lip trembled for a moment. "You've come back to me," she whispered.

"How about you lie down with me? On my good side." He

winced as he shifted over on the bed to make room for her.

"Jeremy, you're in hospital!"

"Am I? I hadn't noticed," he teased, his eyes grabbing hers. "All I can see is you. You're all that matters to—"

"Well, well, this is a good sign! Awake and even coherent from all indications." A doctor had appeared, voice booming over him before taking his wrist to check the pulse.

Jeremy blinked. "Cameron, is that you?"

The doctor grinned. "It is. What's it been, Greymont, ten years?"

"Good God, Cameron, you're a doctor! You've made quite a transformation since university. Never would have thought it possible. I remember you had an aversion to the sight of blood, for Christ's sake!"

"Yes, well I grew out of it." He arched a brow. "Your pulse has steadied. That's encouraging. How are you feeling?"

Jeremy grunted. "Like I've been sat on by an ox."

"Not a surprise," Cameron countered.

"And thirsty. Can you spare a drop of something—anything?"

"Also not a surprise. You're dehydrated from blood loss. Watered wine, broths, and tea will have to do. No spirits for you yet."

"As you say, Doctor." Jeremy grinned and turned back to Gina, grateful just to take in her presence, *safe* and whole next to him.

"You should know I've shared quite a few stories about your dissolute youth with your wife here." Cameron winked at Gina. "And for all your faults, she seems to be blind to them. She is devoted to you regardless. You are a lucky man to have her, Greymont."

"I know. Have always known it."

"No, I mean *lucky* it was her with you," Cameron insisted. "Greymont, you are only alive because of her. She kept your wound from bleeding out and got you here while you still had a pulse. No woman I know could have done all that and remained so focused."

"But I am not surprised." Jeremy kept his eyes on Gina and answered the doctor. "And you are right. My wife is like no other woman. She is brave and strong and brilliant—and I truly couldn't live without her."

# CHAPTER THIRTY~TWO

Three days abed and Jeremy still relished the simple pleasures of life, only now he did have his wife in the bed next to him. His discharge from hospital had come with some strict directives though. For both of them. His old school friend, and now physician, Nathaniel Cameron, had ordered Jeremy unfit to travel for at least a month, so they wouldn't be returning to Hallborough before the New Year, at least.

The good doctor had also been very firm about Gina, declaring her worn out to the point of collapse and in much need of restorative rest. It was still too early to confirm a pregnancy, he'd said, but quite likely for she'd not had her courses since they'd married.

For himself, Jeremy was positive his seed had taken root. He couldn't say how he knew, but he believed it true and for the first time in his life felt as if he had accomplished something worthwhile. Honorable. And he liked feeling that way.

Watching her sleep was something he could do for hours. And as he was confined to bed with Gina stretched out next to him, he could indulge himself. He propped on his good side and tucked his hand under his cheek and just focused on her features.

The dark of her lashes lay on her cheeks, her hair spilled over the pillow. She wore a scant green gown of silk that gave him a cockstand at first sight, even though he was in no shape to act on it. It was sleeveless in the way of a shift and clung to her body like paint. The flow of her breasts under the silk called to him. The impulse to bury his face between the swells before feasting on them got him painfully blue-veined.

Her soft snore punctured the silence of the dawn. Breathing in, he could smell roses blended with her feminine scent, and a small satisfied moan escaped from his throat at the thought of getting his nose right up against her skin.

It was very early in the morning, the quiet time right before the bustling activity of the day began. His woman was safe next to him and he was alive, and Jeremy couldn't resist reaching out to touch…

Georgina woke to warmth radiating into her body and hands on her skin. Jeremy's lips, firm but gentle, kissed her shoulder. She felt the rasp of his whiskers as he swept them across her neck to the valley between her breasts.

She'd missed this—her Jeremy reaching for her, needing her. His mouth burrowed on below the neckline of her gown, closed over a nipple, and sucked the areola far up into a hot, wet, seeking mouth. *Divine.*

She moaned and arched at the shot of pure pleasure that ratcheted all the way down between her legs. He grunted when she thrust up against him, and she realized why.

"Sorry! Oh, dear God, Jeremy, did I hurt you just now?"

"I don't mind. You're very worth it," he mumbled, still

suckling, seemingly undeterred by the pain she'd inflicted.

"But I hurt you!"

"Not quite in top form yet, m'dear, but I'll get there, I promise you." His words muffled by the fact his lips were busy with her breasts.

"Jeremy," she admonished, "I can't be bumping into your wounds and risk hurting you. We shouldn't—you can't—"

"Waste another moment talking about tiresome subjects like wounds when we could be doing other, more tempting things," he interrupted, still laving his tongue over aching nipples that she wanted to push up hard against his mouth, but didn't dare for fear of jolting his injuries more.

"You taste so good I don't think I can stop. I don't want to ever stop, my Gina." He kept his mouth sucking, but his hand had worked its way up her gown and between her legs. "I need to feel you. Inside here. I need this with you right now."

"Ahhh, and the way you touch me." She rotated her hips in rhythm with his finger's very pointed rubbing at her core, trying to be mindful of his wounds but unable to be still. When he did this to her, she couldn't think or do anything but submit to the enslavement of the passion.

"Mmmmm, yesss. It's all for you right now. Come for me. I want to watch you come. Please, Gina. I want to see it happen," he begged, pressing a little harder on her clitoris with his thumb and sinking two fingers up inside. "You're wet and so soft. I love that you're so wet for me."

*Sweet Christ, the things he says!*

His fingers slipped in and out of her slickness, working her into a frenzy of sensation she couldn't escape. She arched toward his hand. Each thrust into her drenched depths was countered by a pass of his thumb over her pearl.

It wouldn't be long now. She recognized a clicking sound was the friction of her wetness spilling out around his fingers, and she didn't care, had no modesty or consciousness other than getting to the glorious end.

He would get her there, as he always had. In this she had complete trust, and her love for him just exploded around her whole body. It pushed the orgasm suddenly up from the depths, boiling over and hurtling her body into ecstasy.

"Look at me, love. Let me see your golden eyes on me when you find heaven."

She did as he asked and shattered apart, crying out her love and her thankfulness for him. Real tears and true sobs. It was the only thing she could do. The fear of losing him, the relief that he had not died, that they were together now, was too much emotion to hold in for a second longer. The last thing she remembered was crying underneath his hands, his gentle voice soothing her with words of love and security so precious she hoped she could keep the memory of it forever in her soul.

When she woke later, he was staring, his eyes alighting on her with a smile. "You drifted back, sweetheart. Finally."

Remembering how she'd cried in her climax, embarrassment flooded through her and she lowered her eyes.

"What is wrong? I see that shuttered look in your eyes."

She shook her head and tried to hold back more tears. How many times would she cry in front of this man? Before he grew utterly sick of her, if he wasn't already.

"Can you not tell me?" He brushed his right hand under her chin to lift it up, but did it gently. She could smell her essence on his hand, and she blushed at the thought of exactly where his hand had been. "You must know you may always talk to me about anything. Don't be shy now. I want you to be at ease to tell me whatever you wish."

"Jeremy..." She croaked out his name, the sound lost, swallowed in her throat. "I nearly got you killed—"

It was true. However their acquaintance had come about,

that—that *creature*, Strawnly, had tried to abduct her. And he almost had done, nearly killing Jeremy in the process. And it was all her fault—her jealousy and the fact she hadn't trusted him enough.

Georgina could hardly bear to recall the swipe of that knife coming down at Jeremy, stabbing him. Any closer to the vein in his neck and he would have bled to death even faster! Because of her. Because she had walked them both right into it, blindly stupid and careless.

"Hush. Listen to me now!" he spoke firmly. "This is not your fault. He hurt you! He caused this! He dared to touch you! Do not blame yourself. Gina!"

"But I do! I know I risked myself and, in the end, your life, but I still have to understand the reasons. Jeremy, how is it that you know that evil man? Why does he know you?"

He reacted to her question with a frown, and his jaw got hard with a clench.

It scared her, and she knew fear in the pit of her guts, even though she was lying down. What would Jeremy say? She turned fully to her side to face him in the bed. He rolled to his back and was quiet for a time.

Georgina stared at his rugged features, his sandy hair, the sharp nose that marked his profile, thinking he was the most beautiful man in the world.

Finally he sighed, looking up and focusing on the ceiling. "I'm going to tell you all of it even though it will hurt you." He started slowly, his words guarded, but she sensed that he didn't hold anything back. He told her how he'd learned of Pellton and Strawnly's intent, Marguerite's knowledge, and how he'd come to hear of it, the extortion letter, their bargain, all of it. The telling seemed painful for Jeremy, his voice cracking at times. Maybe harder than anything he could have ever imagined telling her about the man who'd attacked her, just as it was painful for Georgina to hear it—but necessary. It was the beginning to putting the horrid experience away, so both could start on the healing process of freeing themselves of its burdensome weight.

"...And that is why I went to London. Strawnly had to be stopped before you were hurt any more. I did it out of love. You are mine to protect, and I'd do it again in an instant if you were at risk." His words came out a little harsh. "You are everything to me." He brought her hand to his mouth and kissed it, sending love into her with his earnest blue eyes looking over warm, moist lips pressed to her skin.

Georgina expelled a breath, realizing she'd been holding it in. "I hardly have any words to say. Not only did you save me, but you love me." She was truly incredulous. "Why do you?"

"I do not know the why, but only the truth. For me, loving you has been the easiest thing in the world, sweetheart. I most certainly do love you. You have awakened me to life—literally and figuratively. I am never going to let you go. That is my solemn promise."

Georgina felt her heart pulse deep within her chest, knowing it was absolutely brimming with love for this man. She moved the covers aside and scooted her body down. Finding the hem of his nightshirt, she pushed it up and then lifted her eyes to Jeremy's handsome face.

The hue of his eyes showed only as a slit of blue for they were half closed already in anticipation.

"What are you up to, my glorious sweetheart?" he asked as she took him into her hand and positioned the tip up against her lips.

The skin on his shaft was so exquisitely soft and fine, but when aroused, like right now, could be burning hard and hot. She licked the tip of him and breathed in his male scent. So beautiful—all of him.

He groaned beneath her mouth, but not from pain this time. Power. Love. Need. So many feelings flooded her. Jeremy evoked things in her she didn't know existed until he had showed her.

"Exactly what I want to be doing. This time is for you, so lie back, relax, and enjoy, my husband."

Jeremy picked though a week's worth of correspondence. His wounds were healing to the point that he couldn't bear staying in bed a moment longer, unless of course Gina was in the bed with him, working her magic.

One missive caught his eye though. He'd been anticipating it and ripped open the seal with vigor. From Luc, it was short and to the point:

*Greymont,*

*He boarded the* Excelsior, *eleven o'clock. Tanner and Parkins already on. Cast off midnight. Smooth departure out.*

*Luc*

Jeremy breathed a sigh of relief and shuffled over to the fire. He dropped the note into the flames and watched it burn. Done. Simon Strawnly was done. He would never hurt another helpless woman again.

Frisk looked up from his warm place by the hearth and tilted his head at Jeremy in curiosity.

"He deserved it you know. What he got was earned by him. Earned just as much as you deserve a knighting, Sir Frisk," Jeremy told the dog, stooping to pat him on the head.

Frisk thumped his tail in answer.

What Strawnly had not known was that Jeremy owned the ship, *Excelsior,* he'd boarded that night. The family business was in shipping freight mostly, and occasional passengers, in and out of England. It was how the bulk of the family income was derived.

The added insurance of putting one Mr. Gordon Tanner and a Mr. Joseph Parkins on board was to guarantee that Strawnly wouldn't walk off the ship when it docked on the continent at Cherbourg. He wouldn't walk. He wouldn't breathe.

Mr. Tanner was a successful tradesman in London, and he loved his only daughter, Emma, very much. Mr. Parkins was assistant to Mr. Tanner, and he, too, loved Emma. The young couple was set to marry when the unthinkable happened. She was brutally attacked by two men who hurt her so badly that her hearing was permanently deafened in one ear.

Tanner and Parkins were in the tanning trade in London. The trade was considered base and contemptible by some, but necessary commerce just the same, and a profitable business for one willing to get his hands dirty. And from what Jeremy had heard, Gordon Tanner was acknowledged as the best in the field of his chosen profession of tanning. More specifically, the process of removing hides from carcasses and turning them into leather. Tanner was wickedly skilled with a knife.

And for a man so skilled as Tanner was, with vengeance in his heart toward the beast who had dared to savage his beloved daughter, that degenerate shit, Simon Strawnly, was due a hide-full of hurt before he paid for his sins.

# CHAPTER THIRTY~THREE

*Charity and Mercy. Not unholy names, I hope?*
—Charles Dickens, *Martin Chuzzlewit* (1844)

You know, I think a Yuletide party would be just the thing, dear. Jeremy is recovering so well, and a party would be perfect for introducing you now that he's gone and finally married. We'll invite your family as well." Lady Bleddington patted Georgina's hand affectionately. "There were times I despaired he would ever get around to it." She clucked, pursing her lips in reprimand.

Georgina smiled up at her before focusing back on her book of Keats's poems, of which she had read and re-read the same page too many times to count.

Jeremy's grandmother was a sweet old dear, but she liked to talk. Ruminating over their marriage, his attack and near death, and the possibility of an heir provided more excitement than the woman had experienced in decades, and they all had to hear about it. Still, her affection for her grandson was apparent, and she fussed over her and Jeremy both just like, well, a grandmother, so Georgina didn't really mind.

"What do you think, Georgina dear?" Lady Bleddington

repeated, her voice hopeful.

"Of what, Lady Bleddington?" Georgina snapped her book closed, figuring she might as well give up on the poetry for today.

"Oh, I do wish you'd call me Grandmamma. We are family now after all." She stabbed the yellow rose she was embroidering on the pillow rather fiercely. "I always hoped for a granddaughter, but Clarissa and Henri—there was only Jeremy." She trailed off and seemed a little sad in her remembrances of her daughter before returning to her stitching.

Georgina reached over and touched Lady Bleddington's hand. She squeezed gently. "Thank you for welcoming me so kindly. I never knew either of my grandmothers, so you will be my first." Her voice faltered a bit. "When we were at Hallborough, Jeremy showed me her portrait. His mother, your Clarissa. She was very lovely."

"Lovely it's true. A sweet darling, but unwise in her choice of husband. Sadly, she married a man who cared for nothing save her money." Lady Bleddington covered Georgina's hand with her other one. "Not like you, dear. Our Jeremy loves you. I can see it in his eyes when he looks at you. I can even tell when he speaks of you. Your choice was a good one, and I'm not just prejudiced because he is my grandson. I reckon anyone could know it if they watched you two together." She brought her hand up to cup Georgina's chin. "It makes me happy to see Jeremy so well matched. You ease him and have brought a light into him that's not been there since he was a boy."

Georgina nodded, her lip trembling with emotion. "As he does for me. He is my savior, you know. I love him so very much."

"I know that, too, dear." She embraced Georgina in an affectionate hug, then pulled back and returned to her embroidery as if they had just been discussing something as mundane as the weather.

A moment of silence stretched out before she spoke up again.

"So is that a 'yes' to a party, my dear?"

"Yes, Grandmamma, it is." Georgina cracked a wide grin. "A party shall be just the thing."

Jeremy spooned against her back, his lips at the base of her neck, his hand nestled between her breasts. Cuddled in bed with a warm, clove-scented man, *her man,* was divine, Georgina thought. Her very much alive man, thank the heavenly angels! But was this near miss the end of their worry from that evil Strawnly? Would there be more from him? More extortions for money? She shifted restlessly in the bed.

"What 'smatter?" Jeremy mumbled sleepily, his fingers wandering to find her breast.

"Just thinking." She covered his big hand with her own smaller one. "Sorry for disturbing you. Go back to sleep."

"Thinking 'bout what?" He nestled closer and spoke softly at her ear. She felt his tongue reach out to trace the lobe and shivered into his very hard and prodding erection pressing into her backside.

"Him."

Jeremy froze against her. He sighed. The sound of it sailed through the room like a flaming arrow and the erection so urgent a moment ago lost every bit of its urgency.

"What if he comes back or wants more money? I can't bear the thought—" She rolled to face him so she could see his eyes. If she could look into his eyes, she might be able to read his expression.

It was harsh at first but softened quickly. "Hush now," he said firmly, pulling her close. He stroked her back, kissed her forehead, held her a little tighter. "You are not to worry about him again. I mean it, Gina, don't." He pushed back to find her eyes. Despite his gentle touches, his blue eyes showed a lethalness that made her shiver. "He's not coming back to England."

"How do you know that?" She couldn't hold back the question even though she realized he wouldn't like it—*she* had to know.

Jeremy shook his head and blew out a frustrated sigh. Gina could tell he hated speaking of the man—of giving him even a jot of recognition. "He cannot come back. There are many who would end him if given the chance, and he knows it." He closed his eyes as if his head ached.

"You were not the first woman he hurt. I found a father and a husband of another he attacked, and there is also Luc, the man who went to retrieve Marguerite. Strawnly's time is marked, and has been. He's as good as dead, I'd wager." He frowned at her, and his voice got that harsh edge again. "I don't like you thinking about him—of being afraid."

She took his face in her hands. "You misunderstand. Don't be angry. I do not fear him for myself anymore. My only fear is losing you to another fight or attack should he challenge you, for I know you would defend me. That is the truth, Jeremy. You nearly died, and it was more terrifying than *anything* that ever came before—"

His demanding lips cut her off as they descended on hers, open and warm. It was a possessive kiss. One that told her exactly who she belonged to.

Georgina did not mind as his seeking flesh swept into her mouth and brushed over every surface it could reach. She welcomed the warmth and wet of their tongues mating in a declaration of sorts. An "I love you and you are mine" kind of kiss. One they could both appreciate and recognize.

Jeremy shivered, and it wasn't from the cold of the season. The solarium of Sir Rodney's London townhouse was quite pleasant actually, and the sun's valiant efforts were a bonus for December. No, his shivers were involuntary and happened whenever he allowed himself to think of Gina being groped and terrorized in the paws of that madman, Strawnly. He tried not to fall prey to those horrible images, but the visions popped into his mind at the oddest times—

Jeremy looked up to the sound of the door opening.

"Sir, your scheduled callers are here," the old butler announced.

"Thank you, Wiggins, show them in please."

Wiggins shuffled off and returned eventually with two people in tow, one of which to whom Jeremy was deeply indebted.

"Mr. Ned Smith, Coachman, and—" Wiggins paused in his address, giving the unkempt boy a look of fright, as if the boy might bite at him or do something worse, like soil the carpet.

"Danny." The boy finished the butler's address for him and bobbed his own head.

Jeremy stood and grinned like a devil. Wiggins backed out of the room and shut them all in together, shaking his head in disbelief the whole way.

"Master Danny, at last! I've wanted to thank you, young man! You did us a good turn, helped to rescue my wife, and for that you deserve a reward. What have you to say?" Jeremy asked the boy, thinking he'd send him directly to the kitchens after this interview for a hot meal and a good scrubbing.

"Thank you, Mr. Greymont, sir. It's a right thing to help a lady when she's needin' it. I'm pleased I could help your lady— er...Mrs. Greymont."

"Again, I am indebted to you for your assistance, Danny." Jeremy bowed.

Danny bowed back, a look of awe on his thin, dirt-smudged face. He tried to look Jeremy in the eye, but couldn't help from wandering his gaze around the room, taking in the elegant furnishings, evidence of wealth he couldn't really imagine when all he'd ever known was the poverty and hunger of life on the harsh

London streets.

"Do you have any family that you know of?"

"No, sir. They told me at the work house I've no Mum or Dad."

"You don't stay at the work house anymore?"

Danny frowned. "I run away from there, sir. They was very mean. I get more food fending for myself..." He trailed off and peeked up at Jeremy, afraid he'd said too much.

"I see." Jeremy put a finger to his lips. "Mr. Smith tells me you fancy the horses. You come every day and help with jobs in the stables. He thinks you have potential, Danny."

"Oh." Danny seemed unimpressed at first then looked as if he thought better of his response. "Is that a good thing, sir?"

"Do you know what the word 'potential' means, Danny?"

"No, sir." Danny shook his head.

"It means you have the capacity, the ability, and the hope to succeed, if you've the will and the mind to learn. So here is my offer. You may have a place in my household, as a paid man, and under the tutelage of Mr. Smith here, in the goal of becoming a driver for me. Honest work, mind you, horsemen labor well, Danny, but you'll have a safe and comfortable home for as long as you want, away from the hard streets, and you'll never need worry about your meals again." Jeremy gave Danny a polite nod.

Danny stayed silent, but Jeremy could see a tremor run through the boy, and fear. By Jeremy's best guess, he looked to be around twelve or thirteen and didn't quite know how to take in all the adulation, surely never had any, and was rightly wary of such foreign attentions.

"I can see you need time to consider, Danny, and that is fine. A man must make his decisions wisely and think carefully before rushing to a judgment. Why don't you come back and see me when you have decided what you wish to do."

"I—I—I accept, sir. I don't need no time to think. I want to come work for you," Danny blurted, his voice starting to waver. He twisted his scrap of cloth cap mercilessly in his hands. A tear appeared. And then another. "Th–thank y–y–you, sir. Thank you—"

Danny crumbled under the weight of emotion and buried his face in Ned's jacket. Ned snaked out an arm and patted him on the shoulder. "There now, Danny. I told you it will work itself out," Ned told him. "Buck up, boy, you're a driver's apprentice now!"

Danny swiped the tears away and stood tall before his new master. Ned left his hand where it was, and nodded to Jeremy in thanks.

Jeremy held out his hand to Danny. The solid shake the boy returned seemed a good omen for their future relationship.

Fate brought people together in the strangest ways, Jeremy thought. He owed this discarded boy so very much and felt enormously glad inside his heart to be allowed to make a difference in his, thus far, wretched and lonely life. The funny thing was, it made a difference in Jeremy's life, too.

When the two took their leave, Jeremy kept Ned back. He waited until the stunned but hopeful Danny was sent off for the kitchens, in wonderment of his new station.

"I have a job for you, Ned. Have you any talent for acting?"

"I beg pardon, Mr. Greymont?"

"We have to help right a wrong that's been done, Ned, and I am asking for your help and most likely the help of your new protégé. You may never speak of it once the job is done and if asked, must deny any knowledge of the facts. Do I have your pledge?"

"Never doubt it, sir, I am your man."

# CHAPTER THIRTY~FOUR

*...Remember that thou hast to be thankful and grateful
even for the mere privilege to breathe...*

—Eleazar of Worms, *Sefer Rokeah* (13th c.)

There you are! I was hoping to find you in here, my darling." Gina swanned into solarium, carrying an envelope. Frisk hopped up from his place and greeted her first. She stopped to give him an affectionate pat and a good rub behind the ears. "Hello, Sir Frisk. Are you guarding the master again? I think you've forgotten whose dog you are," she teased, lifting a smirking face to Jeremy.

She looked good enough to eat, he thought, all rosy and glowing in a pale pink gown. He wondered if their baby would be a son or a daughter, picturing light hair and hazel eyes upon a cherub face. In an instant, his emotions bubbled up, and he felt his eyes twitch. He blinked and pushed his sappy agitation down and away, thinking his injuries must have weakened his mind as well as his body. He didn't ever want Gina to see him like this.

Jeremy reached out his hands to her and offered his lips for a kiss. "Miss me?" he teased, making his voice a little naughty.

"Always," she told him, clasping his hands and pressing her sweet lips to his.

"I thought you were buried deep into party plans with Grandmamma, ordering new gowns and other fripperies for the yuletide. She's got Grandfather and me in to see the tailor tomorrow. I know how it works." He pulled her onto his lap and went straight for her neck, his hands wandering up her ribs and forward to the swells of her breasts. "But I'm very glad you came to find me," he murmured, distracted by the softness and scent of her skin.

"Yes, well, I was, but I've managed to escape for the moment. Your grandmother is a very capable hostess and is quite dogged in her pursuit of the perfect festive accruements. She's probably better at party arranging than I can ever hope to be. Actually, we shall be going out this afternoon to have a dress fitting and meeting ladies for tea. Grandmamma is introducing me to her friends, Lady Dorchester and Lady Lampson, and Lady Lampson's recently widowed niece, a Mrs. Golding."

"Well, good luck then. I try to give Lady Dorchester a wide berth and am afraid I cannot help you much with Lady Lampson either. My advice is to paste a content expression upon your face and sit there looking beautiful, which should be no trouble for you. Lady Lampson loves to carry the conversation, so you shouldn't have to say much. Fortitude, Mrs. Greymont."

"Sounds like a treat. I cannot wait," she said wryly.

"Not to worry, my sweetheart, you have many other talents that I adore and appreciate." He quirked his brows teasingly. "To what do I owe the honor of this welcome visit?"

"Two reasons, my darling." She brought a hand up and smoothed back his unruly hair. "That boy, Danny, who helped us the night you were hurt."

"Yes? What about him?"

"Well, according to Jane, Ned has taken quite a shine to Danny and begs to hope you might have something for him—you know, to get him off the streets."

"Some persons prefer street life to that of a more sedentary inclination." Jeremy enjoyed playing with her.

Gina gave her head a little shake, her chin lifting just a fraction. "Not Danny, I'd venture. Jane says he comes every day to help Ned with the horses and do errands and such. Jane and Ned are quite taken with Danny."

"Ah. Are they indeed? And do you think this might in any way be related to Jane taking a shine to Ned Smith? I've seen the way your maid looks at my coachman with stars in her eyes."

Gina cupped his face. "Could be. She looks at him rather the way I look at you."

Jeremy nodded thoughtfully for dramatic effect. "So you want me to indulge the whims of our courting servants, do you? Next thing I know, Ned will be asking for promotion so he can marry her!" He kept his face stoic.

"Well, in this instance, yes, Jeremy, I do," she said imperiously. "I cannot imagine that two loyal servants courting would be much of a bother to you, and since I know you to be the very best of men, and that helping Danny is the upstanding thing to do, I am sure a place can be found for the poor boy."

She waited on his answer, perched so sweetly upon his lap.

"Will you do it?" she asked after a moment, questioning his long silence, the hint of frustration lacing her words.

He kissed her first. "You never asked for anything before. I love that you are asking something of me now. I hope it is just the first of many requests you will make of me. Seeing you happy is my joy. And yes, my darling sweetheart, I will make a place for Danny. In fact, I have beaten you to it. I met with Ned and Danny not one hour ago, and it's already settled. He will come to live at Hallborough and work under Ned, who will groom him as a driver."

"And Ned and Jane?" Georgina asked.

Jeremy shrugged. "Who am I to interfere with Cupid's Arrow

among starry-eyed lovers?"

She giggled at him.

"Does my lordly pronouncement meet with your approval, my lady wife?"

"You know it does, Jeremy. Thank you for helping Danny. It's the right thing for us to do. I owe him more than I can ever repay."

Jeremy thought her declaration odd and rather a bit dramatic. "Well, yes, he made all the difference in helping to rescue you from—"

"No, Jeremy. That is not the reason I owe so much to that boy."

"What could possibly be the reason then?" he asked unbelievingly.

"You. You are my reason, Jeremy." She kissed him on his forehead. "Without Danny knowing the way, we could have never reached hospital so quickly. Ned said he didn't know where to go. Danny directed us straight to Dr. Cameron in time to save your life. You owe your life to him."

"And not just to him. Also to you, my Gina."

Jeremy held onto her for a long time, wondering if he now lived in a waking dream. So much of the foundation upon which his whole life had been built felt like air underneath him. Things that had held importance before meant little now. Self-gratifying behaviors were just that. They entertained the self, but didn't offer anything helpful to the common good.

"Are you all right? You seem very far away."

He smiled at his beloved. "I am well, sweetheart. Just wool-gathering a bit. Thinking about how blessed I am." He touched the tip of her nose. "Mostly because of you." Then he remembered her words from before. "Didn't you say you had two things to see me about?"

"Yes I did. My darling, the post has come, and a letter from— well, this has arrived for you." Her voice betrayed the calm expression she wore as she held out the envelope to him and moved up, off his lap.

He took it from Gina's hand and read the sender's address. *Mdme. T. Blufette.* Dread hit him like a wall, and he was afraid to read it.

He knew fear in the moment. What would it say? *Goddamn!* Did he have an illegitimate child that he'd never known about? How could that be? He'd always used precautions, and he'd never been with Therese in that way. She was the proprietress, not a working girl. He just couldn't imagine whatever it was that Therese Blufette wanted from him, but thought it couldn't be good.

Gina's expression was unreadable as she looked at him from her seat. He shook his head. "I don't know what this is. I cannot imagine what she wants to talk to me about, but whatever it is, I want you to hear it, too. I'll face any news she has to tell if you don't forsake me."

She rose from her chair and walked over to him. He stood up slowly and faced her.

Emotion overpowered him again, and he felt his vision go blurry. "I've never been more helpless and terrified than when you were in Strawnly's grip. I'd die to protect you, and willingly. You are that precious to me." He leaned a little closer. "Whatever this is Therese wants from me, I can solve if I have you safe and by my side and know you'll always be there."

She raised her brows. "You know I will be, Jeremy." She spoke rather severely to him. "Please don't doubt my loyalty, right now or in the future. After all we've been through, you must recognize it by now." Her voice got deeper, the husky sound he adored tempering her chastisement. "I thought we agreed to forgive those things which came before we found each other."

He stared at her for the longest time—her furrowed brows and solemn strength, resolute before him. It was all he could do until the words could form on his lips.

"I never believed in love. Thought it was idiotic fodder for poets and artists. But I was wrong, so very wrong. I knew of my error the day I spied you in the rain at Oakfield. Something snapped inside my chest, and I felt instantly different, changed somehow. I could sense it but had no idea how or why such feelings could be in me. I just knew I wanted you. You. It will only ever be you." He locked on to her clear, serious eyes. "I gave up my disavowal of love in an instant and had no regrets. I wanted to love you, but more than anything I wanted you to love me." He held out both hands to her. She grasped them in hers with strength, and he knew great relief. "And I know that you do."

He pulled Gina into his arms. Solid under his trembling hands, her silent embrace all the reassurance he needed. Yes, his Gina was a gentle woman but stronger than anyone he'd ever known. Courage like an ancient Greek goddess. Artemis came to mind… Bow pulled taut, ready to fly a deadly arrow, steadfast to the end. What a portrait that would make—Gina portrayed as Artemis.

"You were right," he whispered.

"About what?"

"It *does* hurt to love someone so much. And I've learned something else, too. Before you, all the hardness and rough behavior with those others—"

He choked on his words and heard his own voice tremble, but by God he would explain his feelings to her. This was important, and she deserved to know. He took a deep breath and tried again.

"For myself I know now what I was doing was a way to try to *feel* something because my spirit was so very empty. I didn't know it at the time. With you though, all I could do was 'feel.' It was like walking into the light and seeing for the first time in my life. Such a great difference of feeling with you, my Gina. And I felt it right away. Like nothing I've ever known."

Jeremy cupped her face with one hand and brushed her cheekbone with his thumb. "Please don't ever leave me, Gina. I could not live in a world without you. Now that I know the joys of your love, I realize that a life without you would be no life at all."

"You'll never have to worry about that though," she told him, her voice going deep and soft as she leaned into his palm.

"That's the part of loving that hurts."

Gina looked to him in question, her head tilted.

"Knowing that you couldn't live without that person. That you need them so badly, you'd die if they ever left or were lost to you. It's what happened to my mother. When my father left her, she died. Didn't want to live anymore. I vowed never to give my heart away like she did, but history has a way of repeating itself I s'pose." He smiled a little. "For that's exactly what I've done with you."

# CHAPTER THIRTY~FIVE

*Anger and jealousy can no more bear to lose sight of their objects than love.*

—George Eliot, *The Mill on the Floss* (1860)

W alking up to the door, Georgina could feel the tension wafting off of Jeremy next to her. Therese Blufette's private residence stood before them both, and soon they'd know whatever it was that she wanted from Jeremy.

The house itself was part of the elegant Adelphi complex, overlooking the Thames, fashionable and artfully designed by the Adam brothers of Scotland.

A butler admitted them into a cheerful white-and-gold salon with a very frail-looking Therese arranged on the chaise. She was most definitely ill, and if the suggestion had been noticeable before, now it was a surety.

"Welcome to my home, Mr. and Mrs. Greymont. Please excuse my *dishabille* and my improper greeting. I thank you for granting me this audience." She graciously bowed her head.

"You are ill, Madame," Jeremy said. He worded it as a statement. There was no denying the facts, and Georgina understood how it seemed wrong not to acknowledge it honestly.

"Yes. I imagine I'll not see another spring, in this life," she answered gently, her skin so pale it appeared almost translucent.

"Surely not, Madame," Jeremy said.

"I apologize if my condition is uncomfortable for you, Mr. Greymont. I assure you I regret causing distress to you or your wife. 'Tis not my intention. But, my failing health is the impetus though. The reason I have asked you to come. I have so little time left, and my doctors assure me there are no treatments or therapies of any benefit to me at this stage. I am plagued with a cancer that will prove to be the victor in this fight, without a doubt."

She folded her hands in her lap, and spoke carefully. "I have no regrets. My life has been full. I have loved and been loved. I was blessed with motherhood rather late in my life, but no less welcomed. I have a son. A wonderful boy. Twelve years old. Did you know that, Mr. Greymont?"

"We are very sorry for your troubles, Madame Blufette," Jeremy told her. He was calm and dignified, Georgina thought. She could tell he was trying to be sympathetic to this dying woman, but bewildered and uneasy. He cleared his throat. "No, I was unaware that you had a son." He squared his shoulders and set his jaw. "Why, Madame, have you summoned me, and why are you telling me all of this? Tell me why you speak of your son in such ominous suggestion."

"Because apart from me, you are his only family. He is of your blood."

"No." Jeremy shook his head at her. "He could not possibly be my son. Madame, we have never—you and I did not ever—" He held up a palm. "You *know* he could not be mine," Jeremy said quietly but firmly, his other hand reaching out to enclose Georgina's smaller one in a tight clasp.

"Not your son, Mr. Greymont. Your brother." She nodded slowly. "My son's father and yours are one in the same—Henri Greymont. My son is your brother. You share blood and a name.

He is called Revé. Revé Greymont."

Georgina felt her hand get squeezed tighter and breath expel out of Jeremy. He was in shock. Such shock that she imagined Therese could have toppled him with only the tiniest of nudges.

Jeremy leapt up off of the settee all in a rush and then dragged a shaking hand through his hair, making it spread out in disarray. "Can this be true?" Jeremy looked at Georgina first and then back at Therese. There was a tremble in his lip. "I have a brother..." Jeremy sat down again.

Jeremy sat down before his legs gave out and he ended up flat on his own arse. *A brother...* "How is this?" he managed to choke out.

Therese answered him softly. "I met your father in France. He was handsome and charming and vibrant. I did love him, Mr. Greymont. For my part, the feelings were genuine. It was thirteen years ago. I had thought a child an impossibility for me, but alas I conceived Revé much to my surprise. Henri seemed delighted at the prospect, and we were happy, or at least I was."

She paused in reflection, a melancholy expression lighting her gaunt features. "Our marriage was a short one, less than a year. One night he didn't return home. I don't know what happened to him, if he got into trouble with debts and vengeful creditors, or desired to hold on to his freedom, or simply caught up with the wrong crowd. His body was found in an alley behind a gaming house about a week later. He never saw his son."

Therese was seized with a fit of coughing that delayed her story. Her thin shoulder bones made for sharp edges underneath a Chinese silk shawl of deep yellow that gave the illusion of warmth and cheerfulness that wasn't there. A mirage, Jeremy thought, his mind in a daze from the information Therese had shared.

"I took the legacy left me by my father and came to England. Made my life here. Revé is away at school right now. He knows nothing of my life aside from being his mamma and this home. He knows his father is dead, but doesn't know that Henri had another family before. *The Velvet Swan* and its dealings are also unknown to him, and I wish it to remain as such. I have sold my interests in any case. Luc and Marguerite have been set up and are already in France, and situations are being found for the other servants."

"Why did you never tell me? All those years you knew and didn't say anything." He couldn't keep the accusation from his voice and knew it showed how wounded he was by her omission.

"I am sorry for that. Deeply sorry. I believed you would resent Revé and imagine my motives to be other than familial in connection. That is all I want from you, Mr. Greymont, nothing more. There is a generous settlement for Revé. My solicitor has all of the details. His education is already secured, and he will have this house…" She trailed off, her voice stuttering with emotion.

Jeremy lifted his eyes to Therese, still dazed, but sure of his feelings. "I have no resentment for my brother. My father, yes, but never an innocent." He felt Gina's hand return to take his in a clasp. He looked at her and said, "I have a brother, Gina." He smiled.

"You do. Jeremy, 'tis wonderful."

"It is," he whispered in awe.

Therese let out a sob from across the room. "Forgive me, both of you, please. I now know it was wrong of me not to tell you years ago. I have been so afraid, Mr. Greymont. Afraid of leaving my child wholly alone in this world. Only twelve years old, and when I am gone, not one person to call family. No one to care for him and guide him into manhood. No one to…love him…" She broke down then, unable to hold back her mother's tears.

Life presented challenges, and sometimes opportunities. This was an opportunity. Jeremy recognized it and embraced it for what it was. He knew what he would do with it.

All those years of feeling unworthy. Of believing he was lacking. He'd been loved by his mother and his grandparents, yes. But not by Henri Greymont. Jeremy's father had not even been bothered by him, let alone shown a scrap of affection. Why, why, why? No answer would be forthcoming to that question. Nobody knew why Jeremy's father hadn't cared for his wife and son. It simply existed as the painful reality.

But a Henri Greymont Jeremy was not. Suddenly it did not matter anymore that his father had been unfeeling and cold. Jeremy would never be that sort of man. He had a life now filled with purpose. He had Gina to help him. He was a loving husband, and someday, God willing, he would be a father who cherished his children for the gift they were.

And he could be more, too. Jeremy could make sure that his flesh and blood knew the love and support of family. He could be a brother, the guide and mentor that young Revé would need in the absence of his mother.

Jeremy rose from the settee once again and walked over to Therese. He put a hand on her trembling shoulder and waited until she looked up at him, her pale face streaked wet with tears.

"My brother will have *me*," he told her.

With no moon to soften the darkness, only the streetlamps glowed behind their wet, sparkling glass on London's winding paths and byways. It was the perfect night for taking care of business.

On the corner stood a gentlemen's club whose heavy door opened and closed regularly as its well-heeled patrons came and went.

One particular patron was watched as he went out. Unaware of course, he made his way to the carriage waiting. The watchers remained hidden and quiet.

When Ned Smith stepped forward to open the door, the man balked at the driver's strange visage.

"Who the hell are you? Where is Rigby? You are not my driver!"

"No, my lord. I am Smith, sir. I drive for your neighbor, Lord Verlaine. Ribgy took violently ill, quite sudden-like, and sent for me to take his place. I will be driving you home, sir," Ned replied easily. He opened the door and held out his arm. "Your lordship?"

Momentarily taken aback, the gentleman absorbed this strange information and then shrugged, resigning himself to it, just like that, as if pondering the trivialities of servants becoming ill and substituting drivers a mere waste of his more superior and valuable time.

"Dare I pray to hope you know the way to my house, driver?"

"But of course, Lord Pellton. I know exactly where to take you," Ned answered politely.

The instant Pellton stepped into his carriage, John and Tom Russell went to work on their prey. Although they subdued him within seconds, and he hardly made a sound over the din of wheels rolling over cobblestone, Pellton did manage to land one blow, with his signet ring no less, onto the left cheekbone of John Russell's face.

In no time the men had Pellton trussed like a goose for Christmas, gagged and bound on the floor of his own carriage.

"Hello, Edgar. How goes your endeavors of rape and pillage? Been busy have you? I imagine your work to be piling up now that you're down a partner. Your nephew, was it? You know. The one who—raped—my—daughter!" John had difficulty keeping the lethal venom from lacing his words.

Pellton shook his head and emitted a muffled, "No, John."

"Shut up!" Tom kicked him in the ribs. "You're going to listen and not talk."

"Back to your nephew, Edgar." John forced himself to take on an instructive tone of voice. "I think we should talk about him, don't you? I heard he's gone missing. You must be beside yourself with worry over him. The poor lad. I wonder what's happened to him?"

Pellton cringed and closed his eyes.

"Do you take *The London Times*, Edgar? I would imagine you do, being a peer of the realm and all. It is *de rigueur* for a man such as yourself, I suppose."

John turned up the flame on the interior lamp so he could see and held up a newspaper. He gave it a sharp crack.

"There was the most intriguing article today. Well, it wasn't even an article really. More of a snippet. And I had to search carefully to find it being those inconsiderate newsmen at *The Times* crammed it out of the way and down at the bottom of page thirteen."

John cleared his throat.

"Let's see what it says, shall we, Edgar?"

Pellton whimpered like a baby. Tom kicked him on his other side.

"*'Defiled Body Dumped at Sea.'* That's the title line, Edgar. Shall I read more?"

Silent sobs came from Pellton on the floor.

John scanned the article before flinging the paper to his lap in theatrical disgust. "Good God! This is downright revolting! What has the world come to? I am sure I do not know! It says here, a man's body was found in the Channel by fishermen yesterday morn. Dark hair, average height, wearing no identification except for a red waistcoat with the initials S.S. sewn inside. They estimate the poor creature had been in the water for a fortnight in the least, near frozen for the cold temperatures."

Pellton grew quiet, his sobbing ceased. He was listening.

John continued to make his point to his enemy. "Good, Edgar. I am glad you are paying attention to the story. I'm about to get to the interesting part. The paper says his body was defiled, and I quote, 'The male genitalia had been cut off and the anus impaled with a staff of wood.'" He set the paper down on his lap.

"Ouch." Tom whistled. "That couldn't have felt nice." Tom peered at Pellton on the floor. "In fact, it must have been gawd-awfully painful. To think that this S.S. person had to sit there while they cut off his cock and balls and then get buggered up the arse with a sharp stick! Shit, I think a fellow would bloody well *want* to die after all that!"

"Language, Tom," John admonished his son.

"Apologies, Pater." Tom shook his head. "Still, this S.S. must have made some terrible enemies to have wound up fish feed and minus his Nebuchadnezzar."

"Yes, son, you are right about that." John turned to Pellton. "What do you think, Edgar? Do you agree with Tom that S.S. made some vengeful enemies?"

Pellton nodded his head up and down. He now had a dark stain at the front of his trousers.

"I am glad we are of a like mind on this, Edgar, because it is very important that you understand the lengths that fathers and brothers and husbands will go to avenge their womenfolk."

John rapped on the roof to signal Ned.

"I am afraid this visit is nearing its end, Edgar. My son and I are engaged this evening—a Christmas party with my daughter and her good husband's family. In fact, we must fly in order to be punctual. There will be fifty people there at least. Peers, politicians, the crème of society, all witness to our attendance this night."

The carriage turned a corner and slowed.

"Sorry, Edgar, but you are not invited to the party. You must get busy packing, my friend. Well, not really my friend anymore. I guess you never were my friend, or you wouldn't have conspired to hurt my daughter and devise evil abuse on her. My Anne was wise to you, Edgar. She saw right through your thin veneer of gentility straight in to the vile poison that pumps from your monstrous heart. Anne hated you, and she loved me."

The carriage pulled to a stop.

"If you make it through this night alive, Edgar, do go home and pack your things. Leave England and never return. I mean this in all truthful sincerity. If you ever set foot on British soil again, your fate *will* be similar to what this unfortunate S.S. knew. Remember the words of Shakespeare's Hamlet, Edgar, 'Pray you avoid it.'"

Pellton's eyes bulged in disbelief as he comprehended the threat.

"You see, Edgar, it was no trouble to find a father and a husband out for revenge for their sweet girl. I believe the young lady in this case was named Emma and her pater a well known tradesman in Town. Owns a tannery. Good knife skills I hear, but I wouldn't know personally. Given the gift of time, I imagine scores of wronged maidens, and their angry menfolk, can be located."

Pellton started whimpering again.

John and Tom stood up to leave.

"Tom, would you be so kind as to relieve our passenger of his money purse, watch, and signet ring? Take his coat and his shoes as well, I think. We'll find some worthy priory or house of good works and make a donation on our way back."

"My pleasure, Pater."

His son was roughly efficient in his task, and a few extra kicks and blows met their target with no trouble. Tom made sure to tie the bindings extra tight, too.

"Good-bye, Edgar. Our carriage awaits outside to take us to our festive evening. We'll just leave you here in Whitechapel. I'm sure some helpful person will come along eventually. You be careful though. 'Tis a rough sort of neighborhood, and your carriage will stick out like a jewel box atop a rag pile here on this street."

John Russell took one last look, hovering over the squirming, befouled man on the floor. "Be a stranger now," John said, and then he spat in Pellton's face.

# CHAPTER THIRTY~SIX

*A little rebellion now and then is a good thing.*
—**Thomas Jefferson, "Letter to James Madison" (1787)**

tanding beside Sir Rodney at the landing, Jeremy watched as first his grandmother and then his wife descended the stairs. Dressed in a magnificent gown of silver, her mother's pearls, and the pearl and diamond earrings he'd given her, Gina was ethereal to him. Grandmamma looked fine, too, in her gown of dark green. For the first time he could recall, he actually found himself looking forward to the festivities tonight.

"What beauteous wives we have, son! They are a sight tonight, are they not?" Sir Rodney declared, admiring the view.

"An understatement, Sir. I'd say they were a vision," Jeremy murmured, never taking his eyes off the two most important women in the world for him.

He greeted his grandmother first. "Grandmamma, you are most splendid in that green, and thank you for organizing this evening." He kissed her cheek.

"It is my great pleasure, dear. We are so proud of you, Jeremy, for bringing Georgina into our family. I think celebration is due, don't you?"

"Quite." He bowed and stepped forward to claim his wife. He took up her hand and kissed in a lingering brush, inhaling deeply. "You sparkle like the moon and the stars in that gown and your pearls, and will be the talk of the town by tomorrow, I predict, Mrs. Greymont."

"Thank you, Mr. Greymont. I daresay we are lucky ladies to be escorted by such handsome gentlemen, especially in your new jackets. I see that no details have been left dangling." She smiled at Lady Bleddington and Sir Rodney. "Your waistcoats are in hue with our gowns. We shall be matched pairs."

"As it should be, my sweetheart. This way I can stand proudly by your side and growl at the throngs who'll want an introduction and will annoy me greatly in seeking your favor."

"No growling, Jeremy." She laughed at him. "And there won't be any throngs of admirers either."

"Oh, so we don't agree on that point then, for I think there will certainly be throngs. And I promise to refrain from growling so long as you stay close by." He kissed her quickly on the lips. "God, you smell good. It's the most lovely—"

He indulged in another inhale. "You're like a night-blooming rose. My rose in the starlight," he whispered with a wink, plucking at a silvery sleeve of her shimmering gown.

"Clarissa wore the same scent, Jeremy."

He froze. Grandmamma had been listening in. "She—she did?" he stuttered, shocked at what his grandmother had just shared.

"Yes, dear. It was your mamma's favorite. I noticed it on Georgina and thought it a happy remembrance for you. You were so young though..." Grandmamma trailed off in her reminiscence.

"My mother wore it also," Gina reminded him.

Jeremy looked at his beautiful Gina and silently thanked the heavens once again that she was his to love.

"Yet another reason why you were meant for me. It was fated," he told her, thinking back to that strange dream he'd had in hospital. Had his mother come to him a dream? A warm flush spread through him, and he felt something he'd never really known. Full. Filled up. Replete with good feelings and blessings—

"Ahem." Sir Rodney cleared his throat, breaking through the poignancy. "Shall we go forth and greet our guests?"

"Yes, sir." Jeremy came to attention and tucked Gina into his arm, feeling a bit possessive and definitely proud. "Lead us on, Grandfather. Lead us on."

"How's my baby sister?" Tom wrapped his arms around Georgina in a loving embrace. "God, it's good to see you." He held her back and perused her from head to toe. "And looking so smashing. You are a diamond, my dear Georgie!"

"I've missed you, Tommy. We haven't seen each other once since I've been in London," Georgina scolded her brother.

"Sorry, Georgie. Had some unfinished business up in Haymarket, but that's all done now." Tom greeted Jeremy, who took his hand in a friendly shake. "You look good, too, my *brother*. You've hardly changed a bit despite the leg shackles," Tom teased.

"Really, Tommy, you ought to consider matrimony for yoursel—" Georgina lost the rest of her words when she laid eyes on her handsome father stepping toward her. Dressed in his evening clothes, he seemed to stand a little taller, a resolve in his manner that boded a certain poise. He looked well, happy even.

"That's what I keep telling your brother, my dear, to take a page out of his sister's book," he said softly, his hazel eyes a mirror of hers.

"Papa…you came."

"I wouldn't have missed this chance for all the world, my

daughter." Her father kissed her forehead. "To see you looking so beautiful and happy." He touched her cheek. "So like your mother, Georgina. She loved you so much. Mamma wanted the world for you—for all your hopes and dreams to come true. I know she rejoices when she looks down on you from heaven, as I do in this earthly life."

"Oh, Papa!" Georgina embraced him and relished his strong arms returning her clutch. "I'm so happy you are here." She realized how truly she meant her words.

"As am I." He smiled. "You look like a queen in that gown, my dear. With your mother's pearls and those earrings, all you lack is a crown." He bowed. "Walk with me, daughter?"

Georgina took her father's offered arm and walked with him for a bit.

He looked wistful. "Do you remember the picnics we used to have by the old oak tree when you were a little girl?"

Her heart dropped. "I do remember them, Papa," she whispered.

"Your mamma made you a circlet of wildflowers one time, and on that day we crowned you the Fairy Queen of Oakfield."

She gasped. "You recall everything! I had no idea you still think of those times, Papa." Georgina was stunned by his revelations.

"Of course I think about it. I never forget. Those were *the* best days in my whole life, with a loving wife and my children about me." He paused and squeezed her arm. "I lost my path when your mother died, Georgina. I know I wasn't the father I could have been. I wasn't a comfort to you in your hour of need. I let you down, and I am so grievously sorry for my actions."

He pulled them to a stop and looked at her. "You turned out magnificent in spite of my lacking attentions, and I love you very much and am so proud of you. I can now only hope you might forgive your old dad his foolish ways."

Georgina felt the wall of fear that had haunted her crumble to dust. In the acknowledgement of his failings, Georgina knew blessed peace, finally. Papa did not blame her for what had happened to her. He loved her still. *He is proud of me.*

Georgina fell into her father's arms a second time. "I do forgive you. You have restored my heart in this declaration." She kissed his cheek. "More than you can ever know. I am truly happy, Papa."

"I am so relieved to hear it. I have worried, Georgina, over you."

"Worry no more, Papa. I am blessed in my life and very content. Jeremy is the best of men and takes very good care of me. And thank you for this lovely gift of memories tonight. They are most precious to me."

"As you are to me, my daughter. And if you are willing, I want to make more happy memories with you, and your good husband, and your children."

Georgina blushed. "I would love that, very much, Papa."

Jeremy appeared in their midst and stepped forward to greet his father-in-law. "Welcome, sir. Your presence is a comfort to Georgina. Thank you for coming tonight."

"Thank *you*, son. I pledge it shall be only the first of many visits," John Russell answered sincerely. "I was just inquiring to Georgina when you two might see fit to make me a grandpa." He smirked at them both.

"Papa!" Georgina felt the flush spread to the roots of her hair, imagining she must be the color of a strawberry.

Even Jeremy looked a bit discomfited, but recovered quickly and managed a saucy, "I'm giving it my best effort, sir."

In an attempt to steer the topic away from bedroom antics, Georgina touched her father's cheek. "You've cut yourself. Does it hurt?"

"Not in the slightest. I don't notice it a bit. Is it very ugly?" Her father shrugged.

"How did you do it, Papa?"

"Oh, we had a change of carriages—driver got sick—and we made a detour on our way here tonight. I'm afraid I misjudged the height of the roof. I ran right into the door pin and nicked myself right here." John touched his cheekbone gingerly. "I probably should get 'round to see the optical while I'm in Town. It may be time for your old man to don some spectacles, my dear."

Jeremy spoke up. "Did your situation with your driver resolve itself? I hope you didn't find trouble on your way here tonight."

"Oh, just a trifling bit. An inconsequential nuisance, really. Everything worked out in the end and *all persons* got to where they needed to go." Her father smiled cheerfully at Jeremy. Jeremy raised an eyebrow and returned the gesture.

Georgina was so glad for the gift of this night. To have Jeremy and her family all together and to see them enjoying one another's company just filled her heart full to bursting.

"Lord and Lady Rothvale, my wife, Georgina." Jeremy provided the introductions gracefully and turned to her. "Lord and Lady Rothvale come to Kilve in the summers, Gina. Their place, Marlings, borders Hallborough at our south end."

"Delighted to make your acquaintance, Mrs. Greymont, and please accept our heartfelt congratulations upon your marriage," Lord Rothvale greeted kindly.

"Thank you, my lord, my lady," Georgina returned. "I look forward to having summer neighbors. My husband has had nothing but lovely things to say about your family."

"Thank you. Speaking of family, would it interest you to find that I knew your mother, Mrs. Greymont? Anne Wellesley?" Lord Rothvale winked.

"Yes, it would, my lord." Georgina was intrigued.

"Our mothers were best of friends, and thus your mamma and I enjoyed countless hours together. Childhood playmates we were, in our halcyon days of youth."

"What a small world it is, Lord Rothvale."

"True, my dear. You look very much like your mother from what I remember of her. She was tough as nails, Miss Anne Wellesley. I had a beast of an older brother, Jasper, who set out mischief at every turn, and she always bested him. Used to amaze me how she could entangle Jasper in his own devilment."

"I'd love to hear more about my mother from you, Lord Rothvale. You and Lady Rothvale must come to see us at Hallborough when you are at Kilve."

"We will look forward to that, and I'll dig through my drawings. I imagine I have a sketch or two of Anne that I did when we were children. I'll bring them along to give to you."

"Oh, thank you, my lord. I would be so grateful for such a gift and would love to introduce you to my father. He is here tonight, and I know he would find your childhood memories of my mother most endearing."

"It would be my great pleasure, Mrs. Greymont. I should tell you though, I am not here tonight without ulterior motive." He winked again. "I want to talk to your husband about running for a seat in the House of Commons."

"Parliament, my lord?"

"Well, yes of course. Time to put that university education and his talents to good use."

"What do you consider my husband's talents, my lord?" Georgina gave Lord Rothvale a wink of her own.

"He's an upstanding land owner, a successful businessman, and now that he's gone and married such a delightful wife, a settled, family man. Just the good sort of useful person we need in Parliament." Lord Rothvale grinned at Jeremy and then back to

Georgina. "What do you say to my idea of your husband becoming the next MP for West Somerset?"

"I think it is an outstanding idea, Lord Rothvale. I can think of no one better suited than my husband." Georgina beamed at Jeremy.

"What do you say, Greymont? Do your part for God and country and all that? England needs men like you." Lord Rothvale's green eyes twinkled.

"I'll think about it, my lord," Jeremy told him, his eyes wide with disbelief at what the man had just proposed.

Georgina squeezed Jeremy's hand and looked on him with pride before reluctantly turning to greet the next guest.

"Dr. Cameron! Thank you for coming tonight." Georgina held out her hand.

"Ah, the pleasure is mine, Mrs. Greymont." He kissed her hand gallantly. "It is always well met to mix patient visits with festive punch. You looking glowing with good health, I am happy to observe." Dr. Cameron winked at her before turning to Jeremy. "And you, sir, clean up quite smart. You've got some color back, and your strength. It's a well thing, too. You'll need it when you're fighting for the rights of good Englishmen in Parliament." Jeremy took the outstretched hand of his friend.

"Ah. You heard that did you?"

"I did. And, Greymont, I think you should do it."

"Well, I told Lord Rothvale I'd think on it. We'll see." Georgina noticed that Dr. Cameron no longer seemed to be listening to Jeremy. The doctor's attention was diverted elsewhere. Jeremy glanced to look. It was easy to see what captivated the good doctor, too. Dr. Cameron was studying the recently widowed, and very lovely, Mrs. Golding, who had accompanied her aunt, Lady Lampson, to the party tonight. Jeremy nudged the doctor to get his attention. "Shall I have Georgina introduce you to Mrs. Golding?"

"No," Dr. Cameron said sharply. "There is no need. Mrs. Golding and I are already acquainted."

"Ah. Well, have a good time then," Jeremy teased his friend, who ignored him completely.

Jeremy arched a brow at her, and they shared a giggle, hoping to learn more about this acquaintance of Dr. Cameron and the mysterious Mrs. Golding in the course of the evening.

Jeremy and Georgina found themselves staying close by each other's side during the party, chatting with old friends and making new acquaintances. They were together for the entertainment and the singing of carols, and when the more raucous parlor games began, but never had even a second for little more than a word or two.

It was during a game of similes that Jeremy pulled Georgina into the servants' stairwell for a private moment.

"Finally," he whispered, pressing her back against the wall as his lips descended.

Jeremy kissed her wickedly slow, plundering her open mouth with his hot, seeking tongue. He met her hips with his in a slow thrust, and she felt the familiar ridge of an erection push into her.

"I thought I might die if I had to wait another minute to kiss you, sweet wife."

"I know, adored husband," she breathed, pushing right back with a thrust of her own.

Georgina could taste the spices from the wassail on his tongue, and for some reason it made her want to strip him naked. The vision of him in the altogether, stretched out for her, caused a smile to form on her face. She'd have a cup of wassail with her so she could dip her fingers in and splash drops of the fragrant wine down his chest and lower. She could just imagine the taste of the drops mixed with the salt of his skin as she lapped up each and every bead, until she reached his—

"What are you thinking about right now, my Gina?"

"About what a lovely party this has been?" she quipped.

Jeremy shook his head and traced the swell of a breast with his finger. "I don't think so."

"I'm thinking about Lord Rothvale's proposition that you take a seat in Parliament?"

He dipped a finger into her bodice. "Highly unlikely, from the look you were giving me. Try again, my pretty minx."

"Hmm." She put a finger to her lips in thoughtfulness. "I am thinking about what a happy woman you have made me by loving me so much, and about how much I love you?" The giggle she'd tried so hard to suppress was desperately close to erupting.

He waggled a finger through the layers of undergarments until he found her areola and busied himself until he'd raised the center into a hard peak.

Her giggle escaped and then evolved into a moan of desire as she melted into his touch.

"You're getting closer, sweetheart, but haven't quite hit your mark. I think you need to give it one more try—"

His other hand whipped to her waist and tickled.

She managed one shriek before he muffled her with another plundering kiss.

"Tell me," he panted in between kisses. "As your lord and master, I command you to tell me."

Georgina laughed at him and stroked her hand up the front of his formal trousers, and then down inside for a feel of skin on hot skin, taut and ready.

"All right, I recant what I just said," he mumbled into her ear. "As my lady's enraptured servant, I *beg* you to tell me."

"Since you are so humble, I will tell you, but remember that you have a houseful of guests just beyond that door and it'll be hours and hours before we can act on it."

Jeremy nodded, his blue eyes gleaming, anticipating what she would say.

"Well, it involves you stripped out of your fine new suit, and some strategically placed drops of wassail, and my mouth..." She whispered the rest right into his ear.

*The London Evening Standard*
*December 23, 1837*

Lady Lampson, the woman who knows everything worth knowing in London, attended a Christmas party held by Sir Rodney and Lady Bleddington at their Grosvenor Square townhouse last night. Notables such as Lords Rothvale and Verlaine, Lady Dorchester, and Sir Nathaniel Cameron graced the gathering for a festive celebration of the season and shared acknowledgement for the recent nuptials of Sir Rodney's grandson and heir, Jeremy Greymont to Miss Georgina Russell of Oakfield, Wiltshire.

Lady Lampson tells us the party wound down rather quickly after Mr. and Mrs. Greymont were spotted leaving the servants' stairwell rather abruptly. It might have had something to do with the mistletoe catching fire after a candle was lifted to it.

Mr. Greymont remained focused in the urgency of the situation when he doused the flames with a bowl of the Christmas punch, saving the house and preventing any injuries. Not a soul was harmed.

The silk wallpaper, the carpet, and the mistletoe might take exception with the "no harm" assessment though. The mess was quite extensive. And sadly Mrs. Greymont's beautiful silver gown got splashed, necessitating her withdrawal as hostess for the evening.

Mr. Greymont was last seen heading upstairs to check on his lovely wife and had in his hand a cup of wassail for refreshment. The happy couple was not seen again that evening by any person in attendance at the gala event, which along with the Greymont marriage, has been declared a resounding success.

# EPILOGUE

*Oh happy state! when souls each other draw,*
*When love is liberty, and nature, law:*
*And then is full, possessing, and possessed,*
*No craving void left aching in the breast.*

**—Alexander Pope, "Eloisa to Abelard" (1717)**

*December, 1840*
*London*

The love of a good woman was satisfying in a way that nothing else could ever compare. And he'd needed her so badly. She was precisely what he'd required, and he'd found her just in time. It was hard for him to imagine how his life might have turned out if he'd never spied her that autumn day in the rain.

Jeremy stood back and took in the scene around him. He indulged in the feelings of utter contentment and love for his family. Those feelings had been enjoyed for the past three years, and he knew they would only grow stronger with the passage of time.

That was the thing when he was with the woman he loved, knew her better than he knew himself, and intended to keep right

*298*

on loving her for the rest of his days.

Looking around the room, he saw it for what it was. Tastefully done in blue and green silks and filled with the people who mattered to him, gathered together in communion, and in respect, and in caring for one another.

There was his brilliant, two-year-old son, Roddy, sitting upon his Grandpapa John's lap, pouring through a picture book of animals. Both men, young and not so young, looking as if they might succumb to a nap at any moment.

His younger brother, Revé, now a strapping lad of fifteen, and on holiday from the winter term, was taking the finer points of poker instruction from his brother-in-law, Tom, and his grandfather, Sir Rodney, who was still a spry old fox for a man of six and seventy years.

There were new additions and, sadly, departures as well. Jeremy's grandmother, Leticia Bleddington, had died peacefully in her sleep after a garden party at Hallborough in the heat of August this past summer. The party had been just the sort of event she loved to fete, and they all took comfort in the fact that she had gone to her maker swiftly after a rewarding experience from which she took much joy.

Therese Blufette died soon after her disclosure, entrusting her beloved son into his older brother's care. The brothers shared a bond that, be it blood or be it common ground, regardless, drew them together in a way that was a comfort to them both.

Tom Russell had taken a wife. A no-nonsense girl from Somerset that Jeremy had known his whole life. The new Mrs. Russell was scheduled to deliver the much anticipated Baby Russell, sometime in late spring, and was now hard at work knitting a tiny sweater for the young master or miss soon to join the family.

Jeremy had taken Lord Rothvale's suggestion to run for the constituency at West Somerset and had won it by a respectful margin. Politics suited him in a way he never thought possible for himself, when he was younger and self-propelled by actions that did nothing to embolden his service for the common good.

A beautiful person had changed all of that though, was still changing him, for the better, in her support as a wife and a mother, a confidant, a lover, and his very best friend.

His Georgina.

Their eyes met across the room and held a moment. Jeremy mouthed, "I love you."

Georgina returned with, "I know," gave him one of her retiring half-smiles, and then looked down at the infant she held in her arms.

Their sweet baby girl had been born just three weeks earlier, and already he could see Gina reflected in her tiny facial features and diminutive personality. They named their daughter Anna Clare Marguerite in honor of both their mothers and one other person to whom Jeremy would ever be indebted.

Upon reflection, Jeremy accepted that even though it had been a struggle at times, and risks had to be leveraged in the willingness to alter the way he viewed the world, life had done him a good turn. He looked around the room once more before settling his eyes back upon his Gina and smiling. *Yes, a very good turn.*

# *THE END*

# ABOUT THE AUTHOR

Raine Miller is a former teacher and author of the *New York Times* bestseller, *The Blackstone Affair*, but she has been reading historical romances since she picked up that first Barbara Cartland book at the tender age of thirteen. She thinks it was *The Flame is Love* from 1975. And it's a safe bet she'll never stop, because now she writes them too! Granted Raine's stories are edgy enough to turn Ms. Cartland in her grave, but to her way of thinking, a hot, sexy hero never goes out of fashion. Never ever!!

Writing books pretty much fills her days now and she is always busy. Raine has a prince of a husband, and two brilliant sons to pull her back into the real world if the writing takes her too far away. She loves to hear from readers and to chat about the characters in her books.

You can connect with her on Facebook at **Raine Miller Romance** or visit **www.RaineMiller.com** to find out what she's working on now.

*Notes*